ENDLESS OBSESSION

by

Dai Henley

Published by New Generation Publishing in 2021

First Edition

ISBN
Paperback   978-1-80369-979-0
Ebook   978-1-80369-978-3

www.newgeneration-publishing.com

 New Generation Publishing

CHAPTER ONE

March 2018

Flood's receptionist put her head around the office door and said, 'There's a Lisa Black here to see you. Says she's a bit early for her appointment. Is that OK?'

'Sure. Show her in.'

Flood logged off his computer, eased his lean body off his chair and pulled on his jacket hanging on the back of it. He straightened one of several photos on the wall showing his toddler daughters, Gemma and Pippa, splashing each other in a swimming pool as he opened the door.

Lisa entered and Flood shook her extended, sun-tanned hand. On the back of it, he noticed a tattoo of intertwined hearts, each with the initial 'M' in the centre. 'Pleased to meet you,' he said, immediately wondering who the initials referred to.

She flashed him a beguiling smile. 'I've never met a famous private investigator before.'

Flood returned the smile, suspicious of anyone who paid him a compliment. 'Not sure about being famous. Here, let me take your coat.'

She handed him her blackberry-patterned Macintosh. Flood hung it behind the door, noting how unusual it was.

Still smiling, she said, 'I've always been lucky. If a car park's full, someone leaves as I arrive.' Her smile evaporated. 'Luckier still when my bastard of a husband tried to kill me.' The smile returned as she shrugged. 'As you can see, I survived.'

'I assume that's why you are here,' Flood said, as he motioned for her to take a seat in front of his desk. He sat opposite her.

'Too right.'

'Do you mind if we record our chat? It'll be a useful reminder.'

1

'No. Not at all.'

Flood pulled his mobile from his pocket, turned on the voice recorder and placed it in the middle of the desk. 'OK. We're set up. Tell me about it in as much detail as you can.'

Lisa settled her diminutive figure in the chair, crossed her shapely legs and flicked stray hairs from her vanilla-blonde bob back into place. Flood knew what her game was. He'd come across many flirtatious witnesses and learnt not to be seduced by them. In any case, Lisa was roughly the same age now as his eldest daughter.

'Three years ago, I met and married a wealthy guy who lived not far from here. The answer to my prayers, I thought. I'd just turned thirty; reckoned it was time to settle down.

'I had loads of boyfriends before we met, but nothing worked out.' Lisa's eyes opened wide. 'All I wanted was to be with someone kind, generous and fun. You know what I mean?'

Flood nodded. 'That's what everyone wants, I guess.'

'Mike fitted the bill to perfection.' Lisa uncrossed her legs and sat forward in her chair. 'Until we got married. That's when he changed. He believed he owned me; became possessive and mega-jealous. He wouldn't let me go anywhere or do anything unless he approved.' Her eyes narrowed. 'He made my life hell.'

Flood had dealt with many domestic abuse cases; some caused by provocation and most unwarranted, in his experience.

Lisa continued. 'I left him once. But he grovelled, apologised and pleaded with me to give him another chance. Stupidly, I did. After our last argument, he persuaded me to join him on a sailing trip on a rented cabin cruiser in the Gulf of Mexico, starting in Naples, Florida and cruising down to Key West and back. That's his thing. Mike loves being at sea. *A second honeymoon,* he'd called it. Promised he'd never hurt me again. Like an idiot, I fell for it.'

'You're not the first woman to give a man a second chance.'

'I suppose not.' Lisa relaxed back in her chair. 'On the first night, we docked at Everglades City in the middle of the swamps. We had a boozy dinner at the Rod and Gun restaurant and afterwards, Mike insisted that we motored south towards the Keys. In the early hours of the morning, it looked so romantic; shards of moonlight pierced the clouds and glinted off the waves.

'After an hour's sailing, he put the boat on autopilot and went off on a rant, bringing up loads of stuff about my past. He wouldn't let me forget that six months earlier he'd caught me *in flagrante* with a boyfriend I'd been seeing on and off. Then he accused me of flirting with the waiter at The Rod and Gun.

'I know I'm no angel, but when I told him I'd done nothing of the sort, he thrust his mobile inches from my face and flicked through a dozen photos of me having a laugh with him. Mike always got nasty if he felt he'd lost control of me. I could always tell. The veins on the side of his neck looked about to burst, and his eyes glazed over.

'I told him I'd had enough, that our relationship was finished for good. As soon as we reached dry land, I'd find my own way home. It was the worst thing I could have said. The bastard went berserk. He punched me in the face several times and split my lip. I almost passed out.'

Flood grimaced. 'That's horrendous!'

'Then he pushed me over the side of the boat.' She shuddered at the memory. 'Can you believe anyone would do such a thing in the middle of the night? I don't know whether he'd planned this before we left the UK or whether my *flirting*,' Lisa made quote marks with her fingers, 'had pushed him over the edge. I was only having a bit of fun.'

'You must have been terrified.'

'You could say. Plunging into the sea stung my wounds, but at least it brought me round. I watched in horror as the boat accelerated away from me. I screamed after him as the lights disappeared into the distance.

'I wasn't wearing a life jacket – no one does when the sea's calm, do they? I panicked and waved my arms about, trying to keep my head above water, forcing out of my mind the possibility of sharks ripping my legs from the rest of my body. My survival instinct kicked in. Alternately, I floated and trod water. I spotted lights along the coast. Must have been four or five miles away. I'd never, ever swum that far.

'I hoped to continue floating long enough until another boat came along. Someone told me that drug runners regularly made the trip from Cuba to Florida via the Gulf. I hoped they'd chosen tonight. I remember thinking: *Oh, my God, if no one comes, is this where my life ends?'*

Although Flood thought Lisa was overreacting, milking her story, he frowned, imagining himself in her predicament. He was a strong swimmer. His slim but powerful frame was perfect for it, but the thought of providing a shark with supper didn't appeal. 'How did you survive?' he asked.

'The only thing keeping me going was my hatred of Mike. And remember, I told you I'm lucky. Well, after being in the water for what seemed like a lifetime, I heard the humming of an engine and saw lights heading in my direction. I waved my arms and nearly burst a lung shouting at the top of my voice. But the boat sped past me, fifty yards away. Shit! I thought.'

She thumped Flood's desk with her fists. He couldn't help but wonder whether she was putting on a performance. Everything she did was just that little bit over the top.

'So, you can imagine my joy when the boat turned around and headed back towards me. I thought it was Mike – maybe he only wanted to teach me a lesson. I yelled and waved again as it got closer. But it wasn't Mike's boat. I could just make out the name on the hull from the glimmer of light from the moon. *Morning Mist.*

'A searchlight on the boat picked me out and a man threw a lifebuoy in my direction. I grasped it and the man dragged me towards a boarding ladder and helped me aboard. The boat belonged to a lovely, older couple, Scottie and Jean. They got me dry clothes, a hot drink and patched up my wounds.

'They're such caring people. They reminded me of my late mum and dad.' She paused. 'They're dead now. My mum and dad, I mean.' She smiled for a moment at their memory.

'Why were Scottie and Jean sailing at that time of night? They weren't drug runners, were they?'

'No, they weren't. Scottie said they were returning from a trip to the Keys but were running behind schedule. They'd arranged to meet a friend of theirs in Naples the following morning.

'They wanted to know how I'd ended up in the sea and asked if I'd fallen overboard and whether they should try to contact the boat. Being in the water so long, I'd had more than enough time to think about what I'd do if, by some miracle, I survived.

'I told them Mike had pushed me over the side after beating me up. They were shocked, said it was despicable and offered to report him to the police once we'd docked at Naples. That's the last thing I wanted. If Mike knew I'd survived, he'd want to finish me off. I'm convinced of it. Do you know why?'

'Tell me.'

Lisa leaned forward. 'I'll never forget his words. As he kept punching me, he said, "That's for showing me up again. I'm going to kill you, make no mistake about it. I have done it before."' She stared at Flood, pausing long enough for the words to sink in. 'What do you think of that?'

Flood shook his head. He'd been around some nasty people but this Mike sounded particularly heartless. 'Do you think your husband could have said that in the heat of the moment?'

Lisa sat back and pursed her lips. 'You don't know him. He's the most jealous guy I've ever met. When I told Scottie and Jean what he'd said, they were shocked and suggested I get some rest. I couldn't settle, planning my revenge on Mike.

'I woke a couple of hours later. It took me a while to realise where I was. I thought I'd had a nightmare. When I emerged on deck, Scottie had dropped anchor. We were now close to the shoreline and Jean got us some breakfast. I told them my plan.'

'What plan?'

'I thought that if Scottie reported Mike, he'd most likely tell the police that I'd slipped, hit my head on the side of the boat and fallen overboard as he slept below. It would be his word against mine. Or, he could have called the coastguards when the boat was miles away from where he dumped me so the rescuers would be searching in the wrong place. Eventually, they'd give up, assuming I'd drowned.'

'Or he may not have reported it at all, hoping no one discovered your body?' Flood replied.

'True. And Mike would know that if my body washed up somewhere without any form of identification, there'd be no link to him. By the time they found me, he'd be back in the UK.'

'So what did you decide to do?'

'Until I could get back to the UK, I'd find a job in a bar or something and get some money together. Although it would take time, once I was back home, I'd make sure my bastard husband paid for what he did.'

'What did your new friends think about that?'

'Scottie offered to help. He's a wealthy ex-lawyer who worked for the biggest law firm in New York. He'd defended many criminals, including Mafia gangs, before he and Jean retired to Florida. They were unbelievably sympathetic. Said he'd take me to the British Embassy in Miami where I could tell them exactly what happened and issue me with emergency travel documents to get back to the UK.

'I told him that was too risky. I'd have to travel under my real name so Mike would know I survived and come after me again. I wanted him to believe that I'm dead. Scottie took my point and offered to get me a fake passport, lend me some cash and put me up in an apartment in Naples for a while.'

Flood raised his eyebrows. 'Scottie sounds too good to be true.' His scepticism was built on almost forty years of investigating crimes. In his world, rarely did someone do something for nothing. 'Why would he take the risk of breaking the law for someone he didn't know?'

Lisa shrugged and her lips parted in a smile, showing off her evenly-capped, white teeth. 'He took a liking to me, I guess.'

The smile looked rehearsed in some way to Flood. Years of dealing with liars had given him instincts for when someone wasn't being genuine. The disparity between her smile and the look in her eyes was ringing alarm bells.

'And why have you come to me?'

Her smile evaporated. 'I've done my research. I checked out loads of other investigators; no one has as good a record as you. Twenty years as a detective with Hampshire Police and the Met, three commendations and the last eighteen years operating as a successful private detective. That's why I'd like you to investigate Mike, prove he *has* killed before.'

Flood was flattered. Who wouldn't be? But he sensed she was laying it on too thickly. She was a performer. It didn't mean she was lying, but her story sounded suspicious.

'You believe he has?'

'I do and I'll tell you why. I did some digging using Scottie's laptop and I discovered that Mike's first wife had been murdered during a break-in that went wrong. The burglar's doing twenty years for it. Mike never mentioned her murder. That's too much of a coincidence, don't you think?'

'Could be.'

'Once you've proved it, we can go to the police. They'll take my story more seriously if it comes from you.' She focussed her eyes on his again. 'Well, what do you think? Will you help me?'

'You're saying a jury found the murderer guilty and you're asking me to get the verdict overturned?' He shook his head. 'That's highly improbable.'

'I *know* my husband's capable of murder.'

Scottie's generous offer to help a stranger and the astonishing revelation about the murder of her husband's former wife had spooked Flood. He bought time to consider if he wanted to take the case.

'I'll have to talk to my business partner, who happens to be my wife. We only take cases where we believe we can get a result. Let me have your contact number and I'll call you.'

Flood slid a notepad towards her. She scribbled the number down and pushed the pad back towards him. 'How long will it take you to make a decision?'

'I'll get back to you within twenty-four hours.' He looked at the number she'd written. 'You've given me a US number. It begins with 001.'

'It's the mobile Scottie got me in Florida. Once we've got Mike locked up, I'll revert to my original name, get a new phone and apply for a replacement passport. Get my life back on track.'

'What is your name? I assume from the tattoo on the back of your hand, the first one begins with M?'

'I'm impressed with your powers of observation, Mr Flood, but I'd rather not tell you if you don't mind. Not until you take the case. As long as Mike's a free man, I'm Lisa Black. I look forward to hearing from you.'

She stood and held out her hand. Flood shook it before helping her put on her coat. 'I'll be in touch,' he said.

***

Over dinner that evening, Flood discussed the interview with his wife, Laura. She wasn't officially his business partner, but often discussed cases with her. Her insights invariably proved valuable.

They'd met twenty years previously, when she worked for him as a detective sergeant in his Murder Squad, shortly after Flood's first wife was murdered. She now worked as a researcher, specialising in fingerprint technology at a forensics laboratory.

She listened without interruption. When Flood finished, he asked, 'What do you make of her story?'

'God, talk about lucky. What are the odds on that boat turning up in the middle of the night and then finding someone to go along with her plan?'

'Do you believe her?'

'I don't see why she'd lie about something so dramatic. And if her story's true, there's a murderer at large.'

'*If* it's true. What gets me is why *anyone*, let alone a lawyer, would offer to get a stranger a fake passport, a mobile phone, lend her money and put her up; everything to help her exact revenge on her husband.'

'How did she come across to you?'

'She's glamorous, flirty, bit of a drama queen but bright and street-wise.'

'There's your answer. Lisa's manipulated this Scottie chap to fall for her. Some men can be unbelievably gullible. Present company excepted, of course.'

Flood shook his head. 'I've got mixed feelings. Part of me feels sorry for her. What happened was diabolical. On the other hand, there's something which doesn't ring true. For a start, she won't trust me with her real name. She said she would after I agreed to take the case. I don't feel comfortable about it.' After a short pause, he said, 'I'm going to pass on this one. I'll call her first thing tomorrow.'

'Good luck with that.'

When Flood told Lisa his decision, she didn't say anything at first but then shouted, 'What? From everything I learned about you, I thought you had a thing about righting wrongs and doing *anything* in the cause of justice. *Obviously*, I was wrong.' Before hanging up, she screamed down the phone, 'Arsehole!'

Flood felt like he'd dodged a bullet with this potential client.

CHAPTER TWO

A WEEK LATER

As Flood arrived at his office early in the morning, his mobile rang. Laura's breathless voice said, 'Have you seen today's *Daily Echo*?'

'No. Why?'

'I stopped to get petrol and the papers on the way to the lab. The headline on the front page is about a woman who died at a Southampton hotel.'

'So?'

'You remember the interview you had with that woman a week ago? You know, the one who told you her husband beat her up and dumped her off a motorboat in Florida?'

'Yes?'

'It looks like she fell from the top floor of the Sturridge Hotel.'

'What? Bloody hell! How do you know it's her?'

'The police released her name. Lisa Black. That's what you said her name was, right? There's a photo of her in the paper. Taken from her passport, I assume. You'll be able to recognise her. I'll bring the paper home.'

'Can you read out the report?'

Flood heard the rustling of the newspaper. 'Here it is. *Hampshire Police and the Ambulance Service were called to the four-star Sturridge Hotel in Southampton two days ago following a report from a guest. He'd discovered the body of a woman lying on the terrace. Paramedics were unable to save her. The police identified her as 32-year-old Lisa Alison Black, an American citizen staying on the sixth floor of the hotel. The area has been sealed off and police officers are carrying out a forensic search of her room. They are keeping an open mind about the cause of death and appealing for witnesses to call Southampton Police Station or 101.* That's it.'

'If Lisa told me the truth, she's not American. And her surname's not Black. Whoever she is, I can't believe she's dead.' He paused. 'Maybe I should have taken the case.'

'Don't beat yourself up, Andy. You can't solve everybody's problems. I know you *think* you can.'

Ignoring the barb, he said, 'I recorded the interview. I'll replay it now; see if it throws up anything worthwhile. See you tonight.'

He played back the recording twice, concentrating on every word, making sure he hadn't missed a vital clue. It confirmed how little he knew about Lisa. Just her incredible story and her US cell phone number. He didn't even know her true identity or where she lived before her ill-fated trip to Florida.

Flood googled 'Boat registrations in Naples, Florida', to see if a boat named *Morning Mis*t existed. He was directed to the County Tax Collection Office which showed an email address and phone number for all enquiries. He looked at his watch. He worked out that it was 5.00 a.m. in Naples.

He waited the four hours until the office opened and called the number. A sweet-sounding voice said, 'Hi. I'm Carole. How can I help you today?'

'I saw a motor cruiser last week when I was visiting Naples. I'm interested in purchasing it. Can you give me the owner's contact details if I give you the name of the boat?'

'Sure. What is it?'

'*Morning Mist.*'

'OK, let's see. It'll take a moment. Are you OK holding on?'

'Yes. Thanks.'

A few moments later, Carole said, 'I've got a name and address. It's a 2016 Sea Ray 400 registered to a Mr Scott McPherson, 1035 Ibis Quay, Naples Bay Resort.'

'Do you have a phone number?'

'Sorry. No. It must be unlisted.'

Flood thanked Carole, *At least, Lisa had told him the truth so far.*

When he arrived home that evening, Laura poured a glass of red wine and handed it to him as they sat at the kitchen worktop. She passed him the *Daily Echo* showing the woman's photo on the front page and waited while Flood read it. 'Well?' she asked.

'Yes, that's her.'

'Did you discover anything helpful from the recording?'

'No. Not from the recording but the boat and her rescuers certainly exist. I'm sure of one thing. Lisa, or whatever her real name is, didn't commit suicide. She isn't the type. Her falling from a hotel balcony *could* have been an accident. But it's just as likely that her husband found out she'd survived, tracked her down and murdered her. She was scared that might happen.'

'You're always so suspicious, Andy. What are you going to do about it?'

Flood shook his head. 'I feel I've let Lisa down. I didn't believe her story. If I'd taken the case, maybe she wouldn't be lying in the morgue.'

He placed his glass on the worktop and said, 'I've got an idea. Why don't we take a working holiday, go to Florida, talk to Scottie McPherson. I've got his address. I'd like to eyeball him, get his take on Lisa. What do you think?'

'It's tempting, Andy, but I can't. I'm giving expert fingerprint evidence next week. It's taken months to get to court.' She added, 'Why don't you go?'

'Are you sure?'

'I know you. You'll be a grumpy old bastard if you do nothing.'

'It's going cost a few pennies. We'll have to use up some of the money my mother left me.'

'If you think it's important, then go ahead. Of course, you could just inform the police about your interview with Lisa. Let them deal with it.'

'And tell them what? I'll know more after talking to this Scottie guy. See if he corroborates her story. *Then* I'll have something to tell the police.'

Laura looked him straight in the eyes. 'Do you think you'll ever give up your obsession with getting justice?'

'It's all I know, Laura. And anyway, I made a mistake in not believing her. I feel responsible.'

Flood spent the rest of the evening online, arranging a US visitors' visa and checking on flights to Florida. He booked his accommodation and hired a car from the airport. He managed to get one of the last seats on a British Airways flight from Heathrow to Miami departing the morning after next.

***

For most of the ten-hour flight, Flood mugged up on the city of Naples from a Lonely Planet Guide to Florida he'd picked up at WHSmith's at Heathrow. He discovered a prosperous town with twenty thousand inhabitants, a hundred miles west of Miami through the exotically-named Alligator Alley. The population more than tripled in the winter months as thousands of 'snowbirds', mainly retirees, headed south from the northern states to escape the harsh weather, drawn by white, sandy beaches, swaying palms and tropical temperatures.

Flood arrived in Miami at 4.00 p.m. local time, picked up his hire car, drove to Naples and checked in at the Cove Inn, next to a marina, two hours later. Flood called Laura to let her know he'd arrived safely, had something to eat at a local pizzeria and went to bed, feeling jet-lagged.

Flood rose early the following morning fully refreshed and looking forward to getting stuck into the investigation. He'd always had a fascination with the US. He loved the American's 'can do' attitude.

As he passed close by the Inn's café on his way to the car park, the irresistible aroma of cooked breakfasts wafted towards him. He didn't usually do them. Strong coffee and a bowl of muesli usually got him going in the mornings. But now, he could almost taste the yolks. He followed his nose to the bustling café and ordered a full American, complete with eggs, bacon, and pancakes with lashings of maple syrup.

Suitably fuelled, he drove to the Naples Bay Resort, just a mile from the Cove Inn on the road leading back to Miami. Within a few minutes, he'd reached a block of stunning condos, the sun highlighting the pastel shades of yellow and orange stucco plaster.

Despite the early hour, his T-shirt clung to his body as the humidity increased and sweat trickled down his forehead, making it difficult to see through his sunglasses. He wiped his face and neck with his handkerchief before finding number 1035. He rang the doorbell and waited. Nothing. He rang again. Still nothing. Thirty seconds later, he tried once more. Silence.

He knocked on the doors of the neighbours on either side. Receiving no reply from the first one, he tried the other. A bald man in his seventies, wearing a garish, sky-blue, Hawaiian shirt with a green palm tree pattern stretched over his considerable paunch, answered the door.

Flood asked if he knew where Scottie was. 'They're away. Don't see much of 'em. Rarely here this time of year.' He tried closing the door. Flood put his hand against it.

'Do you have a contact number for them?'

'No, sorry.' Baldy added his considerable weight behind the door and shut it in Flood's face.

Flood considered putting a note through Scottie's door but decided against it, wanting to retain the element of surprise when he caught up with him. He walked around the block to the waterfront to see if *Morning Mist* was moored there, but the only access was via steel and wire gates with a security code.

He called Laura that evening. 'I'm getting nowhere. Any developments on your end?'

'Yes. The police released a press release yesterday saying their investigations are continuing. They say there were no signs of a struggle in the room and that the preliminary post mortem confirmed the presence of drugs and alcohol in her body. Nothing so far suggests foul play.'

'The police don't know what happened to her in Naples.'

'I think you should tell them what Lisa told you.'

'It's too bizarre a story, Laura. I'll stay a few more days, hope Scottie turns up. Then I'll go to the police. How did your court case turn out?'

'So far, so good. I'm being cross-examined by the defence tomorrow. After that, I'm done.'

***

From his room at the Cove Inn, Flood noticed a water shuttle, *The Blue Pelican*, which ferried passengers around the bay calling at waterside restaurants. The Inn had produced a timetable together with the route and the stops. One was the Naples Bay Resort, which passed the private moorings at the rear of Scottie's condo. A perfect way to establish whether *Morning Mist* was moored outside.

He took the shuttle once in the late morning and once in the afternoon for the next two days without seeing Scottie's boat.

Flood called Laura again. 'How did you get on in court?'

'Fine. It went well. The defence barrister is chuffed. We got a good result. How are you getting on?'

'It looks like Scottie's away on his boat. He could be anywhere. I'm thinking of coming home. I miss you.'

'I miss you, too, but I know you won't let this rest until you speak to Scottie. Why don't you give it a couple more days? I can deal with anything urgent.'

'Thanks, Laura. I hope it's not going to be a waste of time.'

***

The following morning dawned bright and sunny. Flood took the shuttle's first loop of the day at midday as usual. Tourists heading for lunch packed the boat, which chugged around the bay, dropping them off. As the shuttle glided closer to the Naples Bay Resort, Flood gazed once more at the neat line of gleaming, expensive, state-of-the-art boats moored in the docks at the rear of the condos, checking out the names.

Then he spotted a SeaRay cabin cruiser that hadn't been there the previous day. His eyes focussed on the stern where he saw the name, *Morning Mist*, written in an elegant script. Just the break he needed. Jumping to his feet, he yelled to the skipper, 'Can you let me off here?'

Flood disembarked, raced up the gangplank past the security gate to the dock, towards Scottie's front door. He knocked and heard movement inside. The door opened.

A man wearing a tailored, casual shirt, shorts and sneakers stood in the doorway. With his slim build, lively eyes and neatly-cut silver hair, he looked like a model promoting senior citizens' up-market clothing.

'Yes, can I help you?'

'Scottie McPherson?'

The man looked him up and down. 'Yes. And you are?'

Flood fished his business card from his wallet and handed it over. 'I'm Andy Flood, a private investigator from the UK. I'd like to talk to you about Lisa Black.'

'Who?'

'Lisa Black. She told me how you'd met and how you rescued her from drowning in the Gulf of Mexico late at night. Lisa asked me to prove that her husband tried to kill her.'

Scottie studied the card, looked up and stared at Flood. 'You keep mentioning Lisa. I've never seen or heard of anyone by that name.'

CHAPTER THREE

'You should know her. You saved her life.'

Scottie's eyes looked down at his loafers. He knew her all right. Flood could tell.

'You'd better come in. Mind the cases, we just got back from a trip.'

Flood followed Scottie into an elegantly furnished living room. The floor to ceiling windows opened on to a balcony with a majestic, sun-drenched view of the Bay. A trim, tanned, woman, who Flood guessed to be in her late sixties, was unpacking a bag.

Scottie waved a hand in her direction. 'This is Jean, my wife. Jean, this is,' he looked at the card, 'Andrew Flood, a private investigator from the UK. He's here to talk about the young woman we rescued.'

Jean stopped unpacking and looked up at Flood. 'Mandy? Is she alright? We haven't heard from her in a while.'

'I don't know how many girls you've rescued lately,' Flood said, 'but it sounds like Mandy and Lisa is the same woman. Did she have a tattoo of entwined hearts on the back of her right hand?'

'Yes, she did,' Scottie replied. Flood reached inside his pocket and handed him the photo of 'Lisa' from the *Daily Echo's* press report.

'Is this the young woman you rescued?'

Scottie peered at the photo. 'It looks like her. What do you think, Jean?'

She reached inside her handbag lying on the table, retrieved a pair of glasses and put them on. Flood passed her the photo. 'Yes. That's her, all right. Except Mandy's hair wasn't blonde. She was a brunette. I guess she could have coloured it.'

She handed the photo back to Flood. 'Why are you here?'

'I'm afraid to say, Mandy's dead.'

Jean sucked in a deep breath and put her hands to her mouth. He continued. 'The police are investigating the circumstances. Their initial assessment is that she accidentally fell from a hotel balcony in Southampton, back in the UK.'

Jean blurted, 'That's no *accident*! I bet her husband's responsible.' She took a tissue from her handbag and dabbed her eyes. Scottie put his arm around her shoulder, guided her towards a white leather sofa and sat next to her.

Flood sat in a chair opposite. 'I'm sorry this news is upsetting, but what can you tell me about Mandy?'

Scottie explained the rescue, confirming everything Mandy had said. Jean nodded as he spoke.

Flood asked, 'Did she tell you what her plans were?'

'Yes. Mandy wanted to lie low for a while, let her husband think she'd drowned. She was real scared about him knowing she'd survived. That's why she didn't want us to contact the police. She wanted to make her husband pay for what he did to her. Can't say I blamed her,' Scottie replied.

'Did she stay with you?'

'We put her up here for a week and then she stayed in one of our properties near Wiggins Pass, a few miles north of here.'

'Did you offer to fund her plan to get incriminating evidence against her husband?'

'I told her, if she wanted to get a private investigator when she got back to the UK, I'd lend her the cash. I didn't expect to get it back. Poor kid had no identity. No clothes. Nothing.'

'How much?'

'Enough to pay an investigator plus a few months' living expenses.'

Flood frowned. 'Why would you do that for a stranger?'

Scottie glanced at Jean who, head bowed, sat twisting the tissue in her hand.

She said, 'Two years ago, we lost our only daughter, Ruth, murdered by her controlling husband after years of abuse. She'd have been about the same age as Mandy. Although she didn't look like her, she had a similar personality. Bright, bubbly and vivacious. We felt sorry for Mandy; seems like she was going through the same thing as Ruth. They both had everything going for them but couldn't blossom because of their relationships.'

As her voice trailed away, Scottie filled the void. 'We felt guilty about not spotting what was going on. It's something we'll always regret.' He paused before continuing. 'The only way we can deal with her passing is the belief that everything that happens in life is God's will. He has a plan for all of us.'

He closed his eyes, put his palms together and looked up, as if seeking a divine spirit. His voice trembled and boomed like an evangelical preacher. 'I know the plan I have for you, sayeth the Lord. They are plans for good and not for disaster, to give you a future and a hope.' He opened his eyes and looked at Flood. 'Jeremiah, Chapter 29, Verse 11.'

Flood lost what little faith he had twenty years ago when a gang murdered his first wife and later, abducted and tortured his young daughters in retribution for putting away their leader. He envied those who believed.

Scottie said, 'We *know* the good Lord sent Mandy to us – he gave us a chance to help another soul.'

Flood nodded. 'I can understand that. Is that why you got Mandy a fake passport?'

Scottie shook his head, affronted. 'No. I did not. She asked me to, but that was a step too far. I wouldn't break the law. Not for anyone, even Mandy. It goes against everything I stand for. And as a former lawyer, I have a reputation to protect. Mandy became obsessed with getting revenge against her husband. Nothing else mattered.'

'The photo was taken from an American passport in the name of Lisa Black. How do you think Mandy got hold of it?'

Scottie's eyes narrowed as he glowered at Flood. 'I've no idea.'

'She told me you'd arranged it.'

Scottie scowled. 'Well, she was wrong. I can assure you I didn't.'

'How long did she stay at the apartment you rented for her?'

'About six weeks or so, on and off. Then we heard she'd left. No goodbyes. No note thanking us for helping her. We assumed that, somehow, she may have gotten a passport, returned to the UK and not bothered to tell us. We pray for her every day.'

Jean shook her head. 'I can't believe Mandy's dead!' She wiped away another tear with her scrunched up tissue.

Flood turned back to Scottie. 'Did you discover Mandy's surname?'

'Yes. Bradshaw, Mandy Bradshaw. At least, that's what she told us.'

'Did she give you a UK address?'

'No.'

'How did she spend her time here in Naples? Did she make any friends?'

Scottie shrugged. 'After a few days, she reckoned her husband would have returned to the UK, so she felt safe enough to go out. She got a job working the evening shift in a bar on the edge of town.'

'Do you know the name of the bar?'

'Brad's, up on the Vanderbilt Beach Road towards Wiggins Park. We weren't too happy about it. It's got a reputation for drugs, but with young people these days, it seems to be a way of life.' Scottie shook his head.

Flood scribbled the details in his notebook and stood. 'I'll pay the bar a visit.'

Jean found the energy to say, 'I don't know why you're bothering. You need to find her husband. He's the one responsible.'

***

Flood's mind raced as he drove towards the bar. *If Scottie didn't get Mandy a fake passport, how did she get one in the name of Lisa Black?*

Brad's bar faced directly onto a sun-bleached, sandy shoreline stretching for miles in both directions. Two

20

skimpily-dressed young women were wiping down the tables attempting to make the place presentable again after the lunchtime crowd. Flood made straight for the bar and ordered an iced tea from a bandana-wearing young barman, whose arms were covered in tattoos.

Flood asked, 'Is the manager around?'

'He's in the kitchen. I'll go fetch him. Take a seat.'

Flood sat at one of the patio tables gleaming in the sunlight, gazing out at the families enjoying themselves on the beach and in the turquoise sea. A few moments later, a dark, skinny man with long, black hair tied back in a ponytail approached and sat opposite Flood.

'My name's Mario. I'm the manager. What can I do for you?'

'I'm trying to trace a missing person. Lisa Black. I understand she may have worked here.'

Mario eyed Flood suspiciously. 'Who are you? You're not working for the cops, are you?'

'No. I'm a private investigator.' Flood handed him one of his cards and slid the photo from the press report across the table. 'Do you recognise her?'

Mario studied it carefully. 'Yeah, I reckon that's Lisa. She worked here a while back.'

'Did she make any friends when she worked for you?'

'Yeah. About seven or eight weeks ago, a British girl, Mandy, asked if we had any jobs going. My customers like the Brits so I took her on, paid her cash-in-hand, no questions asked. She looked a lot like Lisa. The only difference was Mandy's got long brunette hair, and Lisa's was blonde and shorter, like in the photo. Oh, and Mandy's accent.'

'How friendly were they?'

'They got real close and worked well together. Then out of the blue, I got a text from Lisa saying that she and Mandy wouldn't be coming back to work. No notice, nothing. They said they were going travelling together.'

'Can you remember exactly when that was?'

Mario laughed. 'You're kidding me. Girls come and go all the time. Especially during the season.'

'Please think, Mario. It's important to the investigation.'

He gazed thoughtfully out towards the Gulf, trawling his memory. He turned to Flood.

'Reckon it must have been on the Tuesday or Wednesday, three weeks ago.' Flood made a mental calculation. Mandy, posing as Lisa, had visited him on the Friday afternoon of that week.

'Did Mandy say where she came from in the UK?'

Mario searched his memory again. 'From the south, I think. She didn't tell me much about her past.'

'Do you know where Lisa lived?'

'The Isle of Capri complex. I had to pick her up once when her car broke down. It's east on the Immokalee Road, 'bout five, ten minutes from here.'

'Thanks for your time, Mario.'

***

He checked his map and drove the two miles inland to the 1970s Isle of Capri two-storey condo block. The area bore no resemblance to the beautiful Italian island or the chic condos in downtown Naples. Quite the opposite. The block was in need of a re-paint and the landscaped gardens hadn't been touched in years.

He parked outside a door marked, 'Community Office' and entered. A forty-something-year-old man bearing a remarkable resemblance to Norman Bates from the movie, *Psycho*, sat on a chair chewing gum as he watched a basketball game on TV. His legs stretched out on a table in front of him. 'Norman' looked up at Flood, turned down the TV and lumbered towards the counter. The enamel badge on his T-shirt read *Pete*.

Flood asked, 'Can you tell me the number of Lisa Black's apartment?'

Pete's eyes lit up at the mention of her name. He pursed his lips and sucked in a breath.

'Ah, the lovely Lisa. When she's here, she's number fourteen, ground floor, block two. Ain't seen her for a couple of weeks. Car's gone, too. She's only paid up till the end of the week. If she don't show up soon, we'll put her stuff in the store and rent out her room.'

'I think something may have happened to her. Can I look in her room?' Flood pulled a twenty-dollar bill from his pocket and laid it on the counter.

Pete shrugged. 'No harm, I suppose.' He picked up the note and stuffed it into his back pocket. He reached for a master key under the counter and ambled towards the door, motioning to Flood to follow him with a flick of his head. The block was the furthest away from the office.

The apartment reminded Flood of the sparsely-furnished rooms he'd lived in at the police college: a tiny bedroom, galley kitchen with a microwave, a sitting room smelling of stale tobacco, and a bathroom. Flood started his search there. Pete said, 'Just close the door behind you when you leave. I'll be in the office if you want me.'

On top of the vanity unit next to the sink, he noticed a rolled-up dollar bill and a mirror lying flat on its side covered with a sprinkling of white powder. He leant towards it and sniffed. The unmistakable whiff of nail polish remover confirmed his suspicion; cocaine.

Next, he checked the drawers and wardrobe in the bedroom. They were filled with women's clothes and shoes, except for several empty hangers, which clanged together as he closed the wardrobe door.

Flood walked back to the sitting room, and noticed marks on the carpet, which he assumed to be coffee stains. Satisfied, he left the apartment and made for Pete's office.

Pete asked, 'Found out whatchya wanted?'

Flood ignored the question. 'Did Lisa say anything to you about leaving?'

'Nope. Nothing. Just disappeared into thin air.'

***

Flood spent the afternoon working on his laptop in his room at the Cove Inn. As a rookie DC back in the 1970s, obtaining information on suspects and witnesses required hours, sometimes days of graft, slogging through mountains of documents and conducting hundreds of interviews. Today, with social media sites and internet access to Electoral Roll registers, he could piece together anyone's life story to a reasonable degree of accuracy with a few keystrokes.

There were nine Amanda Bradshaws registered on the Electoral Roll in the south of England. He checked each entry looking for one married to Michael Bradshaw. It didn't take him long to discover that the couple lived in a house called, 'River Landing' in Hamble, a small town seven miles east of Southampton.

Flood checked Mike Bradshaw's social media next and found a LinkedIn account from which Flood learned that he'd studied civil engineering at Leeds University gaining a First-Class Honours degree. According to his profile, he'd worked for a construction company in the early years before branching out as a property developer. Flood printed a photo of Bradshaw thinking it might prove useful.

Next, he checked Lisa Black on Facebook. Recent photos showed her with friends on Naples Beach. The latest, posted three weeks earlier, showed her grinning, bikini-clad body on the pier with her arms around a tall man wearing a Stetson. Mario was right. Lisa bore a striking resemblance to Mandy. *But why nothing posted since?*

Under 'Friends and Family,' there were over thirty names listed, including a brother called Chris. Flood googled him and discovered that Chris Black owned a real estate agency in Madison, Wisconsin. He noted down the address and phone number from the website.

He called him and, after introducing himself, said, 'I'm following up the whereabouts of a British woman on behalf of her family. She worked with your sister, Lisa, in a bar in Naples, Florida. I understand that they became close friends. I've been trying to trace Lisa. No one's seen her for a while, and the last post on social media was three weeks ago. When did you last hear from her?'

'Directly? Not for ages. I rarely check her Facebook page. I know she wanted to get away from Madison for a while; something to do with her boyfriend dumping her.'

'Chris, I suggest you check whether the rest of your family have heard from her. If not, file a missing person report with the Police Department here in Naples. You can tell them that three weeks ago, she packed up her job, saying she was moving on, travelling with a friend. She's stopped using social media and left her apartment without telling the manager. Her clothes are still there.'

'Do you think something's happened to her?' Chris's voice expressed concern.

'Hard to say. I hope not.'

Next, Flood called Laura. 'I've got all the info I need. I've booked a flight home tonight. Can you pick me up at the airport tomorrow morning?'

'Of course. Can't wait to see you. Have you missed me?'

'I certainly have. I promise I'll bring you out to Naples next year. It's a paradise. You'll love it.'

On the flight, Flood prepared a file of his findings to pass on to the Southampton police.

CHAPTER FOUR

MANDY
EIGHT WEEKS EARLIER

A day didn't pass without me thinking how to take revenge on Mike for what he'd done. I lay awake at night for hours in Scottie and Jean's condo with a raging storm of ideas flashing through my mind. One of them was adopting Scottie's religious belief that God has a plan for all of us. Maybe He had one for me; needed me to survive so I could get Mike put away for a long time. I decided I didn't need God. *I'd* sort it out myself.

Mike's last words, *I've killed before,* reverberated around my head. Needing to find out more, I asked Scottie if I could use his laptop to research Mike's background in more detail. I don't know why I hadn't done it before. With his charismatic personality, good looks, a big house and loads of money, he and I met at a time when I needed stability in my life. After a whirlwind romance, I was flattered when he proposed.

Mike had been married before. I knew his wife's name was Angela, so I googled her. An icy chill ran down my back as I discovered from the newspapers that she'd been murdered at her house in St Albans, a city twenty miles north of London. They reported that she'd disturbed a burglar and that he'd most likely panicked, not wanting to be recognised. He smothered her to death with a pillow and is now serving twenty years.

I rushed to tell Scottie and found him sitting on the balcony overlooking the marina, reading a newspaper and drinking iced tea. When I finished, I asked, 'What do you think? I'm sure Mike had something to do with it.'

Scottie frowned and stroked his chin. 'I suppose it's possible. What do you want to do?'

'When I get back to the UK, I'm going to employ a top-notch private investigator, ask him to prove that Mike murdered his first wife. If he can, the police will take me more seriously. Then I've got the bastard.' I reached forward and gripped his hands.

'I'll need some cash, Scottie. Can you lend me some? I promise I'll pay it back.'

He pulled his hands away, looking sceptical. 'It's going to be difficult to prove, Mandy. I was a lawyer. I should know. Are you sure about your husband being a murderer?'

I shrieked, 'Look at what he did to me! If you hadn't come along when you did, I'd have been murdered, too. I just *know* he killed her.'

Scottie's lips tightened as he thought about his answer. 'How much do you need?'

'I don't know. What do you think?'

He looked across the bay then back at me. 'You'll need money for the private investigator, flights, clothes and stuff. Tell you what I'll do. I'll lend you ten thousand dollars to get you started. Jean and I spoke about helping you financially until you get back on your feet last night. She's happy for us to help. It'll take me twenty-four hours to get that amount of cash.' He reached into his back pocket and pulled out his wallet. Pulling $250 from it, he handed it to me, saying, 'Have this for now. I'll get the rest tomorrow.'

'Oh, thanks, Scottie.' I stood, moved towards him and held his face in my hands this time and kissed the top of his head. 'You're a darling! I'll pay you back, promise.' I sat back in my chair. 'Once Mike's banged up, I'll get a divorce and move back into my house; get my life back.'

I pushed my luck. 'The trouble is, I can't do anything until I get home. I need a fake passport. Can you get me one? You must have contacts.'

'Whoa, hang on, girl! Sorry, Mandy. I can't do that. You know I want to help. But it goes against everything I stand for. If anybody found out, I'd be kicked out of the ABA.'

'The what?'

'The American Bar Association. I sit on several boards. You need to be patient. God will find a way for you to get back home.'

'I can't wait for God!'

I thumped the table with my fist, so hard, Scottie's tea spilt over the side of the glass mug. Storming back inside the condo, I threw myself down on my bed after slamming the door shut behind me.

I lay there, wondering where the hell I was going to get a passport. Then I had an idea. I'd read an article in the local rag that Scottie had brought home about the Mafia, suggesting that 'Associates', as the paper called them, were buying expensive holiday homes in Naples to spend their leisure time away from their 'businesses' in Miami. If I could find one with the right contacts, someone with balls, not like Scottie, surely they'd be happy to help me for a wad of Scottie's cash? It wouldn't leave much for the investigation, but at least I'd be home.

I reckoned the most likely place to meet one of these guys would be in a busy, local bar.

Later that morning, I strode downtown, a mile from the Naples Bay Resort, wearing clothes lent to me by Jean. I visited several coffee shops and asked them which were the liveliest bars and restaurants in Naples. Several came up with the same name: Brad's Bar at Wiggins Pass, a few miles up the coast. While I was downtown, I bought a few clothes and cosmetics with the money Scottie lent me.

As soon as I returned to Scottie's condo, I changed and applied the make-up. I began to look something like my old self. The swelling on my nose and lips had reduced. Looking in the mirror, I didn't look far off my best.

I apologised to Scottie for being angry with him. He'd been thinking about our falling out, too. 'Look, Mandy, I'll still lend you the money, OK? And you can stay in a condo we own uptown. It's vacant at the moment; we're between renters. You can stay for as long as you need.'

'Oh, thanks, Scottie. You're so kind.' I hugged him close. However, when I told him about my plan to get a job at Brad's Bar, he didn't like the idea. Said it attracted a dubious clientele. It sounded exactly what I needed.

I took a taxi for the four-mile trip north to the beachside bar that afternoon. I went inside and asked a server if I could speak to the manager.

'Mario? Sure. I'll get him.'

When he arrived, I took a risk in giving him my real name. Mike would never think of finding me working in a bar. Putting on my sweetest of smiles, I introduced myself and said, 'Hi. I hear you're looking for staff.'

Mario replied, 'Have you worked in bars before?'

'Oh, yes. Back in the UK, I worked in loads of pubs.' I lied, but had plenty of experience on the other side of the bar. How hard can it be?

I fine-tuned my English accent sensing Mario's growing interest in me as we talked. He hired me as a greeter/server and showed me around. He said, 'The money's shit, but you'll earn a bunch of tips, especially if you wear something sexy. Can you start this evening?'

'Yes. That's great.'

'OK. Be here around three-thirty. Happy Hour starts at four. I'll get one of the girls to familiarise you with how we work. Most of the diners are done by seven-thirty. Then the bar gets going.'

I spent an enjoyable afternoon downtown spending more of the money Scottie lent me. I bought skimpy tops, and mini-skirts and the highest high heels possible. A growing sense of excitement gripped me, like an actress making her stage debut.

I arrived at the bar looking every inch a nightclub hostess. The gleam in Mario's eyes told me he approved. He introduced me to Lisa, a smiley, vivacious, vanilla-blonde with chestnut eyes, the same colour as mine. He looked at me, then at Lisa and back to me. 'Gee, you two look so alike. We stared at each other for a moment. He was right. Apart from our hair; she wore a blonde bob, mine was longer, brown and layered. I noticed, with satisfaction, that I was at least a dress size smaller and maybe two inches taller. Later, I learnt she was a year younger.

'Hi, Mandy, let me show you everything there is to know about working at Brad's Bar.' Lisa spent the next quarter of an hour running through my role, which consisted of greeting customers with a smile, checking their reservations and showing diners to their tables. Once I'd started, many commented on my English accent as I peppered my conversations with *lovely* and *brilliant*. Then I'd hand over to Lisa who'd take their drinks and food orders. After the initial rush for dinner, we both helped serving drinks from the bar.

Lisa's infectious zest for life rubbed off on everyone she met, including me. We got two nights off a week. We'd clicked so well, she'd negotiated with the other staff so that we could spend them together, visiting other Naples nightspots. Lisa knew where we could let our hair down. More often than not, I crashed out in her tiny apartment in the early hours.

There, we exchanged our life stories over a margarita or two before going to bed. I told her about Mike throwing me off his cabin cruiser in the middle of the night, leaving me to drown into the Gulf of Mexico.

'I've never heard anything so heartless,' she said, 'He needs castrating. I'd do it myself if I ever had the chance.'

I told her my plan for revenge and the need of a fake passport. 'Do you possibly know anyone who might be able to fix it for me? Anyone at the bar, for example?'

'I don't. Sorry.' Lisa screwed up her face as an apology. 'I'll ask around if you like. Discreetly, of course. Men can be bastards, can't they?' She raised her glass, slightly spilling the contents. 'Here's to bastards everywhere. Piss on you all.' I repeated the toast as we slugged back the drink and fell into each other's arms laughing.

Then Lisa said, 'I've had man trouble, too. My boyfriend broke up with me six months ago. It's why I'm in Florida. We were in a relationship for two and a half years. Two and a half goddamn years! I thought we'd be together forever. Even talked about babies, discussed names. Maybe that's what put him off, I dunno. Anyway, he *dumped* me.'

'That's awful.'

'Yeah. *Awful*,' Lisa said, mimicking my English accent, something she often did in fun.

'I'm over it now. I think. Anyway, I hadn't seen much of the States, so I quit my boring job, packed my bags and started travelling, getting myself together. I want to have *fun.*' Lisa stood and did a jig.

Sometimes, Lisa fired out words like bullets from a machine gun. There were other times when she became moody and sullen. The reason for her mood swings became apparent after another evening's heavy partying. When I had to use her bathroom, I noticed on the side of the basin, a re-sealable, transparent, plastic pouch half-full of a white powder. I recognised it only too well: cocaine.

I'd used before, loving the sensation it gave me. But that was before I met Mike. He was dead against drugs of any kind, so, before we married, I secretly booked myself into a rehab centre. It was bloody hard going, but I did it. I haven't snorted anything since. It was the only good thing to come out of marrying Mike.

Picking up the pouch, I walked back to the living room as Lisa poured herself another glass of wine. Waving the bag under her nose, I said, 'How long have you been using this stuff?'

Lisa threw her head back and laughed. 'Forever! It's my best friend.' She put the wine bottle down and tried to snatch the bag from me. I raised it high above my head as she jumped up, trying to retrieve it.

After several attempts, she cried, 'Mandeee! Don't tease me. You saying you ain't a user?'

'No. Used to be.'

'Don't know whatcha missing. C'mon. This is good shit.'

After the boozy night we'd had and feeling heady, I weakened, anticipating the fantastic, familiar feeling of getting high.

I teased her again by holding the pouch behind my back before letting her grab it. Lisa rushed past me back towards the bathroom. I followed and peered over her shoulder as she tipped out some of the powder onto a mirror she retrieved from the vanity unit.

I watched her reach inside a cupboard under the sink for a safety razor which she used to cut the powder into two short lines. Judging by her technique, she'd had plenty of practice. She took a dollar bill from the back pocket of her jeans, rolled it into a tube and snorted one of the lines, throwing her head back and closing her eyes as the drug took effect.

'Here, your turn.' She stepped aside. As I hadn't used for a while, the powder caused my sinuses to burn and I tasted the familiar chemical tang in my mouth. Then the rush – so powerful, I felt invincible. It beat alcohol hands down.

When we returned to the living room, Lisa turned on the radio and tuned into a reggae music station. She grabbed my hands, and we began dancing and singing to Bob Marley's *No Woman, No Cry* at the top of our voices. After that, drug-taking became a ritual on our evenings off, snorting a line or two every night before going out. Lisa must have spent all the money she earned at the bar on her habit.

***

On one of our nights off, Lisa took me to a karaoke bar, The Yen, at the Mercato Center, a few blocks from her apartment. We arrived around nine o'clock on a typically sultry evening. The Center heaved with young people enjoying themselves in a frenetic hubbub of brightly-lit, flashy restaurants, bars, and shops. Ferraris, McLarens, Bentleys and Porsches lined the streets. Each establishment's music competed with each other; a grown-up's playground for rich kids to hang out.

As we pushed past the crowd of people cheering the latest singer at the karaoke bar, Lisa shouted over the din, 'I love this place. There's a hot guy I fancy, Doug. I met him here a month ago. He's been working upstate for the last two weeks, but he's back soon. He's good at karaoke, too.'

'Not all men are bastards, then?' I shouted back at her. Lisa giggled.

On that first night, I surprised her by taking the microphone and belting out a Whitney Houston number. She sat, open-mouthed, glass in hand, egging me on. Everyone cheered when I finished.

My mother had a beautiful singing voice. As a small kid, I remember her entertaining the family at every opportunity. Made me proud of her. She used to say, *'If you can sing, you'll always be admired.'* She sent me to singing lessons from the age of seven. I've loved an audience ever since.

Mike hated me singing in public. Especially after we got married. He'd snarl afterwards, 'You always have to be the centre of attention, don't you?' I didn't care. If I wanted to sing in front of an audience, I would.

The following evening, as we finished our shift at Brad's Bar, Lisa turned to me. 'Doug's back! We'll see him tomorrow night at the Yen. He's got a fab voice – sings Country n' Western. You know, Johnny Cash an' all that. Can't believe I missed him so much.'

'You're going soft up here, Lisa,' I said, tapping the side of her head.

'You wait 'till you see him.'

***

As we arrived at the crowded Yen, an Elvis impersonator, giving his all, swivelled his hips and curled his lips just like 'The King', much to the delight of the screeching females. Lisa looked around and headed for the bar, stacked two deep. She'd spotted Doug, wearing a white Stetson, sitting on a stool drinking at the counter with one of his buddies.

She fought her way forward with me in her wake and tapped Doug on the shoulder. He turned, eased his six-foot-plus frame off his stool, hugged her and pecked her on the cheek just as Elvis finished.

Lisa turned to me. 'This is Doug. I mentioned him, remember?' She turned back to him and said, 'This is Mandy.' I looked up into his eyes. He removed his Stetson with a grand gesture, revealing a thick mop of blond hair.

'Hi, Mandy. Good to meet ya. Lisa's told you all the good shit about me, I hope?' His deep baritone voice could melt chocolate from fifty yards. He thrust out his hand, and I shook it, holding his gaze. I could see why Lisa had missed him.

She smiled. 'Mandy does an awesome Whitney. I expect you'll hear her later.'

Doug undressed me with his eyes, clearly excited to meet me. Still staring, he said, 'Does she? Can't wait to hear it. Maybe we could do a duet later. What d'ya say?'

'Love to,' I said, imagining what he'd be like in bed.

I grinned back at him and became aware that the smile on Lisa's face had evaporated.

• ▲ •

CHAPTER FIVE

Flood's flight touched down at Heathrow at 07.55, spot on time. He'd been away exactly one week. Despite the nine-hour flight and the four-hour time difference, he felt good. He'd always had a knack of being able to sleep anywhere, anytime. Laura often teased him about his twenty-minute 'power naps', as he insisted on calling them.

When Flood reached the Arrivals Hall, he spotted Laura's smiling face. Heading towards her, he returned her smile, kissed her on the lips and hugged her tightly. He whispered, 'I missed you, Laura.' He often thought that marrying her had been the best thing he'd ever done.

As they made their way to the car park, he sensed her unease. 'Is everything OK?' he asked.

'Sorry, Andy. I was going to wait until we got to the car. I've got terrible news, I'm afraid. I hardly slept a wink all night worrying about it. It's about your daughter. Gemma's been arrested.'

Flood stopped and turned to face Laura. 'Arrested? What for?'

'I don't know how to tell you this.'

'Laura, for God's sake! What's happened?'

'Late last night, she called me from Southampton Police Station. She told me she'd stabbed Simon with a carving knife in a pub they used to visit. He's in the General Hospital Intensive Care Unit. As you can imagine, she's beside herself.'

'Christ! Why would she stab her husband, for God's sake? What was she thinking? They've only been married a couple of months.'

'I spoke to a DS Potts. He said it happened in a pub near the docks, the Blue Anchor. She made an initial statement saying that Simon groped her outside the ladies' loo and she reacted, pushing him away, but he came after her again. She drew a knife she had tucked down inside her boot and lashed out in self-defence, stabbing him in the chest.' Flood stopped walking, bowed his head and slowly shook it from side to side.

'I can hardly believe what you're saying! What on earth was she doing carrying a knife?'

'I've no idea.'

They started walking again. As they reached Laura's car, Flood said, 'Has she been charged?'

'No. Not yet. Potts told me they're still investigating the circumstances. I knew you'd want to call him. I've got his direct number.'

'Were there any eyewitnesses?'

'None, so far. Potts said they've put out an appeal.'

'I'll call him from the car.'

As Flood sat in the passenger seat, his mind flashed back, as it often did where Gemma was concerned. She'd never held down a 'proper' job. Her intense mood swings and erratic nature caused her difficulty in maintaining relationships, mainly because she didn't trust anybody – especially men. Therapists had diagnosed borderline personality disorder.

When she was 'up', she could be a joy to be with: bubbly, effervescent and charismatic. But the 'lows' were the opposite: dark, moody and petulant.

Gemma married Simon Saltus after a whirlwind romance. Flood and Laura remembered how lovely she looked on her wedding day. His heart had swelled, seeing he look so happy and beautiful after years of heartache. They hoped Simon would bring stability and joy to her life.

Before they'd married, Flood checked Simon's background. He couldn't help it. Being suspicious was embedded in his DNA. He found nothing untoward – a thirty-two-year-old, well-educated director of an advertising company based in the outskirts of Southampton. He didn't have so much as a speeding ticket to his name. Flood and Laura's only contact with Simon's parents was at the registry office wedding and afterwards at the reception.

Clipping on his seat belt, he said, 'I still feel guilty about what happened to the girls when they were so young knowing

Gemma never got over being abducted and tormented by lowlife arseholes after I was responsible for putting away their leader.' He gazed out of the window as his stomach cramped at the recollection; a familiar feeling whenever he thought about what had happened.

As Laura negotiated the early morning traffic towards Southampton, she said, 'You shouldn't blame yourself, Andy. You were only doing your job.' She passed her mobile to Flood. 'Here. Call Potts. I saved his direct line in my list of contacts.'

'Thanks, Laura.' Potts answered on the first ring. Flood turned up the speaker so that Laura could hear. After introducing himself, he asked, 'How is Gemma?'

'Fragile, I'd say.'

'Do you know about her mental health issues?'

'Yes. Gemma's told us. She's not in a good place. We've asked a psychiatrist to assess her condition.'

'What are the chances of bail?'

'Not good. It depends on the charge. We're cracking down hard on people who carry knives. The number of stabbings in Southampton has doubled in the last five years.'

'How is Simon doing?'

'The last we heard, it's touch and go whether he'll survive. We've got an officer at the ICU. He's keeping us informed.'

Flood looked across at Laura and mouthed, *Ugh!* before saying, 'OK. We're on our way down to the station.'

'Ask for me. I'll update you.'

Flood ended the call and turned to Laura. 'Can you believe Gemma's capable of stabbing Simon?'

'She's still mixed up. What happened to her all those years ago was unforgivable. It was a lot to take on board for a young girl.' Laura changed the subject. It was a sore point with Flood. 'I know it's difficult to think about anything else, but what else did you discover in Naples?'

Flood updated her then asked, 'Have you heard whether the police have made progress?'

'There's nothing in the papers. An accidental death doesn't excite the media as much as a murder case. The police only know half the story. Are you going to tell them the other half?'

'I've got to. It changes everything.'

***

They walked into the deserted reception area of the police station and asked a uniformed officer to see DS Potts. Flood handed over his card saying, 'He's expecting us.'

Potts, solidly-built, the wrong side of forty and with a receding hairline, arrived after a few minutes. He introduced himself and showed Flood and Laura into an interview room off the reception area where they sat around a table.

Flood asked, 'Can you tell us any more about what happened?'

'Nothing that I haven't already told you both. The investigation is ongoing. We need to get your daughter's full account but can't formerly interview her until the psychiatrist gives us the go-ahead.'

'What's the latest on Simon's condition?'

'We received a report an hour ago saying there'd been no change. He might make it, he might not.'

Potts looked intensely at Flood's face. 'You look familiar. You were one of us once, weren't you? Based here in Southampton?'

'Yes. You're talking about a long time ago.'

Potts looked pleased with himself. 'I thought so. I remember, I was starting out as a constable. You were a DI here in Southampton before you moved to the Met.'

'You've got a good memory.'

Laura asked Potts, 'Look, is there anything we can do for Gemma?'

Potts shook his head. 'You know the rules. You won't be able to see her until she's charged and remanded. I suggest you get her a lawyer, unless, of course, you want to use the duty solicitor.'

Flood resisted the urge to run out of the interview room, find Gemma, storm out of the police station and take her home. She wouldn't be comfortable being interrogated and banged up in a cell.

Instead he said, 'Thanks. Can I talk to you about something else? Who's investigating the Lisa Black case?'

'You mean the woman who fell from the hotel balcony about two weeks ago?'

'Yes. That's the one.'

'Why do you want to know?'

'I have some information about the incident.'

'OK. It's DI Ashford. If you stay here, I'll go and tell him.'

After Potts left, Flood turned to Laura. 'You realise Gemma could be charged with murder if Simon dies. That's a minimum of fourteen years inside.' He let out a sigh. 'It doesn't bear thinking about.'

'Yes, but we don't know the whole story, do we?'

'I know. I know.'

Flood slumped forward and placed his head in his hands.

Laura said, 'We won't be able to see Gemma today. There's not much point in me staying, is there? Unless you want me to?'

'No. That's fine.'

'OK. If you're sure. I've got a meeting at the lab later, so that would suit me. Call me if you need picking up later.' She leant across and kissed Flood on the cheek before leaving.

Within a few minutes, a uniformed officer arrived and led Flood to DI Ashford's office on the first floor. When he entered, Ashford stood and offered a hand over his desk covered in files.

He wore a long-sleeved, white shirt and a loosely-knotted, dark blue tie which hung around his neck emphasising his slim physique. Flood put him at no more than forty. Even so, the dubious joy of being a senior police officer showed in his dull eyes. Sixteen-hour shifts with a never-ending number of cases arriving on your desk had that effect, Flood recalled. At least as a private investigator, he could pick and choose the ones he needed to give him a good living.

As they sat, Ashford said, 'I understand you have information about the Lisa Black accident?' His superior tone grated with Flood.

'You're still convinced it was an accident?'

'Unless I have hard evidence proving otherwise, yes.'

Flood began by telling him about Mandy's visit posing as Lisa Black and claiming that her husband had dumped her overboard in the Gulf of Mexico. And about her belief that her husband had killed his first wife.

Ashford, who'd been making notes, stopped. Placing his pen down on the desk and asked, 'Why didn't she go to the US police or the British Embassy?'

'Because she was worried that if her husband knew she'd survived, he'd come after her again. She wanted him to believe that she'd drowned. That's why she used the name Lisa Black as her alias. She wanted to get revenge by hiring me to investigate her husband, prove her allegation. I've got a tape of the conversation.'

Ashford picked up his pen and scribbled another note as Flood continued. 'I didn't buy her story at the time, so I declined the job. But when I heard about her death, I felt guilty that I hadn't taken her seriously. That's why I went to Florida to interview the couple Mandy said had rescued her. Find out if she'd told me the truth.'

'And?'

'I traced them. They confirmed her story. So the victim is not Lisa Black. It's Mandy Bradshaw. I discovered that they worked together, became friends and looked alike. I believe Mandy travelled to the UK using Lisa's passport. I don't know how she got it.'

As Flood spoke, he realised how ridiculous the story sounded. Ashford pursed his thin lips tightly together causing then to almost disappear into his face. He said in a supercilious tone, 'So you think the woman in the hotel room is not Lisa Black?'

'I know it sounds crazy, but listen to me. I visited Lisa Black's apartment in Naples, Florida. The caretaker told me he hadn't seen her for nearly a month. She'd left most of her clothes, and posted nothing on social media since. I also spoke to the manager of the beach bar where Mandy and Lisa worked. He told me he got a text from Lisa's mobile saying neither of them was coming back to work. They were going travelling. I think it was Mandy who sent the text from Lisa's mobile.'

Ashford flicked over several pages in a file on his desk and stopped at one. 'We checked the airlines. A Lisa Black flew into the UK on 26th February on a BA flight. We found her passport, driving licence and seven thousand dollars in her purse and Class A drugs in the hotel room safe. The forensic team crawled all over the place and sent a report to the coroner.' He flicked over another page.

'We interviewed the hotel employees and guests in the rooms adjacent to Lisa's. We also checked the hotel's CCTV. Unfortunately, it's pretty crap. Not much coverage and the low resolution and lighting makes recognising faces impossible. There's nothing to suggest foul play.' Ashford folded his arms and leaned back in his chair. 'There's no doubt in my mind that the woman who fell from the hotel room is Lisa Black.'

'I'm saying it's Mandy Bradshaw.'

'You can *say* what you like.'

Flood fought to control his anger at Ashford's intransigence. 'There's something else you should know. I spoke to Lisa's brother, Chris, based in Wisconsin. Given what I'd found out about his sister, I suggested he report Lisa as a missing person to the Naples, Florida police.'

Ashford spoke slowly, as if addressing a three-year-old. 'She went *missing* because she travelled to the UK, stayed at the Sturridge Hotel and fell from the balcony, off her head with drugs and booze. We've passed Lisa's details to the American Embassy so they can inform her next-of-kin and handle the funeral arrangements when her body is released.'

Flood shook his head. 'There's just too much surrounding this case to assume that Mandy died accidentally. You need to interview her husband. I've got the address. It's in Hamble, twenty minutes away. Ask him about what happened to his first wife. It would only take a morning of your time.'

Ashford raised his eyes. 'I've told you, there's nothing to suggest that the victim is anyone other than Lisa Black.'

A thought struck Flood. 'Have you discovered her mobile phone? Checked her calls, texts?'

'No. We haven't.'

'Isn't that odd?'

'I'm confident there'll be a valid reason for it not being in her room.'

'What did the initial post mortem show?'

Ashford shrugged. 'Everything you'd expect from a fall from a sixth floor. She had cranial-cerebral trauma to her head, a punctured lung and broken bones. The pathologist found alcohol and drugs in her system. We're waiting for the full toxicology report, but we found a couple of empty wine bottles and a small stash of cocaine in her hotel room. It all points to her being "coked up" and delusional, which led to her losing her balance and falling. I'm confident the final report will confirm this is the most likely explanation.'

Flood opened both his arms, pleading with Ashford. 'C'mon. Won't you at least investigate the possibility that it's Mandy Bradshaw's body in the morgue? It's easy to check. You could contact the US authorities, get Lisa's dental records. I can give you her brother's contact details. He'll know Lisa's dentist. It's a couple of phone calls, take no time at all. Or if that's too much to ask, check out Mandy's dental records. She probably used a dentist in Hamble.'

Ashford leant forward again. 'I'll say this, you've been thorough. DS Potts tells me you were once one of us. Bit of a local hero, I hear. Went on to serve with distinction in the Met.'

Flood forced himself not to react to Ashford's condescending tone. 'Yes. I started here as a rookie PC, made it to DCI and transferred to the Met twenty years ago.'

'Well, things are a bit different from when you were in the Force. We don't have the resources to follow up half-baked hypotheses.'

Flood glared at Ashford. 'You're making a big mistake.'

'I don't think so. It's pretty clear cut to me.'

'So you won't mind if I follow up this case then?'

'Who's paying you?'

'No one.' Flood stood and leant towards Ashford. 'This is personal.' They eyed each other like professional boxers at the weigh-in before Flood strode out of the room.

CHAPTER SIX

MANDY
EIGHT WEEKS EARLIER

The first time me and Doug sang a duet at the karaoke bar, the customers went wild. I'd not experienced anything like it. They sensed the intense chemistry between us.

Doug suggested adding more songs to my repertoire. He sent me a playlist together with notes about how to synchronise our voices. I devoured them, couldn't wait to meet up and harmonise with him.

On karaoke nights, we poured our hearts out to each other, singing romantic love songs. When Doug sang, *I Walk the Line,* by Johnny Cash, and reached the lyrics about his lover being on his mind every day and night, he made a point of staring at me. Sitting on a barstool knocking back margaritas, I stared back with my *come to bed* eyes. Mike would have been incandescent with rage. Now I could enjoy myself and flirt with any man I fancied.

I teased Doug after a particularly boozy evening by singing Whitney Houston's, *Saving All My Love for You.* Purring the words about making love the whole night through, I looked at Doug the entire time. Out of the corner of my eye, I spotted Lisa scowling.

As we all left the bar in the early hours, Lisa confronted Doug. 'Suppose you want to take *Mandy* home tonight?' she whined.

'Don't be silly, honey. Why would I do that when I've got you?' Doug, still wearing his Stetson, tried scooping her towards him.

Lisa resisted, and pushed him away. Jabbing a finger at him, she yelled,

'You've spent more time with Mandy than me in the last few nights. Admit it; you fancy her, don't you?'

Doug smiled and spread his arms out wide. 'No. It's only an act for the punters.'

'Lisa, Doug's right,' I said. 'There's nothing else going on, I assure you.'

Lisa mimicked my English accent, saying '*I assure you.*' Reverting to normal, she said. 'You can *assure* me of nothing.' She turned away and stomped off in the direction of her condo, a block away.

Doug shouted after her, 'C'mon, Lisa. Don't be like that.' She turned and faced him. 'Screw you, Doug. If you want her, you can have her.' She began running, her high heels clicking on the sidewalk.

I shouted after her, 'Come back, Lisa!' Turning to Doug, I said, 'I'd better go after her.'

He gave me a cheesy grin. 'Don't bother with her. Come back to my place.'

Tempting though it was, I said, 'I can't,' and ran as fast as I could, catching up with Lisa as she reached the front door.

'Please don't be upset, Lisa. Doug loves you. He told me so,' I lied.

Ignoring me, she turned the key in the lock and angrily kicked the door open. I followed her inside. She made straight for the bathroom, locking the door behind her. I hammered on it.

'Lisa. Listen to me. What can I say? Nothing's going on between me and Doug. We sing together, that's all. I don't want to lose you as a friend. We're good for each other. Please... Let's talk.'

'Piss off!'

'I'm not leaving until we sort this out.' I walked into the sitting room and sat on a chair next to a marble coffee table.

After a few minutes, she emerged from the bathroom, a trace of white powder sticking to her nose. She stood in the doorway to the sitting room, crossed her arms and glared at me. 'How long have you been taking your panties off for Doug?'

I stood up to face her. 'What? What are you talking about? I'd never do that with a friend's boyfriend.' I had once, but wasn't about to admit it.

Lisa's eyes bore into mine. 'Don't lie to me, you bitch.'

'I'm *not* lying, I swear.'

'Yes, you are!' She rushed towards me and whacked my cheek with her open palm, yelling, 'You cow!' I fell back on the chair and put a hand to my face. My eardrums throbbed. Incensed, I staggered back to my feet and slapped her back with as much venom I could muster. Her cheek turned red. She stood motionless, her mouth wide open, surprised that I'd do such a thing.

She made a lunge to grab my hair with both hands, but lost her balance. Lurching forward, her left temple smashed against the corner of the unforgiving marble table with a sickening thud. She was out before she hit the floor.

Rolling her onto her back, I knelt beside her, not knowing what to do. I shrieked, 'Oh, my God! Lisa! Lisa!' She didn't respond. Blood began oozing from her nose and ears as well as from the gash on the side of her face. I rushed to the bathroom, grabbed a towel, and scrambled back. Kneeling beside her again, I pressed the towel firmly against her wound.

'Lisa. Lisa. Can you hear me? Open your eyes. Please.' Still no response. After five minutes, I realised she'd drawn her last breath. To make sure, I felt her pulse. Nothing. It had all happened so quickly.

In a blind panic, I took my mobile out of my bag to call 911. As my thumb hovered over the numbers, I thought, *what's the point?* The emergency services couldn't bring her back. I sat with the mobile in my hand for what seemed an age, trying to process what happened.

As my mind began to clear, another thought came to me. Didn't Scottie say things had a way of working themselves out? That I had to be patient? That God would find a way for me to get a passport so that I could return to the UK to deal with Mike? I switched off my mobile, a plan quickly forming in my mind.

I went to Lisa's bedroom. In the bottom of a wardrobe, I found an empty holdall which I filled with a few of her clothes. They'd be a bit loose on me, but they'd serve my purpose. In a drawer, I found Lisa's passport, flicked through it to make sure it was in date and placed it into the holdall.

Lisa had left her handbag in the bathroom. It held makeup, car keys, her mobile phone, her wallet containing a credit card and a hundred dollars in cash. I put the car keys in my pocket and dropped the handbag and its contents into the holdall to sort out later.

I opened the front door, peered into the pitch-black darkness to make sure no one was around, and then carried the holdall to Lisa's car. Her beaten-up silver Toyota Camry was parked thirty yards away out of sight of the other condos.

I clicked open the doors and threw the holdall onto the front passenger seat, got in the driver's side and parked outside Lisa's condo. Leaving the engine running, I got out of the car, opened the boot and went back inside.

Placing my arms under her armpits, I pulled her up until she was almost standing and dragged her body through the door towards the car. With considerable effort, I lifted her inside the boot and quietly closed it.

Returning to the condo, I picked up the towel I'd used to staunch the flow of blood from Lisa's wound and mopped up the blood on the carpet as best I could before turning off the lights and gently closing the front door.

When I reached the car, I tossed the bloody towel onto the rear passenger seat and drove the mile-and-a-half to the apartment Scottie had set up for me.

I wasn't going to leave behind what remained of his generous loan of ten thousand dollars.

I'd sobered up considerably by now, but knew I'd be over the legal limit to drive. Shooting red lights and speeding were off the menu.

At the apartment, I picked up Lisa's holdall from the rear passenger seat, carried it inside and dashed to my bedroom. Retrieving the brown envelope with the money in it, I scooped up an armful of underwear from a drawer and dumped everything into the bag. Now I had everything I needed.

Kicking off my high heels, I changed into a comfortable pair of trainers and dashed to the car, opened the front passenger door. I threw the holdall back onto the seat. Before heading the hundred miles to Miami airport. I glanced at the fuel gauge which showed three-quarters full, more than enough to get me there. The digital clock read 3.15 a.m. Given what I planned to do, I'd be at the airport by early afternoon.

**

As I drove, I processed the events of the last hour. My feelings veered from the horror of what had happened to Lisa, to the practicalities of putting my plan into action. I questioned how I could live with myself using my friend's death to my advantage. But then Lisa's demise wasn't my fault. I could do nothing to change it. I grew convinced that God, or fate, had intervened.

Another thought zinged through my mind: *did I have the balls to carry out the rest of my plan?* Then I recalled the terror of Mike dumping me overboard in the Gulf of Mexico, miles from anywhere, assuming I'd drown. *Too bloody right, I did.*

I chose the route, the Tamiami Trail, because it skirted the Everglades National Park, a wetlands and mangrove jungle renowned for its swamps, wildlife and conservation area. I'd learnt all this from one of the servers, Al, at The Rod and Gun Club in Everglades City where Mike had taken me for dinner on the night before he dumped me. Al told me he'd hiked on many of the trails through the swamps and said his favourite was the Fakahatchee State Park because of its remoteness. Sounded like the perfect place to dump a body.

Heading out of Naples, I shuddered when the car's headlights picked out signs along the road warning drivers to be aware of the dangers of encountering alligators and black panthers.

After three quarter-of-an-hour's driving on the deserted trail, I took a left turn signposted, 'Fakahatchee Preserve'. The tarmac soon gave way to a deeply-rutted dirt road. The undercarriage of the car slammed into the track every few yards, bouncing me up and down, almost knocking me out my seat.

I didn't want to risk being stranded if the suspension collapsed, so after three hundred yards, I pulled over to the edge of the track and parked.

I remembered that Lisa kept a pocket torch in the glove box. We'd used it once when she'd dropped her keys in the road outside her condo a week earlier. I turned it on, put it in my mouth and directed the beam ahead of me.

Walking around to the boot, I clicked it open in the inky-black darkness and recoiled in horror as the torchlight reflected Lisa's death stare; her wild eyes locked onto mine accusingly, as if judging my actions. Bloody spit had oozed from her gaping mouth.

I'd never seen a dead body before. My stomach clenched and I almost threw up. Sucking in a deep breath through my nose, I hauled her out, trying to avoid looking at her face. Her stiffening body made it difficult, but I managed to get her into an upright position by putting my arm around her waist and placing one of hers over my shoulder and holding it tightly with my other arm.

The mangrove hummed with the sounds of nocturnal wildlife. Tree frogs croaked, cicadas chirped, and the occasional swishing sound I heard above my head must have been bats. A pungent smell of damp earth, stagnant water and putrefying woodland caught in my nose.

Lugging Lisa through the thick bracken, taking care not to trip over the mangled tree roots crisscrossing each other, the unfamiliar noises rustled on both sides of me. I turned to look, the torch in my mouth making breathing more difficult. The beam highlighted trees looking like skeletons festooned with giant spiders' webs.

I fought hard to keep my emotions under control and staggered forward in a straight line. That way, I hoped I could easily find my way back to the car once I'd ditched Lisa's body.

My breathing became more erratic. A mixture of fear and exertion in the humid air caused dribbles of sweat to run down the sides of my face.

After fifty yards, a swamp halted my progress. Fearing alligators could be lying in wait, I said to myself, *this'll do,* and found a slight hollow in the ground to my left. I unwound Lisa's rigid body from mine and gently dropped it, face down, to avoid having to see her staring at me again. I couldn't bury her, I didn't have the tools, and the shallow tree roots would make it impossible to dig a grave.

Feeling an illogical need to cover her, I dragged several fallen cypress tree branches over her body, adding ferns yanked from the ground.

When I finished, I took the pocket torch out of my mouth and pointed it in front of me, carefully retracing my steps in the straight line I'd picked, hoping it would lead me back to the car.

As I got within twenty yards of safety, I heard a rasping bellow behind me. It sounded like a motorbike starting up. An alligator sensing blood, maybe? I quickened my pace.

Finally, I reached the car, got in, and slammed the door shut. I sat for a few seconds to regain my composure.

I couldn't believe what I'd just done; dragging my best friend's cold and stiff body through a mangrove swamp. The only thing that kept me sane was focussing on my plan.

Delving into the glove compartment again, I found some wet wipes, and used them to clean my mud-caked hands and trainers, then U-turned and re-joined the Tamiami Trail.

An hour later, I could hardly keep my eyes open. My head boomed as the buzz of the alcohol and drugs I'd consumed earlier wore off. I pulled into a deserted rest stop in darkness about twenty-five miles short of Miami. The café was closed. The digital clock on the dashboard read 5.15 a.m. I chose a parking space well away from the café, leant my head back on the headrest and drifted into a fitful sleep.

***

I awoke with a start to the sound of a persistent tapping at the driver's door. Trying to remember where I was, I fumbled to find the window switch. The glare of the sun didn't help. The brown uniform of a state trooper wearing sunglasses and a wide-brimmed Smokey Bear hat, peered through the window. My heart rate accelerated off the scale.

The officer drawled, 'Sorry to wake you, ma'am. Do you know that you've left your lights on? Hate for you to be stranded here with a flat battery.'

'Oh, thank you,' I muttered. With the trooper watching me, I switched off the lights and immediately turned the ignition key. The engine sprung into life. I uttered a silent prayer. 'Thanks, so much, sir. I'll be OK now.'

He touched the brim of his hat. 'No problem. You have a good day now.' He turned away and headed for the now open café with a sign outside saying, 'Early Bird Breakfasts. $4.99'.

Looking behind me as I reversed the car, I noticed the bloody towel I'd thrown onto the back seat. Thank God the trooper hadn't seen it.

Although desperate for a coffee and something to eat, I drove on into Miami. I didn't want to get into a conversation with law enforcement officers. There was a lot I had to do.

CHAPTER SEVEN

Flood took the train to get back to his office in Winchester. On the journey, he tried to understand why Mandy's fate had affected him so personally. Was it because in some ways, she reminded him of Gemma? They both needed his protection. There wasn't much he could do about Gemma but maybe he could get justice for Mandy.

When he reached his office, Flood called his friend, David Montgomery, known to everyone as Monty. Flood had known him for twenty years. He'd built a reputation as one of Winchester's finest solicitors. They'd met at the golf club Flood had joined when he returned to the city after resigning from the Met and struck up an immediate friendship. They'd worked together, too. Many of Flood's investigations involved taking legal advice which Monty supplied with his usual calm efficiency.

Several years previously, Flood shared the details of the abduction of his children and the murder of his first wife when they were young and the effect it had on them, especially Gemma. Monty had shown extraordinary empathy, having two daughters of his own. Flood regarded him as the closest thing he had to a best friend.

After explaining Gemma's situation, Monty said he'd immediately visit the police station and represent her during the interviews.

When Flood arrived home later that evening, the first thing he did was to have a shower and change his clothes. Just as he finished, Laura arrived home from the lab. She hung up her coat and entered the kitchen. Flood had poured out two large glasses of wine and handed one to Laura, saying, 'After the day we've had, I thought we needed this.'

She asked, 'How did it go at the police station?'

'Don't ask. Ashford's a cynical bastard. He won't take anything I say seriously. He needs to get his arse in gear and follow up my leads.'

'What did he say?'

'He's certain it's Lisa Black's body in the morgue.' He spat out, 'Prick!'

'Calm down, Andy. You always get like this when you don't get your own way. You need to consider Gemma's situation. Put Mandy's case on hold for now.'

'Gemma's constantly in my mind, but there's nothing I can do until she's been charged or released. Until then, I'll do what Ashford should be doing. I'll visit the Bradshaw's house tomorrow, question Michael Bradshaw, see what he has to say. Then I'll visit the Sturridge Hotel where Mandy died. Talk to the staff.'

'Can I do anything?'

'Yes, you can. Could you run a check on Angela Bradshaw's murder? That would be a great help.'

***

Driving the six miles to the Bradshaw's house in Hamble, Flood's mind constantly drifted back to Gemma, imagining her in a prison cell. Ever since her abduction, she'd hated confined places. It didn't help when she'd once been stuck in a lift with other children on a school visit to the Tate Modern Gallery on the South Bank. It took the engineers over an hour to rescue them.

He'd last visited Hamble years ago and forgotten its quaintness with its four pubs practically next to each other on the cobbled streets leading towards the harbour.

The Bradshaw's house was situated in Saunders Lane, which stretched for over a mile, parallel to the river. Flood found the house easily and parked fifty yards away in a lay-by.

He opened the boot, pulled on his coat and reached for a small holdall. It contained a lock-picking device, known in the trade as a bump key, and other useful items; latex gloves, a change of clothes, bottled water and snacks. He always carried it with him in his car as a force of habit. He slung it over his shoulder and made his way towards the house.

The gate, with 'River Landing' engraved in silver letters on granite stone, led to a modern property with white-rendered walls and tinted glass.

Fixed to the walls under the eaves, Flood spotted CCTV cameras covering the entrance and noticed the absence of the blinking red lights. *Odd,* he thought. Flood pressed the intercom next to the gate. No reply. He rang again. Still no reply.

He walked to a side gate, lifted the latch and pushed. To his surprise, it opened, revealing a landscaped garden with a path leading towards a decking area and a private jetty stretching into the Hamble River. A sleek *Sunseeker* cabin cruiser with its trademark navy-blue hull bobbed in the water.

He approached the rear of the house and, shielding his eyes with his hands, peeped through the windows trying to spot movement.

Looking up into the eaves at the back of the house, he noticed a BT alarm box connector, which he knew from experience, would be linked to a receiving centre. Again, no blinking lights.

Certain there was no one at home and thinking it suspicious that the side gate was open and CCTV seemingly turned off, he decided to break in, hoping to find clues to Bradshaw's whereabouts. Flood used the bump key from his holdall and waggled it in the lock. Within moments, he heard a satisfying click and pushed open the door which led in to a pristine, open-plan kitchen full of high-tech appliances with a large island worktop. Full-height windows showed off the stunning views of the riverfront.

He didn't hang about, knowing that if the alarm *was* live and not reset on entry, the receiving centre would contact the named key holders and send a text to the owner notifying them of the alarm going off. If it hadn't been reset in ten minutes, the centre would inform the police.

He swiftly checked out the four ground-floor bedrooms first. The wardrobes and drawers contained only women's clothes and shoes. In the en suite bathroom, he found the same thing; women's toiletries and a drawer full of jewellery.

Looking at his watch, he guessed he had five minutes remaining if the alarm was working. He sprinted up the steel spiral staircase to the south-facing living area situated on the first floor, designed to take advantage of the magnificent views of the river.

Flood checked the drawers of a desk in the corner of the room. Empty. No laptop either. With a minute remaining, he dashed down the stairs and left the house the same way he entered.

Moving round to the front, he peered through the small windows of the detached double garage. It was empty.

Cautiously retracing his steps, he dashed out into the lane and made his way back to his car.

He drove back towards the village, parked opposite the post office and entered. He said to the man behind the counter, 'I'm trying to trace a Michael Bradshaw. I've been to the house and can't get a reply. Do you know if he's on holiday?'

'Haven't seen Mike for a while. He normally pops in for some stamps about once a week.'

A female voice behind Flood said, 'Did you say Michael Bradshaw?' He turned and looked down on an elderly lady clutching several parcels she'd retrieved from her trolley.

'Yes. Do you know him?'

'I live a few houses down on the opposite side of the lane. It's funny you should be looking for him. A few weeks ago, my daughter was driving me home after a trip to visit my other daughter in London. It must have been about half-past ten by the time we got back. As we passed the Bradshaw's house, a white van raced out of the driveway and almost collided with us. My daughter had to swerve to avoid it. I thought it must be

Mike but then his BMW edged out of the driveway, driven by a woman.'

'I don't suppose you got the van's registration, did you?'

'My daughter did. She wanted to call the police, but I said I'd have a word with Mike in the morning.'

'Can you remember when this happened ... Mrs?'

'Crompton. Mrs Crompton.' A pained expression crossed her face. 'Yes. It was the anniversary of my late husband's death. God rest his soul. 7th March. That's why me and my daughters got together.'

'And you haven't seen either of the Bradshaw's since?'

'No. It's all a bit odd, now, come to think of it. The last time we spoke was in the corner shop a couple of months ago. Mike told me Mandy had left him. Apparently, she'd met someone else when they were travelling in America and wasn't coming back.'

The man behind the counter nodded in agreement. 'Yes. Mike told me much the same.'

Pieces of the jigsaw began to fall into place in Flood's mind.

***

His thoughts switched to Gemma again as he returned to his car. He couldn't get his head around why she felt compelled to not only carry a knife but to use it. And what if Simon died? He quickly pushed the idea to the back of his mind.

From Hamble, he drove to the Sturridge Hotel and made his way to the reception desk.

A squat, well-dressed, dark-haired man with designer stubble and in his mid-thirties, Flood guessed, asked, in a Latino accent, 'Can I help you?' According to the badge on his blazer, his name was Carlos.

'Yes. I'd like to talk to someone about one of your former guests, Lisa Black. She's the woman who fell from the balcony of one of your rooms two weeks ago. I'm a private investigator working on behalf of her family.' Flood handed over his card.

'I know the police are investigation what happened, but the family have employed me to make sure they haven't missed anything.'

Carlos studied Flood's card for a moment before looking up. 'Lisa Black? I remember her. A bad accident, yes?' He shook his head. 'The police were here most of the day. They inspected her room, took away her things and copied the hard disk of our CCTV system. There's nothing else I can tell you.'

'Is it possible to see Lisa's room?'

'I don't see why not.' Carlos reached under the counter and retrieved a key card, saying, 'It's not occupied. I'll get someone to cover me. Uno momento.' Picking up a phone, he made a brief call and seconds later, a bright-eyed, blonde girl, aged around twenty, appeared from a room behind the reception area.

'Can you cover for me? We shan't be long, Susan,' Carlos said, as he led the way to the lifts and pressed the button for the sixth floor.

Flood asked Carlos, 'Were you working that night?'

'Yes. We had a big party going on in the bar. I worked the night shift and left at seven in the morning. One of our guests found her after I'd gone home.'

The lift pinged as they arrived at the sixth floor. Carlos led the way down a corridor to the room. Flood asked, 'Is the only way into the rooms via the lifts from the reception area?'

'Yes, apart from the fire escape stairs which are alarmed.'

'You said the police copied your CCTV footage and took it away to examine. Which areas are covered?'

'The entrance doors to the hotel, the reception and the bar area.'

'Nothing covering the lifts or the corridors?'

'No. Boss says it costs too much to install. Here we are.' They'd stopped outside room 621. Placing the key card in the slot, Carlos pushed open the door.

'The Health and Safety people spent days here looking at all the balconies in the hotel. They say we can't book out any of these rooms until they've completed their report. The boss is not happy.' Carlos raised a hand in the air and rubbed his index finger and thumb together. 'He's losing money.'

Flood strolled around the room, his eyes darting into every nook and cranny. Sliding open the balcony door, he stepped outside. The sound of traffic thrummed beneath him. He looked across at the other balconies and wondered if anyone could have witnessed what happened. *Except,* he asked himself, *who'd be out there on a chilly evening at midnight in early March?*

Flood noticed Carlos watching him through the balcony windows with his arms crossed. He re-entered, closing the door behind him, surprised at the effectiveness of the glazing system.

He asked Carlos, 'Do you know if Lisa had visitors that night?'

'Only one that I noticed. A man followed her into the hotel lobby about 11.30 p.m. She didn't look happy to see him. I asked if everything was OK. She said, yes. He left but I noticed he came back a few minutes later and took the lift.'

Flood raised his eyebrows and showed Carlos the photo of Bradshaw he'd downloaded from his LinkedIn site. 'Is this the man?'

Carlos studied it with a puzzled look on his face. After a short while, he said, 'Si. I think it may be.'

'Did you see him leave?'

'No. I didn't.'

'So this man would have been captured on camera as he entered and left the hotel?'

'Yes, should be.'

'Did you tell the police about this?'

Carlos looked affronted. 'Yes. Of course I did.'

'Is there anything else you can tell me about Lisa Black?'

Carlos's dark eyes gleamed. 'She liked to chat. Is that what you say? Chat? She's pretty, too.' Flood imagined Mandy flirting with him as she'd done with him when they first met.

'Can I see the CCTV footage?'

Carlos screwed up his face and stroked his beard. 'I'll have to check with the boss.'

'That's fine. Can you call him?'

'OK. I'll do it when we go back down to reception.'

When they arrived, Carlos gestured to Flood to follow him into the back office. He called the owner and after a brief conversation, hung up and turned to Flood. 'He's happy for you to look at the CCTV. He wants this matter sorted so he can let out the rooms as soon as possible. Start making money.'

Carlos sat in front of a 42-inch monitor mounted on the back wall of the office. The screen showed four black and white, fixed-view sections: two covering the entrance via the revolving door, inside and outside, plus the reception desk and the bar area.

Flood asked, 'Can we start with a search of the entrance from say, 11.30 p.m. to 1.00 a.m. on the 8th March? That's less than two weeks ago. Hopefully, you still have it.'

Carlos typed the search parameters onto the keyboard as Flood looked over his shoulder. A minute later, he stopped and turned to face Flood. 'Here it is. I'd better get back to my reception desk. I'll leave you to go through it.'

He vacated the chair as Flood removed his jacket and took his place. He methodically worked through the tapes, starting with the entrance area, placing the photograph of Michael Bradshaw next to the monitor.

Carlos was right; it had been a busy night with many comings and goings. A mixture of poor lighting and grainy film resulted in murky, grey images. It proved to be impossible to clearly identify Bradshaw. Or anybody else for that matter.

CHAPTER EIGHT

That evening over dinner, Flood told Laura about his visits to the Bradshaw's house and the Sturridge Hotel. He closed with, 'It looks like Michael Bradshaw visited the hotel the night Mandy died. That's exactly what Mandy was afraid of. Now it looks like he's done a runner.'

'Surely Ashford must look at the case again?' Laura replied. 'When are you going to tell him what you discovered?'

'I'd like to get more information. Did you find out anything interesting about Angela Bradshaw?'

Laura referred to her notebook sitting on the kitchen top. 'I scrolled through the online Electoral Rolls for the past ten years. She lived in St Albans with Michael Bradshaw from 2009 to 2013. That's when she was murdered in her home. A guy called Sam Wharton is doing twenty years.'

'So Mandy was right about that.'

Laura continued. 'As you'd expect, there was stacks of local press coverage regarding her death. A local journalist, Nick Smithers, covered the case for the *Herts Advertiser.* He had some interesting ideas about the investigation. Thought you might want to talk to him. I've got his contact details. If you like we could go to St Albans tomorrow? It's my day off. We can have a look around and talk to the journo.'

'Sounds good. There's nothing we can do about Gemma for a couple of days. Monty told me the custody officer has refused her any visitors until she's been interviewed. I'll call him after that.'

Flood called Nick Smithers and arranged to meet him at the White Hart pub in St Albans at 12.30 p.m. the following day.

***

They found the charming 16th century inn on Holywell Hill, a short walk down from the high street. A man, aged around thirty-five, Flood guessed, wearing jeans and a T-shirt was sitting in a window seat typing on his laptop. Flood walked over to him. 'Nick Smithers?'

'Yep, that's me.' He stood, closed the lid and pushed the laptop to one side of the table. 'You must be Andy Flood. Good to meet you.' They shook hands as Flood introduced Laura.

Spotting Nick's half-empty pint glass, Flood asked, 'Can I top you up?'

'That would be good. I'll have another pint of Best please.' Nick drained the remainder of his pint and handed Flood the glass.

Once he'd returned to the table with drinks for all of them, Nick said, 'So, you want to know more about the Angela Bradshaw murder?' He reached for his fresh pint, took a sip and licked the foam from around his lips.

'Yes. We're following up a case involving her husband, Mike Bradshaw, which we believe may be linked. What can you tell us?'

'I remember the case well. It was the first one I reported on for the paper. On the face of it, the incident looked like a straight-forward burglary gone wrong. Hertfordshire Police believe Angela discovered the burglar, a taxi driver called Sam Wharton, and got a good look at his face. He panicked, suffocated her with a pillow on her bed. An eyewitness saw him driving his cab away from the crime scene shortly after the time of death. They arrested him the next day.'

Flood pursed his lips. 'Did he have any previous?'

'Yes. He was a tearaway when he was young. He'd been convicted a couple of times for burglary and spent six months in a Young Offenders' Institute. The judge allowed this to be disclosed to the jury.'

Laura asked, 'Any fingerprints linking him to the crime?'

'Nothing on the tools he'd allegedly used to gain entry. It looked as if either the user wore gloves or they'd been wiped clean. But Wharton's prints matched those on a rucksack found in the boot of his taxi. It contained a crowbar, drill and Angela's jewellery. His prints were also found on the front door of the house.'

Flood looked puzzled. 'An experienced burglar would surely have worn gloves. How did he plead at his trial?'

'Not guilty. Wharton's defence was that he was having an affair with Angela. That's the reason he gave for being there. He said her husband must have found out and set him up. Wharton claims that in a fit of jealousy, it was Mike Bradshaw who suffocated her with a pillow before he'd arrived.

'It came out in court that Angela and Mike were going through a tough time in their relationship. They'd decided on a trial separation. Bradshaw had moved out and lived with his brother. Angela remained in the marital home. Interestingly, Mike admitted in court that he'd kept a key and said he occasionally visited to collect some of his stuff.' Nick took another gulp of his beer before continuing.

'Wharton denied breaking into the house. His defence barrister suggested that it was possibly Michael Bradshaw who'd used the crowbar to force open a conservatory door at the back of the house earlier in the day. Then he pushed it back into place so that his wife wouldn't notice anything wrong. He could also have used the same crowbar to crank open a metal safe, located in the wardrobe of the master bedroom. That's where Angela's jewellery was kept.'

Laura asked, 'Did Wharton say how he gained entry?'

'He said that when he arrived, the house was in darkness apart from a subdued light in one of the bedrooms. He noticed the front door slightly ajar. He pushed it open, entered and went upstairs to the bedroom. In the dim lighting, he saw Angela's body sprawled on the bed. Drawers had been left open and the contents strewn all over the floor. As he got closer to Angela, he realised that she was dead. It must have been a hell of a shock if he's telling the truth.'

Laura stopped making notes. 'What happened next?' she asked.

'He panicked. Ran off. It didn't exactly help his case.'

'What about the time frame?' Flood asked. 'I assume Bradshaw had an alibi?'

'The pathologist couldn't pin down the precise time of death. All he could state with certainty was that Angela died between 8.00 p.m. and 9.00 p.m. Bradshaw's brother said Mike was with him at that time.'

Flood asked, 'Did the police discover any proof of the affair and whether Bradshaw knew about it?'

'No. Wharton said they took exceptional steps to cover it up. They never used social media or mobiles. The prosecution laid into Wharton saying that his defence was a feeble attempt to shift the blame away from him and onto Bradshaw.'

'How did Bradshaw come across in court?'

'He played the wronged husband for all the sympathy in the world. The jury were only out for two hours. They found Wharton guilty and he got twenty years. He still maintains he's innocent.'

'I'd like to see him. Do you recall the name of the solicitors who acted for him?'

'Lamont and Partners. Their offices are in the high street.'

Flood stood and said, 'Thanks, Nick. That's been most helpful.' Laura closed her notebook and asked, 'Before we go, do you think the jury got it right?'

'To be honest, I'm not so sure.'

If there was one thing that wound up Flood, it was the thought of someone being banged up for something they didn't do. He'd lost count of the cold cases which proved the point. He didn't know how he'd react if it ever happened to him. Probably top himself.

***

Flood and Laura found the solicitor's office easily. Flood handed his card to the receptionist and asked to speak to the solicitor who'd dealt with the 2013 Angela Bradshaw murder case.

'I'll check. It was before my time.' She scrolled through her computer and looked up. 'It was Mr Lamont himself.'

'Good. Is he in? Can we see him? We only need a few minutes of his time.'

'He's got clients with him at the moment.' She checked her computer and said, 'He hasn't got another appointment this afternoon. Shouldn't be long. Please take a seat. Can I get you a tea, coffee?' Flood and Laura both declined.

After twenty minutes, Craig Lamont's office door opened. He ushered a young couple towards the reception area, shook their hands and said goodbye.

The receptionist nodded towards Flood and Laura, saying to Lamont, 'These are private investigators wanting to talk to you about the Angela Bradshaw case.'

Flood's first impression was that Lamont was the least likely looking solicitor he'd met. His open-necked denim shirt, stonewashed chinos and thick, silver hair tied back in a short ponytail wouldn't have looked out of place at Woodstock.

Lamont turned to them. 'Now that's a case I'll never forget. Please come through to my office.'

Flood handed over his card and introduced Laura as Lamont gestured towards them to sit at his desk. Once seated, Flood outlined his interest in the case, starting with the visit from Mandy Bradshaw passing herself off as Lisa Black and about the conversation they'd had with the journalist, Nick Smithers.

'When Mandy came to see me, she told me that her husband had tried to drown her, and said he'd killed before.' Lamont leant forward with his eyes firmly fixed on Flood's, concentrating on what he was saying.

Flood carried on. 'I didn't take her seriously. Anyone might say that in the heat of the moment. However, Mandy has since died in suspicious circumstances. It seems too much of a coincidence that Bradshaw's first wife was murdered.'

Lamont sat back in his chair and nodded. 'I can see that. Have you spoken to the police?'

'Yes, we have. They don't believe us. What did you think about the case against Wharton?'

'The evidence provided by the prosecution was compelling. Our defence was that the reason he visited the house that night was because he was having an affair with Angela. Not because he was burgling the place. You could almost hear the judge and jury laughing it out of court.'

Laura interjected, 'Do *you* think he's guilty?'

Lamont didn't hesitate. 'Despite all the evidence against him, I believe he's innocent. I feel uneasy about the conviction. It's hard to explain why. It's a gut feeling. It didn't help that in court, Bradshaw came across as erudite, educated and played the victim brilliantly. Wharton's testimony was not convincing. That, and his criminal record, counted against him.'

'I'd like to hear Wharton's account first hand. Could you arrange for me to visit him?' Flood asked.

'He's in Pentonville Prison. I'd like to come with you. Make it a legal visit. That way, we can get a private interview room. It'll take me twenty-four hours to fix.'

'Thanks. I appreciate that. I'll meet you there, whenever you say.'

***

Laura drove back to Winchester, while Flood called Monty to check on the latest situation with Gemma. He turned up the speaker so that Laura could hear Monty talking.

'I thought you'd call,' he said. 'Gemma hasn't been interviewed yet. The police are seeking eyewitnesses. They want to be certain about Gemma's *intention*s. That'll affect the charge.'

'How is she?'

'Not good, Andy. She's feeling guilty for what's she's done. She's all over the place; jittery, anxious and tearful. The police doctor has given her something to calm her down. Sorry to tell you this, but I know you'd want the truth.'

Flood looked across at Laura who shot him an expression of sympathy.

'What's the latest on Simon?'

'Still hanging on the last I heard.' A silence hung between them as both men knew what was going through each other's mind.

Flood turned off his mobile and thumped the dashboard with a fist, making Laura jump. She concentrated on the road as Flood sat quietly brooding for the rest of the journey.

***

As soon as they arrived home, Flood went to his office to check his emails as Laura prepared dinner. An hour later, his mobile buzzed. Monty.

'It is bad news, I'm afraid. Simon Saltus died from his injuries. I'm sorry, Andy.'

'Shit! Have the police told Gemma?' Flood walked into the kitchen, looked at Laura, pointed at his mobile and mouthed, *Monty*. Laura stopped laying the table and stared at Flood, concerned at his expression.

Monty replied, 'Yes, they have. In the absence of an eyewitness confirming she was provoked, they're considering a murder charge. The psychiatrist has said that Gemma's now fit to be interviewed. It's taking place this evening. I'll call you as soon as I know more.'

Flood rang off, sat on a stool and closed his eyes so tightly, lines creased the sides of his face. He let out a sound like a wounded animal. Laura said 'What is it? I've never seen you like this.'

'Simon's dead. Gemma could be facing a murder charge.'

'Oh my God, no!' Laura said, turning off the hob.

'I had no idea Gemma was capable of using a knife on anyone, least of all Simon. She's more disturbed than we thought. And it's my fault. I should have protected her more.'

Laura's face tightened. 'You can't take all the blame, Andy. The last time we saw them together, she and Simon didn't seem that close. You'd think after only being married for a matter of weeks, there'd still be a spark between them. I didn't see it.'

'Why didn't you mention it?'

'I didn't want to worry you. You were so convinced that marrying Simon would be good for her.'

'Something must have triggered her action. But *killing* him? Bloody hell, Laura! What the hell caused her to do that?'

CHAPTER NINE

Flood was tempted to call Monty several times during the evening, images of the police interviewing Gemma flashing his mind. Eventually, Monty called him at 9.30 p.m.

'How did it go?' Flood asked.

'It was pretty tough. She can't believe Simon's dead. The most worrying thing is that she told the police they'd decided to separate a couple of weeks ago and that she'd taken it badly. Worse still, she admitted going to the pub as part of a hen party, armed with a knife, knowing Simon would be there. The police say there's a clear case for premeditation.'

'Did she say he provoked her?'

'The police asked her about that. She said he did, groping her breasts and forcing himself on her outside the pub's loos. Unfortunately, no one can confirm it. They've only got her side of the story.'

'So she hasn't been charged yet?'

'No. The file is with the Crown Prosecution Service. We should hear something soon. I'll call you the minute I hear their decision.'

Flood ended the call, slumped down onto his chair and sat motionless, thinking about how Gemma would cope spending the next fifteen years or so in prison. *And there's nothing I can do about it.*

***

The following morning after breakfast and feeling powerless to help Gemma, he called DI Ashford. 'I've got more information on the Lisa Black case. Can I come and see you?'

Ashford heaved a sigh. 'I've told you. Lisa Black's death was an accident. There's no evidence suggesting anything else.'

Flood snorted. 'Are you saying you haven't checked out dental records yet?'

'We don't need to. The case is closed.'

'You'll regret it if you don't investigate what I've discovered.'

'Are you threatening me?'

'No. I just happen to know more about this case than you do. For example, there's something on the hotel's CCTV you may have missed. Can you spare me half-an-hour?'

'How did you get access to it?'

'The hotel owner gave his permission.'

Ashford uttered another sigh before saying, 'OK. Come to the nick at 11.30 this morning.'

***

Flood entered Ashford's office and the DI stood. He nodded towards a detective sitting at another table with a TV monitor on top and said, 'This is DS Bobby Bridges.'

With his earnest expression, mop of dark hair and shirtsleeves tightly rolled up, Flood thought he looked like a younger version of himself. Bobby nodded towards Flood.

Ashford said, 'My team have been all over the CCTV footage. It's a crap system. It revealed nothing. What have you seen that's so important?'

'Something that proves the victim is not Lisa Black.'

Ashford glanced at DS Bridges and rolled his eyes. 'Let's humour Inspector Clouseau here.' Bridges smiled, delved into an evidence box lying next to the monitor on the table, pulled out a disk and placed it into the player.

'This is a copy of the CCTV footage. What do you want us to look at?' DS Bridges said, as Flood and Ashford stood behind him, looking over his shoulder.

Flood referred to his notebook. 'Can you fast forward to 11.00 p.m. on the 7th March? You'll see a young woman wearing an unusual blackberry-patterned raincoat entering through the glass doors of the hotel.'

69

Bridges peered at the screen and scrolled through the footage until he'd found the frame. 'OK. I've got it. What's so interesting?'

'The woman who came to my office wore the same raincoat when she visited me. Her name is Mandy Bradshaw.'

Ashford leant forward and stared at the screen. 'It looks like Lisa Black to me. We matched her face to the passport found in her room.'

'The woman who came to my office and the one staying at the hotel wearing the same patterned coat is one hell of a coincidence, isn't it? You can easily check. The raincoat was probably hanging up in her hotel room so should be in the evidence store.'

Ashford and Bridges exchanged a glance as Flood continued. 'You'll also remember that I told you the manager of the bar in Naples where the girls worked confirmed that Mandy and Lisa looked uncannily alike, except Mandy was a brunette and Lisa was blonde. To me, it's obvious; Mandy dyed her hair and somehow obtained Lisa's passport.'

Ashford turned to Bridges. 'What do you think, Bobby?' Bridges shrugged.

Flood groaned in exasperation. 'Look, you're not listening. I'm telling you that the victim isn't Lisa Black. If you won't follow up dental records, here's something else you can check. When Mandy came to see me, I noticed a tattoo showing a pair of entwined hearts on the back of her right hand. The hearts had the initial M in each one. Call the pathologist. I'm certain he'll confirm that the body in the morgue is Mandy Bradshaw.'

Bridges looked at Ashford and shrugged again as if to say, *he has a point.*

Before Ashford could reply, Flood continued. 'Carlos, the hotel reception manager, told the police that he saw a man arguing with Mandy in the lobby around 11.45 a.m. The man left, but returned a few minutes later and got into the lift. Carlos said he didn't see him leave. Unfortunately, there's no

CCTV coverage of the lifts so his statement can't be confirmed but this man *must* be a suspect.'

Ashford turned away from looking at the monitor and returned to his desk. 'If we arrested every man who visited a woman in a hotel, we wouldn't have enough cells available to hold them. And, in any case, identifying him from the crap CCTV system is impossible. DS Bridges had a team looking at over a hundred males entering or leaving the hotel between midnight and 3.00 a.m. We only had the reception manager's description to go on.'

Reaching inside his pocket, Flood retrieved a photo and placed it on the desk so both Bridges and Ashford could see. 'This is Michael Bradshaw. Mandy's husband. I showed Carlos this photo. He can't be certain, but he thinks he's the man. Mandy told me that if her husband found out she'd survived, he'd come after her again. It all makes sense.'

Before he could answer, Flood added, 'I've checked Bradshaw's background.'

Ashford stared at Flood and folded his arms. 'And what, *exactly*, did you discover?'

Flood explained the circumstances of Angela Bradshaw's death, adding, 'Hertfordshire Police carried out the murder investigation. As a result, a guy called Wharton is doing twenty years. In court, he claimed Michael Bradshaw had set him up. I spoke to a local journalist and Wharton's solicitor. They both have reservations about the conviction.'

Ashford unfolded his arms and glared at Flood. 'Reporters and legal eagles always take that line. It's what sells papers, gets the lawyers more fees.'

Flood placed both hands on Ashford's desk and thrust his head forward. 'I visited Bradshaw's house, had a good look around. I found nothing belonging to him except his boat, which is moored on the jetty. No car, clothing, laptop or mobile phone. Only women's clothes. I'd say he's done a runner.'

'Are you telling me you broke in?'

'That's not important. It's obvious he no longer lives there. Now, why do you think that might be?' Ashford, looking unsure, didn't answer. Flood had Ashford on the ropes. He went for the knockout blow.

'I asked some people in the village if they'd seen Bradshaw recently. A Mrs Crompton told me that around 10.30 p.m. on March 7th, she and her daughter were driving past the Bradshaw's house when she saw a white van emerge driving erratically. It almost hit them. She thought it was Bradshaw driving. A BMW followed, driven by a woman.

'Mrs Crompton's daughter wanted to report the driver of the van, so she memorised its number plate. You should speak to her, see if she still has the registration number of the van. It may show up something important.'

Ashford placed his elbows on the table and clasping his hands and fingers together as if about to pray, he said, 'Let's get this straight. You're suggesting that this ... this Mandy Bradshaw ... impersonated Lisa Black, used her passport to enter the UK and was murdered by her husband, who is now on the run?'

'Yes, and I'm *suggesting* you need to follow up all these lines of enquiry urgently.'

Ashford's silence and grim expression confirmed that Flood had finally sown a seed of doubt in the DI's mind.

Ashford turned to his detective sergeant. 'We need to cover our backsides. Contact the American Embassy. See if you can put a hold on the next of kin form we sent them. If Mr Flood is right, and I'm not saying he is, we'll look worse than stupid if they've contacted Lisa Black's family and told them she's dead.'

'OK, Boss. I'll get on to it right away.' Bridges nodded at Flood as he left the room.

Flood rammed home his advantage. 'I suggest you also speak to the Hertfordshire Police SIO who handled the Angela Bradshaw murder. Ask him to reopen the case.'

Ashford looked up at the ceiling, considering Flood's request. 'That's a big ask. I'll tell you what I'll do. I'll call the pathologist. OK? Get him to check for the tattoo. And I'll contact dentists within a twenty-mile radius of Hamble. See if they've got Mandy's records, get them checked, too. That's where you said she lived, wasn't it?'

'Yes. River Landing, Saunders Lane, Hamble.'

Ashford scribbled down the address. 'This'll prove who's right, you or me. If I'm satisfied that Lisa is Mandy, I'll interview her husband. In the meantime, leave the investigation to us.' Ashford paused before adding, 'I hear you've already got a lot on your plate. Sergeant Potts tells me your daughter is suspected of stabbing her husband.'

'Yes. She is.'

'I got a call from the Senior Investigating Officer. Potts must have told him about your police service and your involvement in this case. The SIO asked me to pass on a message. He made it abundantly clear that he doesn't want you to get involved in your daughter's case. You're biased. That could undermine his investigation.'

Flood knew he was right. He'd have issued the same warning in similar circumstances. *But it's not the SIO's daughter we're talking about.*

***

Flood had barely stepped inside the hallway of his house when he got a call from Monty. 'It's bad news, Andy. The police have charged Gemma with murder and possession of an offensive weapon.'

'What? Murder?' Flood slumped down onto the bottom stair. 'I can't believe Gemma would kill someone deliberately.'

'I know it's not something you needed to hear. The mental health team have sectioned her and taken her to the Psychiatric Intensive Care Unit at the Royal South Hants Hospital for her safety. They're concerned about the possibility of her doing something silly.'

'Can we see her?'

'Not for twenty-four hours. They'll carry out further tests to establish her current medical condition, see if she's capable of receiving visitors. After that, as she's technically on remand, you can visit her for up to three hours, two days a week.'

Flood ended the call feeling as if a ten-ton truck had run over him. The words *sectioned* and *on remand* tumbled in his mind.

After sitting on the bottom stair for several minutes, thinking about this latest development, he walked through to the kitchen where Laura was preparing supper. She looked up from her preparations.

Flood collapsed onto a kitchen stool and explained what Monty had said, finishing with, 'I can't imagine what Gemma's going through.'

Laura put down the knife she used for cutting up the vegetables. 'She's probably in the best place right now. If she were home with us, neither of you could handle it.'

She walked behind Flood and placed her hands on his shoulders and began massaging them. He moved his head back far enough to make eye contact.

'I don't know what I'd do without you, Laura.'

She leant forward and kissed his lips. 'We'll get through this, just like we've got through every other crisis in our lives.'

CHAPTER TEN

MANDY
FOUR WEEKS EARLIER

My throat felt like coarse sandpaper, and I'd not eaten anything for over twelve hours. I turned off the Tamiami Trail towards Doral, a Miami suburb, a couple of miles from the airport.

At the first shopping precinct, I parked and took out a top, jeans and fresh underwear from Lisa's holdall and packed them carefully into my bag together with Lisa's purse, credit card, passport, make-up and cell phone. I remembered to transfer the bloody towel from the rear seat to the boot.

Starving, I walked to a Denny's fast-food joint in the corner of the precinct and made my way to the restroom where I washed, changed clothes and renewed my make-up. Feeling better, I found a quiet table and a waitress took my order of omelette, fries and black coffee.

To explain our absence from the bar, I texted Mario, the manager, using Lisa's cell phone. *Mandy and I have decided to go travelling. U know what she's like. Sorry, won't be coming back to work.*

He replied, *That's great. Thanks for the notice.*

I couldn't resist texting back, *U don't have to be so sarcastic. U can keep the money you owe us.*

The food arrived, and I wolfed it down as the waitress refilled my mug. I paid with Lisa's credit card, scribbling 'L Black' on the receipt, copying her signature on the back of the card as best I could. The waitress barely glanced at it before stuffing it in a pocket of her apron. It amazed me that the most technologically advanced country in the world hadn't yet introduced chip and pin. Another lucky break.

I needed a hair salon and found one five doors down from Denny's. Two young Hispanic girls worked on customers while another with long, curly, raven-black hair, sat at the reception desk reading a magazine. She put down it down as I entered.

'I want this,' I said, running my fingers through my shoulder-length, mid-brown hair, 'to be shorter and blonde.' I made a chopping motion with my hands to demonstrate how much I wanted cut off. 'Can you do that?'

She nodded and handed me a folder containing a portfolio of styles and colours on beautiful, air-brushed, Caucasian models. 'You look through this. We do anything you want.'

I flicked through the folder and stopped at an elegantly-cut, blonde bob similar to Lisa's. Pointing to it, I said, 'This one. I want it the same colour, OK? How much will it cost?'

'Shouldn't be no more than a hundr'd and fifty dollars.'

'That's fine.'

By mid-afternoon, she'd finished. 'What d'ya think?' she said, moving a hand mirror behind and to each side of my head.

'Looks great.' I was delighted to see that I now bore an uncanny resemblance to Lisa's passport photo. I paid her in cash with a good tip.

I drove to one of the many airport car parks and used Lisa's credit card to gain entry. At the terminal, I booked an economy return ticket to London Heathrow leaving at 7.45 p.m., three hours' time. I'd worked out that my chances of getting through Border Control would be better if it looked like I planned to return to the USA.

I paid with Lisa's card again, hoping it had enough credit on it. If the airline had rejected the card, at least I had Scottie's cash on me.

Sitting at the departure gate, one question worried me: *What if the police found Lisa's body and identified her as the girl who worked in the beach bar in Naples?* Mario, the manager, would tell them about our friendship and show the police the texts I sent from Lisa's cell phone. They'd think that I'd murdered her, dumped her body and used her passport to get to the UK. I'd be toast.

My head ached, racking my brains to come up with a plausible explanation. I concluded that my only hope of achieving my plan rested on no one finding her body. The waiter at the restaurant in Everglades City told me the Fakahatchee State Park was a dangerous place and plenty of people had gone missing over the years. Their bodies had never been found. I hoped that was true.

My mind raced through the rest of my plan. When I got home, I'd exchange Scottie's dollars for sterling and use the money to get a private investigator to prove Mike had murdered his first wife. That would get him put away for a long time.

Then I'd apply for a replacement passport; claim that I'd lost the original. Once Mike was out of the way, I'd move back into our home in Hamble. It's in joint names. I'd insisted on it. He was so loved-up with me in the early days, he agreed. Later, I'd start divorce proceedings. Who wants to remain married to a convicted murderer? Under the circumstances, I'm sure I'd get a decent settlement. I'd look up a few ex-boyfriends, have some fun. Get my life back. I deserve it.

***

During the flight, a handsome American businessman sitting next to me tried to engage in conversation. The previous night's exertions had left me shattered, so I told him I needed to catch up my sleep. Pity. He looked like fun.

With an hour-and-a-half to touchdown, the smell of breakfast and coffee being served by the flight attendants brought me round. I visualised my next challenge; passing through UK Border Control and began to doubt myself. *Could I really pass myself off as Lisa?* Butterflies fluttered in my tummy.

Before we landed, I went to the toilet, used Lisa's make-up and brushed my hair. Then, I pulled her passport from my bag and compared her photo with my face in the mirror. *Pretty good likeness, I'd say.* It gave me confidence. I practised speaking with an American accent, drawing on my last six weeks' experience. The butterflies took a break.

After disembarking, I walked through the terminal with hundreds of other passengers. A sign directed EU passport holders towards automatic gates with no border officers. Another sign directed non-EU travellers, to a queue snaking back through the aisles. I turned to a fellow traveller I'd heard talking with an American accent. 'How come the Europeans don't have their passports checked by an officer?' I asked.

He drawled, 'EU countries use face recognition software. You look at a camera and place your passports into a machine. If they match, you're through. It'll be in use everywhere soon.' He added, 'We *foreigners* have to be checked in by an officer. They're bringing in fingerprint checks next year.' I hadn't given that level of security a thought. Another lucky break.

After twenty-five minutes shuffling through the aisles, I reached the front of the line. With clammy hands, I opened Lisa's passport to the photo page and handed it, together with the landing card, to the unsmiling officer. He picked up the passport and glanced at my face. The butterflies returned.

With a bored, monotone voice and steely eyes which locked onto mine, he asked questions, most of the answers to which were on the landing card. Trying to catch me out, I guessed.

'What is the purpose of your visit?'

Hoping my American accent didn't sound too false, I kept my answers brief. 'Visiting relations in the UK.'

He nodded. 'And where are you staying initially?'

'The Sturridge Hotel in Southampton.'

'For how long?'

'Four weeks.' He looked me directly in the eye and paused. *Oh, God. Did I say the right thing?*

'OK,' he said, as he stamped the passport with a three-month visitor visa. 'Have a good trip.'

I mouthed, 'Thank you,' hoping the officer didn't notice my sense of relief as I picked up the passport and hurried to the baggage reclaim area.

After collecting Lisa's holdall, I dropped it in a trolley and headed towards the exit. Once outside, I caught the National Express, and arrived in Southampton at lunchtime. I checked into the four-star Sturridge Hotel, which I'd booked online using Lisa's cell phone and her credit card, while waiting in the departures terminal of Miami airport.

A dark-haired, fit-looking, guy called Carlos checked me in. Looking me up and down, he said, with a Latino accent and a sickly smile, 'Welcome to the Sturridge, Madam. We hope you enjoy your stay.' He'd fiddled with his keyboard and added, 'I've upgraded your room to a suite. No extra cost. It's ready now.'

'That's kind of you,' I answered, returning his smile.

'I'll take luggage to your room. Please, you follow me.'

As we travelled in the lift to the sixth floor, he asked whether there was anything else he could help me with. I sensed him flirting with me. I declined. Although exceptionally good-looking, I found him too smarmy for my taste. And I had things to do.

When we arrived at the door to the suite, Carlos unlocked it with his master key card and ushered me into the room, dropping the holdall onto a rack. He showed me how the lights, air conditioning and TV remote worked. Then he opened the balcony door and insisted I take in the view. 'It's good, yes?' I agreed.

We returned to the room. He ogled me with suggestive brown eyes and repeated his offer. 'If you need *anything, anything* at all, you ask.' As he turned to leave, I rummaged inside my handbag and handed him a ten-dollar bill. He beamed and nodded his thanks.

I catnapped for a couple of hours and, feeling much better, spent time in the hotel's business centre, researching private investigators in the area. I settled on Andrew Flood, an ex-Metropolitan Police Detective Chief Inspector who had an office in Winchester, a twenty-minute train ride away. His website included impressive reviews and glowing police commendations. I called his office and asked for an appointment on the first available date. He could see me on Friday, two days' time.

●▲●

CHAPTER ELEVEN

Flood waited twenty-four hours before calling Monty again. 'I've *got* to see Gemma,' he said. 'She'll be in a hell of a state.'

'I'll call the hospital now, see what I can do.'

Fifteen minutes later, Monty called back. 'You're all set. Can you be at the hospital this afternoon at three o'clock?'

'No problem.'

'Good. Ask for Doctor Rogers. He's her Responsible Clinician, fancy name for a therapist. He'll update you. Then you'll be able to speak to Gemma.'

***

Flood checked in at the hospital and after being searched by a security guard, a nurse led him to the doctor's office at the end of a corridor. A series of doors with keypad entry led to the wards.

The nurse tapped on Doctor Rogers' office door and opened it. The doctor unfurled his white-coated, giant frame from his chair, smiled and shook Flood's hand. His brown, thick-rimmed, glasses, greying hair and moustache gave him the aura of a professor or a university don.

'Good to meet you, Mr Flood. Please take a seat. You must be worried about your daughter.'

'You could say that. How is she?'

'Considering the circumstances, not bad. I've had one session with her already. We're trying to find out *why* she did what she did. There would almost certainly have been a trigger. Right now, she has a pathological feeling of guilt, which is feeding her lack of self-worth. We're especially concerned about her self-harming and having suicidal thoughts.'

'That's what I'm afraid of.'

'She's under a high level of supervision. Someone's with her 24/7.'

Tapping a file on his desk, he added, 'I see from her records that Gemma's had a great deal of therapy to combat her borderline personality disorder. I'm sure you're aware of the symptoms: an inability to handle stress, dramatic mood swings, insecurity, and having intense but unstable relationships.'

Flood was only too well aware. He'd witnessed some of the symptoms first hand and her many setbacks after therapy. He'd always thought it a waste of time.

'Obviously, it hasn't worked, has it? What makes you think you can help her?'

'I can't give you any guarantees, but I'll be personally involved. We have an excellent track record here.'

'I'll need convincing.'

Holding up his palms towards Flood, Doctor Rogers said, 'I understand your scepticism.'

'It's nothing personal.'

'I'm sure it isn't.'

Doctor Rogers leant back in his chair. 'It would be helpful if you could describe *your* relationship with Gemma. Tell me more about her life right from childhood. I know a lot of it is in the file, but I'd like to get the family background into context. You were a police officer, weren't you?'

'A DCI in the Met.' Flood went on to tell him that that he had two daughters and described their early experiences, starting with the devastating hit and run killing of their mother by a gang intent on seeking revenge after he'd helped put away their leader.

'How old were they?'

'Pippa was three and Gemma, five. My mother looked after them while I carried on working. She died a couple of years ago, after the girls had left home. As if losing their mother wasn't bad enough, a vicious gang abducted and tortured them four years later. The gang wanted me to hand over incriminating evidence in exchange for the girls' release and threatened to kill them if I got the Met involved. I believed them, so dealt with it on my own. Not the best decision I've ever made.

'I found out where the gang were hiding and after a violent altercation, rescued the girls. The gang treated them badly; locked them up and shaved their heads. It must have been terrifying for them.' Flood's body shook with anger. More with himself than the gang.

He regained his composure and added, 'I *completely* underestimated the effects this would have on my daughters. I blame myself for what happened to them.' Flood's words caught in his throat. 'And now it's come to this.'

Doctor Rogers paused for a moment, allowing Flood to recover. 'Being abducted and tortured is possibly the worst thing that could happen to someone so young. I'm sorry to have to tell you that in my experience, most never fully recover. Especially without a mother to nurture and console them. For many, it's a life sentence of fear and insecurity.'

Flood wanted to run from the room. He didn't need to hear this. *My guilt is a life sentence too.*

'What about your other daughter? Pippa?' Doctor Rogers asked. 'How has she dealt with it?'

'She was always the feisty one, despite being younger. Pippa seemed to put it all behind her. She went to uni and got a good degree. Gemma struggled at school and left as soon as she could. She's had loads of jobs, working in bars, coffee shops that sort of thing.'

'What's her relationship like with her sister?'

'Not good. After what happened, they were never the same together. Gemma grew jealous about the way her younger sister dealt with it and Pippa thought Gemma was weak.'

'And how is *your* relationship with Pippa?'

Flood looked down at the floor and up again to meet Doctor Rogers' eyes. 'Non-existent. Pippa always accused me of favouring Gemma. We had a major falling out a few years ago. She emigrated to Australia and got married. We never hear from her and she never returns my calls or texts.'

Doctor Rogers scribbled more notes. 'And what about Gemma's other relationships?'

'She has a few girlfriends and had a succession of what I thought were totally unsuitable men. None of them lasted long. She got married only a couple of months ago after a short romance. My wife, Laura and I, were surprised but pleased; thought it might help her cope with her disorder. That didn't turn out too well, did it?' Doctor Rogers didn't reply.

Flood broke the silence and asked, 'What's next for Gemma?'

'We'll start by providing her with coping strategies until we think she's in a good enough place to be transferred to prison.' He tapped her file again. 'There's a history of alcohol and drug abuse which is not unusual in these cases. We'll address those issues, too. She's not the first person to go down that route.'

It didn't surprise Flood. He'd seen some of the effects but didn't regard her addiction as excessive. *Am I kidding myself?*

'But she stabbed her husband to death!' he said. 'That's not Gemma. Something else is going on in her mind.'

'I agree. We need to get to the bottom of it. She's in good hands here. I'll do my best to see her through this.' Flood, impressed by the doctor's sincerity, mouthed *Thank you.*

The doctor continued. 'One thing's for sure. She's going to need a lot of support from you, Mr Flood. From my initial chat with Gemma, it's clear that you're an important figure in her life.'

Flood was pleased. Many times, he thought he meant nothing to her. 'When can I see her?' he asked.

'Right now. I'll have one of the team bring Gemma through to a private room. I'll sort out some tea and biscuits.'

A nursing assistant showed Flood the way to a sparsely-furnished, brightly-lit room along the corridor from Doctor Roger's office. As he waited, he thought about his conversation with Doctor Rogers and concluded that if anyone can help her, he can.

Within a few minutes, an orderly arrived, carrying a pot of tea, two mugs and a plate of digestives. She left them on a table next to a vase of sweet-smelling flowers, smiled at Flood then left. Soon after, a nurse led Gemma into the room. 'Here we are,' she said. 'I'll leave you two to chat. When you've finished, press the buzzer next to the door and I'll come and collect her.'

Gemma stood still, arms by her side, looking down at the floor like a naughty schoolgirl. He stepped forward and hugged her. Gemma didn't reciprocate.

Flood couldn't disguise his look of concern at Gemma's appearance. Her normally flawless skin now stretched tautly over her pale, waxy complexion. The clothes she wore, hung loosely from her body. Her normally auburn, lustrous hair hung limply around her face. He felt a wrench in his stomach. He hated seeing her like this.

Flood noticed a bandage on her right hand. After ushering her to sit at the table, he sat opposite her.

'What happened to your hand, Gemma? Is it painful?'

Still avoiding looking at her father, she ran her good hand gingerly over the bandage and mumbled, 'It's OK. The knife didn't have a hilt. My hand must have slipped over the blade.' Gemma slowly raised her head and looked at Flood with cheerless eyes. 'I can't believe I've killed Simon.' She started shaking.

'Why did you do it, Gemma? We assumed everything was fine between you two.'

'It was, at first. Simon seemed to be the only man who understood me. We had a lot of fun together, but that all changed when we got hitched.'

Flood leant forward. 'Doctor Rogers told me you feel guilty about what you did and that you might do something stupid. Promise me you won't?'

Gemma shook her head then sat motionless, staring at the floor again. Flood reached across the table, reached for her good hand and squeezed it tightly.

'Laura and I love you. We're going to do everything we can to make sure you get through this. And the doctor says he's confident he can help you.'

Gemma slowly slid her hand away from Flood and stared at her father. 'Did he?'

'He's going to treat you himself.'

'He's got a hell of a job then. How's he going to sort out my shit life that's just got a whole lot shittier? Did you know that Simon and I had split up?'

'Yes, Monty told us. Why didn't you mention it? Maybe we could have helped.'

'There's nothing you could have done. It's me.' Gemma twisted a tissue in her hand into a tight knot. 'You know I can be pretty intense, full-on. I can't help it. Simon seemed to like that about me. But once we were married, he dominated my life and became brutally demanding. Especially, in the sex department. I don't want to go into details, Dad. It's too upsetting. We rowed almost every night. I don't think he realised what he'd let himself in for marrying me. We had one almighty bust-up a couple of weeks ago. He became incensed; called me a "fridge" and an "Ice Maiden" before kicking me out. Something else I managed to screw up.' Gemma bowed her head.

'You didn't screw up. This is down to Simon. You should have told us. We could have spoken to him.'

She looked up. 'It's not the sort of thing you discuss with your father and stepmother, is it? And if he found out I'd told you, I was fearful how he would retaliate.'

'Tell me what happened that night at the pub. Did you know Simon would be there?'

'He's always at the Blue Anchor. There's no way I'd avoid going there because of *him*. I went with some girlfriends on a hen do. I bumped into him outside the loos. He started harassing me. Here we go again. I thought. I lost it, pulled the knife out of my boot and lashed out in self-defence. He still wouldn't stop so I lashed out again. I wanted him to stop.'

'Did you notice anybody who might have witnessed him coming on to you?'

'Dad, stop it. You're interrogating me. I don't like it when you do that.'

'I'm sorry, Gemma. I'm trying to understand what happened, that's all. Let me ask one more question. Why in God's name were you carrying a knife?'

'It's my way of coping. After the way Simon treated me, it reinforced my fears about what men are capable of. I don't trust them.'

'How long have you been carrying it?'

'Since we separated, two weeks ago.'

'So you didn't go to the pub armed with a knife *specifically* to exact revenge on Simon?'

Gemma looked deeply into her father's eyes. 'I don't know what I was thinking. I was all over the place. I'm disgusting. My life is over.'

'You mustn't say that, Gemma. Laura and I are here to help.' Flood stood, walked around the table and put an arm around her shoulder. She brushed it off.

'I don't think I'm capable of living a *normal* life. I hoped getting married would be the answer. It wasn't.' She looked down at the floor.

'Listen to me, Gemma. If you carry on like this, you're facing fifteen to twenty years in jail. Is that what you want? Think about it. It's not a very nice place.'

Gemma stayed silent, shrugged, and looked around the room, anywhere but up at her father. A few seconds passed. Flood noticed a tear sliding down her cheek. She wiped it away with her sleeve. Like most fathers, he hated seeing his daughters cry. He wanted to scoop her up in his arms and whisk her away to somewhere safe.

'I don't know what to say, Dad. It was so humiliating at the police station. They removed my clothes for analysis and put me in overalls. Then they slapped on handcuffs, locked me up in a stinky cell and interrogated me for two days and nights. It reminded me of when Pippa and I were abducted.' She wiped her eyes with her sleeve again. 'And now I've *killed* my husband!'

The reference to her abduction fired up a raw nerve in Flood's mind.

He countered its effect by saying, 'You know you'll be having therapy while you're here?'

Gemma huffed. 'Yes. But you know what? I've had a gutful of it. Most of the shrinks had no idea what I went through. Who's to say this lot will be any better?'

Flood recognised the intensity in the expression on her face. She used it every time she threw down a challenge, usually with good reason. He recalled her frustrations with the psychologists who'd treated her in the past. She had a point.

Flood replied, 'We don't have a choice though, do we? Gemma, I know you must be going through hell, but you've got to trust these people. This could be the last chance we'll have to help you. Promise me you'll co-operate with Doctor Rogers and his team?'

'OK, Dad. I will. But how am I supposed to deal with stabbing my husband to death?'

Flood didn't have an answer, but said, 'We will get through this, princess.' She gave him a weak smile at the mention of his pet childhood name for her.

'I'll come back to see you as soon as I'm allowed. Probably in a couple of days.' Flood stood, put his arms around her and pulled her close to him. She barely responded. Then he pushed the bell to summon the nurse to take her back to the ward.

As Flood walked to his car, the familiar, overwhelming feeling of guilt stuck to him like Velcro. Then he remembered Doctor Rogers' words about how important he was to Gemma. A sliver of guilt evaporated.

***

When Flood arrived home, he went to his study and, with nothing more he could do for Gemma, called DI Ashford. 'Have you got the results of Mandy Bradshaw's tattoo and dental records?'

'They're due this afternoon.'

'I'll bet my house on the fact they'll match the body in the morgue. If they do, you'll need to find Michael Bradshaw.'

'I don't need you to tell me how to do my bloody job. Even if the body is Mandy's, there's little evidence to suggest she was murdered. I believe she fell to her death, coked-up and delusional.'

'I can't believe you're saying that! Why aren't you following up the stack of leads I've given you? There could be a man banged up for a murder he didn't commit.'

Ashford spat back, 'Look, Flood, you're getting on my nerves. I'm doing nothing until I hear from the pathologist. And aren't you forgetting something? There was a trial *and* a jury *and* a judge. I rely on the justice system to get the right verdict.'

'If you won't do anything, I will.'

'You can do what you like, as long as you don't get in my way.' Ashford hung up.

Seconds later, Flood's mobile buzzed again. 'It's Craig Lamont, Sam Wharton's solicitor. I've arranged for us to visit Sam at Pentonville tomorrow morning at ten. You'll need to get there earlier to go through security. Bring some ID. Is that OK?'

Flood didn't hesitate to reply. 'I'll see you there.'

CHAPTER TWELVE

Flood met Lamont under the alcove outside the prison entrance. Once inside the reception area, a prison officer checked their IDs against his list, ticked a sheet and directed them towards a coin-operated locker where they left their coats and mobile phones.

Another officer carried out a thorough body search and inspected the inside of their mouths with a pocket torch. After he'd checked the contents of Lamont's briefcase, he passed Flood and Lamont over to yet another officer who escorted them through two sets of steel doors leading to a sparsely furnished interview room off the visitors' hall.

Wharton looked up when they entered. Lamont said, 'Sam, this is Andy Flood, a private investigator. As I mentioned to you, he's looking at your case.'

In his prison-issue maroon jogging bottoms and grey T-shirt, Wharton was taller than Flood expected, broad-shouldered, too, with a square jaw and dimpled chin. A severe prison haircut emphasised his massive head. He spoke with a gravelly voice, probably the result of a forty-a-day habit, thought Flood.

Unsmilingly, Wharton said, 'Glad someone's finally looking at my case. I shouldn't be in here.'

Flood and Lamont sat opposite Wharton and Flood said, 'We haven't got much time, Sam. I'll get straight to the point. Talk me through, in as much detail as possible, the events of the evening Angela Bradshaw died.'

Wharton's eyes narrowed. 'Why are you doing this? I can't afford a private investigator.'

'There's no cost to you. As I've explained to your solicitor, I'm investigating another case involving Michael Bradshaw. There may be a link. I don't want to get your hopes up, but it could prove that your conviction for murder isn't safe. I must warn you, though; it's going to be hard to come up with something new after the police investigation and your trial.'

Wharton glowered at Flood. 'I didn't do it. I was fucking stitched up.'

Unfazed, Flood continued. 'I have a golden rule. You have to be straight with me. If I find out that you've told me *anything* of significance which I later discover to be untrue, that's it, I'm off the case. Look at me. Did you kill Angela Bradshaw?'

Wharton eyeballed Flood. 'No. I bloody didn't.'

Flood took out his notebook, opened it and placed it on the table. 'OK. Good. Now, tell me everything about that night ... from the beginning.'

Wharton took a deep breath. 'Angela and I first met 'bout two months before. I was a licensed taxi driver. She used me once when she left a pub a bit worse for wear. We hit it off straight away and agreed to meet the next night. To be honest, I didn't think she'd show up, but she did. From then on, I couldn't get enough of her. She said the same about me. She was a real sexy lady.'

He shook his head before continuing. 'She told me she was unhappily married. Said her husband was the jealous type, wanted to control everything she did. I think that's why she got drunk on a rare girls' night out. I didn't care. I was bored, wanted a bit more zizz in me life. I was married with two kiddies, so we agreed not to use mobiles or social media in case her husband found out about us. We planned our meetings from one to another. Mostly, we ended up in my taxi, in a lay-by or in a field. After a month or so, she told me that her husband had given up on her and moved out.'

Flood jotted a note as Wharton laid his hands on the table, and clasped his fingers so tightly together, his knuckles turned white.

'Is that why you went to her house?' Flood asked.

'It was her idea. She said now they were separated, she could invite whoever she wanted to her house. She loved being free of him.'

'How did you get there?'

'I drove and parked in the front of the house.'

'What time?'

'Around eightish.'

'How did you get in?'

'Angie had said she'd leave the front door on the latch and told me to go up to the bedroom. She'd be waiting for me with a glass of bubbly, give me the night of my life.'

Wharton swallowed hard. 'When I got to the house, it was in darkness apart from a light in a bedroom window. I pushed the front door open and went upstairs. I knew something wasn't right immediately. The room looked like someone had done it over; clothes scattered on the floor, drawers left open. It was a right bloody mess.

'Angie was lying on the king-size bed with her eyes closed. She wore heavy make-up and a sequinned, low-cut, mini-dress. One of her high heels lay on the carpet beside the bed. I thought she was play-acting. I shouted, "Get up, Angie. Stop fucking about." I slapped her face, gently at first. She didn't rouse. I grabbed her shoulders with both hands, shook her and shouted at her again. When she didn't respond, I felt her wrist for a pulse. Feeling nothing, I realised she was dead.' Wharton held his head in his hands.

Flood stopped writing and asked, 'What did you do next?'

Looking up at Flood, he said, 'I panicked, legged it down the stairs and out of the house. I ran to my car and drove to the nearest pub. I sat there until closing time, trying to work out what the bloody hell had happened.'

'What did you think?'

Wharton looked at Flood as if he was stupid. 'Obvious, isn't it? Bradshaw must have found out about me and Angie meeting up at their house.'

'How?'

He closed his eyes, shook his head and frowned hard, deep lines appearing across his forehead. 'I don't know. It's a question that's been bugging me for the past four years.'

'Did you tell the police about your affair with Angela?'

'I didn't want to, but Mr Lamont suggested I did. He said I needed a reason to be at the house. My wife wasn't best pleased.'

Lamont, who'd been listening carefully, turned to Flood and spoke for the first time. 'That was an important part of our defence, but we couldn't provide any evidence supporting Sam's story.'

Flood nodded and asked Wharton, 'How did you explain how the rucksack, containing burglar's tools and Angela's jewellery, had your fingerprints on it?'

'That's easy. About six that evening, I picked up my last fare of the day from St Albans train station. I needed to finish then because of seeing Angie later. He asked to be dropped off in the high street, a seven-minute ride away.

'It was a cold day and the fare wore gloves and a scarf pulled up around his face. He carried a rucksack on his shoulder and threw it onto the rear passenger seat in the back of the taxi before climbing in.

'Thursday's market day. Traders were loading up their stuff in their vans, ready to go home. I couldn't find a place to drop the man off. Eventually, I double-parked and he thrust a ten-pound note in my hand. He didn't hang about for the change. When I got home, I realised he'd left his rucksack on the back seat. I picked it up and threw it into the boot. As I was seeing Angie later, I planned to take it to the station's lost property office the next morning. I didn't have time to take the rucksack back immediately.'

'Did you recognise the fare?'

'I had no idea at the time. But when I saw him in court, I *knew* it was Bradshaw. I'd recognise him anywhere.'

Lamont interjected. 'The prosecution dismissed Sam's allegation saying that he'd made it up. Again, we couldn't produce evidence to prove it was true.'

Flood turned back to Wharton. 'What happened next?'

'Before I could return the rucksack, the cops came to my place early the next morning. They said an eyewitness had taken down my registration number as I sped away. That's how they knew where I lived. They arrested me on suspicion of murdering Angie and impounded my car. Once they found the rucksack with my fingerprints on it, I was done for.'

Wharton pushed his head towards Flood and Lamont. 'What really clinched my conviction was my fingerprints on Angie's body. I explained how they got there. They *never* took my side of the story seriously. Bradshaw fooled 'em. *Mister nice, grieving, straight-up guy.'* Wharton scowled, 'More like a scheming shit. I told you, he stitched me up.'

Flood had experienced many suspects who denied their offence but had turned out to be guilty as hell. But there was something about the way Wharton spoke that made him think again.

'Who discovered the body?'

As Wharton slumped back in his chair, Lamont answered. 'A next-door neighbour popped round to get Angela to witness a signature on a legal document at around 9.00 p.m. Finding the front door ajar, she went in, discovered Angela upstairs and immediately dialled 999.'

'Were there any other eyewitnesses?' Flood asked Lamont.

'Yes. Two in particular. One neighbour confirmed that they saw Bradshaw arrive at the house in his red Range Rover at around ten that morning and leave about an hour or so later. Angela was at work that day and a neighbour confirmed that she saw her return home about six.

'We believe Bradshaw returned to the house on foot at about 7 p.m. and entered through a conservatory door that he'd jemmied open earlier in the day and left the same way. That's when we think Bradshaw suffocated Angela with the pillow and made the place look as is if it had been burgled. Unfortunately, no one has come forward to say they saw him return later that evening.'

Wharton leaned forward again and snarled, 'He *must* have done it then. I told you; when I felt for a pulse, Angie's wrist was still warm.'

Flood asked Lamont, 'And the second eyewitness?'

'A female driver using a webcam spotted Sam's taxi leaving the crime scene in a hurry at around 8.30 p.m. We've got a copy of the footage back in the office if you want to go through it.'

'I'll do that. Thanks, Craig.' Flood ran the timeline of Bradshaw's movements through his mind. Something didn't add up.

'Let's get this straight.' Flood looked at Wharton. 'You maintain Bradshaw left your taxi in St Albans at what, around ten past six?'

Wharton nodded. Flood turned to Lamont. 'Where was Bradshaw's car at this time?'

'Michael Bradshaw alleges that he stayed with his brother, Barry, who lives in Hemel Hempstead, about twenty minutes away. Another eyewitness stated that Michael's Range Rover was parked next to Barry's car in the driveway of his house from midday on the day of the murder. It was in exactly the same position until 10 a.m. the following morning. And Michael Bradshaw's phone records show that his mobile remained at Barry's address throughout the same period. That went a long way to confirming his alibi.'

Flood frowned. 'So that means if he's responsible, he must have used public transport or driven another car to get back to Barry's house. Did you check that out?'

'Yes, we did. We ruled out the train. It's a poor service from St Albans to Hemel Hempstead. Needs two changes and takes over an hour. The bus service runs every half-hour and takes seventeen minutes. Once we realised that Bradshaw might have been responsible, we asked the police to check the bus company's CCTV footage but drew a blank. Their video records are overwritten after seven days.'

Flood asked, 'How long would it take to walk from the high street to the Bradshaw's home?'

'Forty-five minutes at the most.'

'So, after Bradshaw got out of the taxi he could have walked to his house, entered the conservatory door he'd previously jemmied open and murdered Angela. Then he could have walked back to the high street to catch the bus back to Hemel Hempstead.'

Lamont replied, 'It's eminently possible, except for his alibi.'

'What about forensics? Any fingerprints or DNA evidence presented at court?'

'Yes. They didn't help our case. As Sam's told you, his prints were found on Angela's face and shoulders, the front door and the rucksack. Bradshaw's fingerprints were discovered in the house, but that would be expected. He'd only moved out three weeks previously and had visited the house a couple of times since.'

'What about the pillow?'

'Nothing. We can only surmise that Bradshaw wore gloves.'

'Did the police question Bradshaw about his movements?'

'They did. He admitted going to the house in the morning to pick up a few things he'd left behind. He said he'd OK'd it with Angela and would account for him carrying a rucksack. Unfortunately, it wasn't distinctive enough for the eyewitness to confirm that it was the same one found in Sam's taxi.'

Flood scribbled a note; Bradshaw visiting the crime scene just hours before the murder was a red flag. Taking a moment to process everything he'd heard. He asked Wharton, 'Did you have any other affairs?'

'Why? Is it important?'

'If you did, it might make your story slightly more plausible.'

'No. Angie was a one-off. My wife, Janet, has never forgiven me for being unfaithful. She's more pissed off about the fling than me being found guilty of murder. God knows what she's told my kids. I'm really missing them.'

Flood flicked over the pages of his notebook and skimmed through them. 'There's so much evidence against you, Sam, I have to say; I can see why the jury believed you were guilty.'

Wharton stood and pushed his face close to Flood's. 'Except for one thing.'

'Which is?'

'I. Didn't. Do. It.' He thumped the table with the bottom of his fist in time with each word.

As they left the prison, Lamont asked Flood, 'Do you think Michael Bradshaw's responsible for Angela's murder?'

'It's all down to the alibi. I'll visit Barry, have a chat.'

CHAPTER THIRTEEN

MANDY
THREE WEEKS EARLIER

Prior to seeing Andy Flood, I became paranoid that Mike would discover I'd survived and returned back to the UK. I *know* he'd want to finish me off.

During the day, I exchanged some of Scottie's dollars for pounds, walked to Southampton's shopping areas and treated myself to some designer clothes and shoes. Not wanting to be recognised, I tied a scarf around my head and turned the collar up on my coat.

That first evening at the hotel, I watched mindless TV and finished off a bottle of wine. So boring. I had the now familiar craving for happy powder and remembered Carlos, the hotel reception manager, saying that if I needed *anything,* anything at all, I only had to ask. I assumed this might include drugs.

I went down to the reception desk and began chatting to him. Although I didn't like the way he fawned and grovelled over me, his dark, close-shaved head, long black eyelashes and Latino accent made me warm to him.

'You know you said I could ask you for anything. Did you mean "medication"?'

'Sure. What's your preference?'

'Charlie?'

He smiled. 'No problem.'

He reached into the inside pocket of his jacket and handed me a small envelope. It looked like I was receiving my mail. 'For you, pretty lady.'

'That's what I call service. How much do I owe you?'

'Nada. It's a gift. Maybe we come to some arrangement?' I couldn't believe he actually winked. His meaning was clear. I wasn't sure I wanted to sell myself for drugs. *A step too far.* Something I'd have to think about.

When I returned to my room, I opened the envelope. It contained five distinctively packaged, two-gram baggies of white powder, each worth at least £50 to £100, I guessed. A nice gift. It turned out to be good stuff, too. The high was better than anything I'd experienced previously.

During the night, I fantasised that I'd already moved back into my house on the Hamble River, and hosted drunken, drug-filled, wild parties with my friends.

All I needed was for that private eye to prove that Mike had killed his first wife and to get him locked up for a long time. Then I would be free to do exactly what I liked.

CHAPTER FOURTEEN

Flood googled Barry Bradshaw's Facebook page. Four years younger than his brother and divorced with no children, he worked as a salesman for a BMW dealership in Watford, twenty miles north of London.

Flood called and made an appointment with the receptionist for the following morning, saying that he and his wife were interested in buying a new car. He added that someone had recommended dealing with Barry.

He also decided to visit Wharton's wife, Janet. She lived in St Albans, around seven miles from Watford. He wanted to obtain more background to the case against Sam Wharton.

At first, Janet was suspicious. 'There's nothing more I can add,' she said.

Before she put the phone down, Flood said, 'Someone's come forward and suggested that Angela Bradshaw was murdered by her husband, Michael. I'd like to chat to you about it.'

After a short pause, she replied, 'Alright. But I can't see my opinion changing anything. Come if you want.' They arranged to meet at her home the following afternoon.

Laura said she could take a day off work and go with Flood if he liked. 'Good,' he said, valuing her insights as an ex-detective sergeant, especially in questioning women.

The next morning, they drove the ninety miles to Watford. The BMW dealership wasn't hard to find. A huge, glass-fronted building dominated the entrance to the trading estate.

Second-hand BMWs, looking as if they'd never been driven before, surrounded the entrance to the showroom. Flood and Laura made their way through the latest pristine models with eye-watering price labels on the windscreens to a smartly-dressed receptionist at the rear of the showroom.

Flood loved his ten-year-old Honda. Every time he got in it, he likened it to putting on a comfy pair of slippers. But now, surrounded by these stylish, shiny, automobiles smelling of leather and polish, he thought it might be time to change.

The receptionist made a brief call and a man wearing a smart jacket and tie approached them with a beaming smile and firm handshakes. 'Good morning. I'm Barry Bradshaw. Mr and Mrs Flood, I presume?'

His lack of hair and chubby face made him look older than his brother. 'How can I help? Do you have any idea of which model you're interested in?'

Flood handed over his business card. 'I'd love one of your cars, but first, I'd like to talk to you about your brother, Michael Bradshaw.'

Barry looked at the card, then back at Flood and Laura. 'My brother? You've come to talk about my brother? You told my receptionist that you were interested in buying a car.'

'I did, but I needed to make sure you'd see us.'

Barry glowered at Flood. 'That's a bit sneaky, isn't it? We'd better discuss it in my office. Follow me.' He turned and strode to a room at the rear of the showroom and pointed at two chairs opposite his at a table with a PC on top. 'Take a seat,' he said, curtly. 'What's this about my brother? Is he OK?'

'That's the problem. We don't know. It's important we speak to him. I've visited his home. He's not there, and his clothes are missing. No one's seen him for three weeks and he hasn't used social media since then either.'

'Why do you want to speak with him?'

'We represent the family of your brother's wife, Mandy Bradshaw,' Flood lied. 'Are you aware that she died recently in suspicious circumstances?'

Barry's draw dropped. 'Mandy? Dead? My brother told me she'd left him. Run off with someone when they were on holiday in the US.'

'I can assure you that she's dead. Her family have asked us to contact your brother to tie up some loose ends regarding their finances. Have you any idea where he is?'

'Sorry. If he's not at home, I can't help you. We don't keep in touch as much as we used to.'

'Really? I understood that after your brother's first wife, Angela, was murdered, he stayed with you for a while. You even provided him with an alibi covering her time of death. It sounds to me like you were pretty close.'

Barry huffed. 'That was four years ago.'

Laura spoke for the first time. 'When were you last in touch with your brother?'

Barry shrugged. 'Oh, I don't know. Ages ago.'

Laura raised an eyebrow as Flood said, 'Before Mandy died, she told me that your brother had tried to kill her and implied that he'd killed someone before. That's an amazing coincidence, don't you think?'

Barry opened his mouth to say something but the words never materialised. Flood noticed his leg twitching.

He added, 'You'll know that a guy called Sam Wharton is doing twenty years for Angela's murder, mainly because of the alibi you gave your brother. I've spoken to Wharton's solicitor. He believes his client is innocent.'

Barry let out a nervous laugh. 'That's total crap.'

Laura, watching Barry intensely, said, 'There are a couple of things that aren't clear. You might be able to enlighten us. Did your brother ever tell you about Angela seeing someone else before she was murdered?'

Barry looked at Laura, then Flood, considering his reply. Eventually, he said, 'No. Never.'

Flood asked, 'Do you think your brother *could* have been responsible?'

Barry regained his composure. He snorted, 'Don't be so bloody ridiculous!' He leant forward and placed his palms on the table in front of him. 'I'll tell you what I told the court. Michael stayed home with me that night. We watched a soccer match on television. As far as I'm concerned, that scum-bag burglar murdered Angela. The jury agreed.'

Flood nodded. 'You're right. They did. But I'd still like to talk to your brother about it. If he gets in touch, would you call me? You've got my card.'

'I don't see the point. The case is closed. You should go now. I don't like the inferences you've made about my brother. I'm busy, got proper customers to talk to.'

He got up from behind his desk, walked to the office door and opened it. He didn't offer a handshake as Flood and Laura passed him in the doorway on the way out.

As they got into their car, Flood turned to Laura. 'What do you think?'

'I'm thinking it's odd that Barry said he knew Mandy had left his brother two months ago. Unless Michael had told him, how else would he know? Then he went on to say that they don't keep in touch as much as they used to. In fact, he evaded the question about the last time he was in contact with his brother.'

Flood nodded. 'I'll let Ashford know about our suspicions. Let's hope he'll get his arse in gear for once.'

***

In the afternoon, they visited Janet Wharton's run down, terraced Victorian house, located a mile and a half outside St Albans town centre. Janet opened the door as far as a brass chain would allow and anxiously peered through the gap. Mousy-haired, bespectacled and diminutive, she wore an anxious look. After they'd introduced themselves, Janet invited them inside.

Picking their way past two kiddies' bikes parked in the hallway, Janet led them to a neat and tidy living room. She motioned to Flood and Laura to sit on a sofa which had seen better days as she sat opposite in an armchair. 'I hope this won't take long,' she said. 'I've got to collect the kids from school at quarter past three.'

'That's fine, Janet,' Laura said. 'Thanks for agreeing to see us. We'll come straight to the point. As we mentioned to you

103

on the phone, someone's alleged that Angela Bradshaw was murdered by her husband, not Sam. We've already spoken to your husband and his solicitor. It must be difficult, but can you tell us about the case from your point of view?'

Janet sighed. 'One thing's for sure. He didn't go the house to burgle it. If he'd still been thieving, I'm sure I'd have known about it. And as for suffocating that woman ...' She shook her head vigorously from side to side. 'He's never, ever shown a violent streak to me. It's not him.' Then she spat out, 'Perhaps it was to do with the sex. Some women like it rough. Maybe it got out of hand.'

'Did you know about your husband's affair with Angela Bradshaw?'

'Not at the time. No. But there were others.'

'How do you know that?'

Janet lowered her voice as if revealing a deep secret. 'I scratched around a bit after he got sentenced and found out he'd been chasing women ever since the kids were born. There's at least three he's shagged. It was easy for him, being as he's a taxi driver. He had plenty of opportunities.'

Laura glanced at Flood before asking, 'Is Sam aware that you know about this?'

Janet shook her head. 'No. He doesn't. The first time I heard about him screwing *that* particular woman was in court. You've no idea what that felt like.'

She looked at Flood and Laura in turn, a pained expression on her face. 'Humiliated. Totally humiliated. Whether he murdered her or not wasn't important to me. The main thing was that he cheated on the children and me more times than I care to think. How could he do that? For Christ's sake, the kids were only three and five when he got done. Once I found out, I didn't want to have anything more to do with him.'

Laura leant forward. 'That must have been awful for you. What have you told your children?'

'Not much. They're too young to understand. They'll learn what he did soon enough. I've told them that their father's done something wrong and he's got to pay for it. I don't like taking them to Pentonville every two weeks. It's affecting them. But even convicted murderers have the right to see their children. To be honest, it's not good for the kids or me – only for him.'

Despite Flood noticing that Janet was close to tears, he said, 'Sam told me he's really missing his kids. He's pinning his hopes on the authorities realising there's been a colossal mistake and will set him free. Free to come back home to his family.'

Janet scowled. 'Oh, does he? Well, he'd better think again. Even if he's acquitted of murder, he's totally guilty of messing with other women.' She smacked a fist on the side of the sofa. 'I'm not having it. The only reason I didn't divorce him is because of the effect it would have on my kids. It would be something else for them to cope with. I'll do it when they're older.' She glanced up at a clock on the wall. 'Look, I'd better be going. I can't be late for the kids.'

Laura stood and offered her hand. 'Thank you, Janet. We hope things turn out OK for you and your children.'

Flood added, 'I hope so, too,' and offered a sympathetic smile.

Walking back to the car, Laura, noticed Flood's grim expression. 'What's up?'

'Their stories don't match. Wharton told me his affair with Angela was the only time he'd been unfaithful. One of them is lying.'

'What are you thinking?'

'I'm thinking that if Wharton is a serial love rat and the affair with Angela was just another notch on the bedpost, it might have supported his defence that he wasn't a burglar, just a randy git.'

'In which case, why didn't he admit to having the other affairs in court?'

'That's what I'd like to know.'

'Are you going to tackle Wharton about it?'

'Yes. As soon as possible.'

As they drove back to Winchester, Flood's mobile rang. He put the call on the speaker. Monty sounded excited. 'Hi, Andy, I've been investigating barristers to represent Gemma. There's one I'd highly recommend, Robin Porter QC. I've worked with him before. He's expensive but one of the best.'

'OK. If you think this guy's good, go ahead. I trust you, Monty.'

'Good. We'll go through the evidence and statements together to decide on her plea. I'll let you know the outcome.'

Flood hung up and turned to Laura. 'It sounds like it's going to cost a lot of money. We'll have to use more of the money my mother left me. Are you OK with that?'

'Of course, Andy. We've got to do what's best for Gemma. That's all there is to it. Don't you think you should let Pippa know what's going on?'

'Yeah, I should.' Flood looked at his watch. 'It's the middle of the night in Oz now. I'll call her this evening.' He took his hand off the steering wheel, reached across and squeezed her hand. 'I love you, Laura.'

Next, Flood called Craig Lamont to arrange another legal visit to Sam Wharton in prison. The earliest date was the day after next.

He rang Pippa from home that evening. He got an answerphone message, as usual and explained Gemma's situation in detail. *Surely she'd call me back?*

***

When Flood and Lamont visited Pentonville prison, Flood asked Wharton, 'Do you remember me telling you that if I found out something important that you'd not told me, I'd drop your case?'

'Yes.'

'Angela wasn't the only affair you'd had, was it?'

Wharton remained silent for a moment. Eventually, he replied. 'OK, there were others, but I couldn't tell anyone that, could I? Once I'm out of here, I'm determined to start again with Janet and the kids. I know she's pissed off with me. If she knew about the others, she'd blow me out, big time.' His voice trailed away.

'Yes, but if the jury knew about your affairs, it might have helped your case. They nailed you down as a burglar caught on the job.'

'I know. I thought I was doing the right thing.'

'By the way, you should know that your wife is aware of your affairs.'

Wharton groaned. 'Oh, shit, no!'

'Do you remember my golden rule? I have to consider whether there's anything else you haven't told me.'

Wharton spat out, 'I swear to you, there's nothing else. I have to get out of this place. It's doing my head in. You've got to believe me. I didn't murder Angie.'

CHAPTER FIFTEEN

As Flood drained the last of his black coffee after lunch at his office desk, his mobile rang. He picked it up and recognised the international number on the screen.

'It's Chris Black. Remember me? Lisa's brother in Wisconsin.' Flood guessed from his trembling voice that maybe the American Embassy had wrongly informed him of his sister's death.

'I've got bad news. Alligator hunters found Lisa's body in the Fakahatchee region of the Everglades National Park, between Naples and Miami.'

'Bloody hell! Are they sure it's her?'

'Yes. The police checked dental records and DNA against missing persons in the area. Remember, you told me to register her? They found her necklace and watch close by, but no purse or cell phone. I thought you'd like to know.'

Flood felt vindicated in not believing Mandy's story. She'd implied that Scottie, her rescuer, had arranged her fake passport. Scottie had denied it. *It looks like she could have stolen it.*

'Thanks, Chris. I'm so sorry. Have the police said how she died?'

'No. They told me it's impossible to say at this stage. Her body parts were spread all over the place. It looks like the alligators and panthers had a feast. We weren't close, but she was my sister.' Chris's voice faded away, fighting back a sob.

'Do the police know how she came to be there?'

'No. But I told them you're investigating the whereabouts of a British woman and discovered she'd become friendly with Lisa. The detective would like to talk to you. His name's Chuck North. He's left me his number.'

'Good. Let me have it. I'll call him right away. Please accept my condolences, Chris.'

Flood dialled Chuck North, introduced himself, and said, 'I understand you've found Lisa Black's body.'

'Yes, we have. Can you tell me your interest in Lisa and why you travelled to the USA?'

Flood explained his investigation into Mandy's death, starting with her visit to his office using Lisa Black as her alias and finishing with Mandy's demise. He added, 'Do you know the cause of death?'

'We're not ruling out homicide. It's unlikely she went to the Everglades voluntarily. There's no abandoned vehicle in the vicinity, which suggests someone drove her there. Of course, it could have been an accident, but we're asking, why the heck she'd be there? It's a dangerous place to be on your own unless you're prepared. We haven't found her purse or cell phone, and we're short on leads. What else can you tell me?'

Flood told North about his meeting with Mario, the bar manager, adding, 'He told me they looked extraordinarily alike and got on well. A month ago, he got a text from Lisa, saying that she and Mandy were quitting their bar job and going travelling. I visited Lisa's apartment. It's number fourteen, Block D in The Isle of Capri complex near Wiggins Pass. I didn't find anything incriminating but there's a creepy community manager there. Pete. He may be worth interviewing.'

'Thanks. I'll follow that up.'

'Can you keep me posted?'

'Sure thing.'

Flood called DI Ashford next and told him about his conversation with Detective North ending with, 'Lisa Black is dead. There's no doubt now.' He waited for Ashford's reaction. None came.

'Are you still there?' Flood asked.

Ashford's voice crackled with emotion. 'Christ! This is a game-changer.'

'So now we know the body in the morgue is not Lisa. You need to confirm that it's Mandy Bradshaw. Have you chased the pathologist's report?'

'I'll get on to it right away, but we still don't know whether her death was accidental or not.'

'For Christ's sake! When are you going to take me seriously? I think you owe me that at least. I imagine the US Embassy wouldn't be too impressed with you telling them Lisa had died in an accident in the UK and having to retract it. Makes you look pretty stupid.'

Ashford remained silent for a moment before saying, 'OK, I owe you that.'

'Good. I've got more information about the Angela Bradshaw murder. Is it possible for me to speak to the Senior Investigating Officer who handled the case? Maybe arrange a conference call?'

'OK. I'll get a name. I can't promise he'll cooperate.'

'Tell him if he doesn't, he'll look pretty stupid, too.'

'Alright, you've made your point. I'll be in touch when I've spoken to him.'

***

A day later, Flood received a call from Ashford. His friendly tone of voice came as a welcome surprise. 'I've received the pathologist's report. Dental records confirm that it's Mandy in the morgue. She also has the tattoo you described.'

Flood made a conscious effort not to gloat. 'I never had any doubt. So, what now?'

'I spoke to the Hertfordshire Police about the Angela Bradshaw case. The original SIO in charge, a DI Cunningham, retired shortly after the trial. The Super at St Albans has asked a DI Wells to have a look at the files and he's agreed to hear what you have to say. I've set up a FaceTime call in my office at 3.15 this afternoon. Can you make it?'

'I'll be there.'

***

Ashford's transformed attitude showed in his face as Flood entered his office. He gave Flood an apologetic, almost thankful smile as he greeted him and shook hands.

'I'm interested to see what DI Wells has to say,' Ashford said, as he set up the call on his laptop and moved it to the side of his desk so they could both watch the screen. Within seconds, a bespectacled face appeared, showing the unflattering effects of a thirty-year veteran police officer.

Ashford made the introductions and DI Wells said, 'OK, fire away.'

Flood started with Mandy's allegation that Michael Bradshaw had tried to kill her and told her during an argument that he said he'd killed before. 'I'm looking into the possibility that he might have murdered his first wife, Angela. I've spoken to Sam Wharton, the guy convicted of her murder and his solicitor. I also spoke to Michael's brother, Barry Bradshaw. You'll see from the files that Barry gave Michael an alibi for the time of the murder.'

DI Wells constantly fiddled with a pen in his hand as Flood continued, 'Several things concern me about this case. I think it's possible that Michael Bradshaw set up Wharton.'

'What makes you think that?'

'When the police found the rucksack containing the burglary tools and Angela's jewellery in Wharton's taxi, it had his fingerprints on the straps.

'Wharton says it's possible. It would have happened when he transferred the rucksack from the rear passenger seat to the boot before planning to return it to the lost property office at the station the following morning. My first question is, did you check the rucksack for other fingerprints?'

Wells flicked through a file on his desk. 'Yes, of course. There were others. We ran them against the fingerprint identification database. One of the sets matched Wharton's.'

'Were they *specifically* compared to Bradshaw's prints?'

Flood waited while Wells checked his file again. 'It doesn't look like it,' he said. 'DI Cunningham interviewed him and cleared him as a suspect.'

'It sounds like he'd already made up his mind about Wharton being responsible. I assume you'll still have the rucksack in your evidence store?'

'It should be.'

'Can I suggest you get your forensic unit to re-check it, see if Bradshaw's prints are present? All you'd need is the *slightest* trace to put doubt in a jury's mind and support Wharton's allegation.'

DI Wells took off his glasses, pulled a handkerchief from his pocket, breathed on the lens and began polishing them. 'I don't buy that. Bradshaw's not stupid. If he'd planned the whole thing, he'd have worn gloves when handling the rucksack.'

'Exactly. But it's just as likely that Bradshaw purchased the rucksack before he planned the murder, so he wouldn't have been wearing gloves. And it doesn't matter how long ago. You know as well as I do that fingerprints last forever if the fabric's been stored in a dry place. Surely, it's worth a shot?'

'As it's a cold case, I'll need to get special authorisation.' Wells studiously put on his glasses and thrust his handkerchief back in his pocket.

Flood pressed on. 'There's something else which needs explaining. Wharton's solicitor allowed me access to the eyewitnesses' statements which I've checked thoroughly.' He looked down at his notebook. 'One of them came forward after you'd appealed for help. She was driving towards Wharton's taxi as it sped from the crime scene at 8.40 pm.

'According to her statement, she said that although it was dark, her car's headlights showed the driver hunched over the steering wheel with his *fingers* gripping the top of it. That could imply the driver wasn't wearing gloves.' DI Wells opened his mouth to respond, but Flood got in first.

'Her car had a dashboard camera which captured the incident. You'll have the film in your evidence store. Again, can I suggest you re-check it?'

'How will that help?'

'You'll remember, the police found Wharton's fingerprints on the front door. He says it's because he was invited there for a romantic dalliance. Angela told him the door would be on the latch. Surely, if he intended to *burgle* the house, he'd have worn gloves from the onset and have no reason to take them off when he drove away.'

Wells made a point of carefully placing his pen on the table before peering back into the camera with a determined look. 'Wharton's allegations were ludicrous. There's not a scrap of evidence supporting his defence that he went to the house for a bit of nooky with Angela. And his explanation about Bradshaw leaving the rucksack in his taxi is laughable. The jury was out for less than an hour before coming back with a unanimous guilty verdict.'

Flood always enjoyed the cut and thrust of comparing hypotheses. He bent forward towards the screen. 'Wharton told me he and Angela went to great lengths to keep their relationship secret. That's why there's no evidence of it. In court, he said his affair with Angela was a one-off. His wife told me the opposite; her husband was a serial love rat. This is important because it increases the probability that Wharton was telling the truth about his affair with Angela. When I asked him why he didn't reveal it in court, he said he was trying to protect his marriage and his kids.'

'That's circumstantial in the extreme,' Wells snorted.

'Maybe. But it paints a picture. What about Michael Bradshaw's alibi? Are you entirely happy with it?'

'Yes, we are.'

'I think you should interview Barry again. He mentioned something which didn't ring true.' Flood explained Barry's contradiction about not being in contact with his brother for ages, but then admitted that Michael had told him that he and

Mandy had split up. 'That only happened recently, after Michael returned from Florida.'

Wells looked thoughtful. Flood continued, 'I visited the Bradshaw's house. It looks like Michael's scarpered. All his clothes and personal effects are gone. No sign of a mobile phone or laptop either. You have to ask, why would he go missing?'

Flood left the question hanging in the air for a moment before adding, 'There's another eyewitness statement in the file confirming that Bradshaw's car was parked next to Barry's car at his house from midday on the day of the murder until late the following morning. That doesn't mean he didn't visit his former matrimonial home. He could have gone there by public transport or borrowed a car.'

Wells put a hand up in front of the camera. 'I'm sorry. I don't know where you get your ideas from. That's pure speculation.'

'It may be speculation, but hear me out.' Flood explained his theory, including a timeline, proving that Bradshaw could have used buses to travel between St Albans and Hemel Hempstead and walked to his house and back that evening. 'I've checked the timetables. It's perfectly feasible.'

Wells flicked through the pages of the file once more, presumably looking for something to prove otherwise. 'For that theory to work, you'd need to produce CCTV footage from the bus company showing Bradshaw travelling in both directions at the appropriate times. Better still if it showed him carrying the rucksack into St Albans and *not* having it with him on the return journey to his brother's house. That's what I call proper evidence.'

'No chance. I've already checked with the bus company. We're talking over four years ago. They overwrite the footage every seven days.'

'That's a pity. Look, Flood, all I can say is, that when we presented our evidence, the CPS were happy for us to charge Wharton. We weren't looking for anyone else.' Wells sat forward in his chair, put his hands together and placed them on the table in front of him. 'So what do you expect me to do?'

'Let's face it; DI Cunningham's investigation was sloppy. He should have checked the CCTV on the buses much earlier in the investigation. It seems to me that he decided Wharton was a shoo-in for Angela's murder, wanting to end his career on a high. I believe there's enough here to at least consider re-interviewing the key witnesses, re-visiting the fingerprints and the dashcam footage. And much more importantly, Bradshaw's alibi.'

'You can't put all this on Cunningham. Wharton fitted the bill. He had previous and couldn't deny he was at the crime scene at the time of Angela's death. Add in the rucksack containing the tools and her jewellery being found in his taxi. It's a strong case.'

DI Ashford, who'd silently watched Flood present his case, interjected. 'I've worked with Mr Flood for the last few days on another case involving Michael Bradshaw. I've found him to be an excellent investigator. I told you he was one of us a few years back. Despite what you're saying, I think his points are worth following up.'

Flood almost fell off his chair, grateful for Ashford's support, even if it sounded patronising. Wells scribbled a note, looked up at the camera and scratched his cheek, considering the request.

Heaving a resigned sigh, he said, 'I'll tell you what I'll do. I'll apply for the authorisation for Bradshaw's fingerprint check. If I get it, no promises, mind, I'll assign a senior officer, a DC, and an analyst to do the legwork, prioritising the points you've made. I can only spare them for three days, max.'

Flood sat back in his chair. 'Thank you. I appreciate it.'

As Ashford ended the video call, he turned to Flood. 'Happy?'

'I'll be happier still when Wells confirms my suspicions.'

115

CHAPTER SIXTEEN

MANDY
THREE WEEKS EARLIER

What a waste of space Andy Flood, turned out to be. According to my research, he had the best track record by far. I thought about approaching another private investigator but I don't like being rejected. I reasoned, if I can't get Mike out of my life legitimately, I'll do the bloody job myself. I'd need someone to help me, though. I knew just the man.

Up to now, my plan had worked well. To the world at large, Lisa Black is alive and kicking and having a ball in London. It's me who's missing, and as far as I know, Mike never reported it. I suspect that he'll tell everybody we split up ... again, and that I'd met someone in Florida and ran off with him. He's such a jealous arsehole, although I admit that he had just cause to be pissed off.

A few months before out trip to Florida, he found out I'd been seeing one of my ex-boyfriends, Gary. I've known him for years, well before I got married. Mike didn't like losing control of anything, most of all me. He gave me hell for a few days, then begged me to stay.

Gary works as a boatyard attendant at the Ocean Village Marina. Not exactly a high flyer, but he always seemed to be in my life. Trimmer and more muscular than Mike as a result of working out three or four times a week, he loved showing off his body. His dark and broody looks matched an insatiable sexual appetite. Talk about letting his dick rule his life. I could get him to do anything if I did what he wanted.

Gary often called, begging me to go back with him. Pathetic really. But the sex was fantastic. That's the reason we met up every three or four months or so in our favourite hotel in the New Forest, a national park west of Southampton.

Every time we met, he'd get all sentimental; say he wanted to spend the rest of his life with me. Fat chance. He's immature and not in my league. Mike was the opposite. But apart from the early days of that relationship, when he couldn't get enough of me, he controlled my life. I vowed it would never happen again.

I called Gary to arrange to meet up at our usual place. When he heard my voice, he said, 'Bloody hell, Mandy! I've been calling you for weeks, couldn't get a reply. I thought you'd dumped me.' There was no doubting the excitement in his voice. I explained that I'd been travelling in the US and changed mobiles, which is sort of true. I'm convinced that Mike would have destroyed my UK mobile shortly after he'd dumped me in the Gulf.

Gary sat at the bar drinking a cocktail when I walked into the hotel wearing my latest purchases; a low-cut, mini-dress with a zip running its entire length and Jimmy Choo high heels. As I slinked into the bar, he looked up and peered at me, not sure whether it was me or not.

'Hi Gary,' I said, pecking him on the cheek before he had a chance to stand up. I did a twirl and ran my fingers through my now blonde bob before sitting down on a stool next to him at the bar. 'Well, what do you think?'

His dark brown eyes, shielded by unbelievably long black lashes, widened. 'Wow! I like it. Blonde suits you. Tell me more?'

'I've changed my name to Lisa.'

Gary laughed. 'Lisa? I like it. Why did you change it?'

'Finish your drink, Gary and I'll tell you everything. We can talk in your room.' I stood and dragged him to his feet. He grasped his glass, drained it and replaced it on the counter as I pulled him towards the lift.

Gary called room service and ordered a couple of bottles of Cabernet Sauvignon. He kept asking me what I wanted to chat about. 'I'll tell you later,' I said.

The bottles arrived, and Gary poured two large glasses. We sat on the sofa, drinking and catching up on our news. He couldn't take his eyes off my exposed, tanned legs, and within minutes, he started snogging and fondling me with increasing intensity. We yanked off each other's clothes until we were naked, then I pulled him onto the king-size bed.

I'd forgotten how much I'd missed sex. And Gary is good, very good. I knew what he liked, too. And I did a good job, judging by the noises he made.

The first time didn't take long. When we'd finished, we pulled on the hotel's fluffy white dressing gowns and Gary topped up our glasses. He lay his head on the back of the sofa. 'That was so good,' he said, as he rolled his head to look towards me. 'Come on, Mandy ... sorry, Lisa. What's going on.'

'You probably won't believe me, but I swear everything I'm about to tell you is true.'

'Oh, yeah?'

I told him about Mike pushing me off the boat in the middle of the night, leaving me to drown. The memory of it sent a shudder down my spine. With a look of horror on his face, Gary snarled, 'The bastard!'

I told him, too, about being rescued and meeting Lisa, and that we'd become great mates. 'Apart from our hair colour, we looked so alike. When I told her what happened to me and that I wanted to take revenge on Mike, she agreed. Even offered to lend me her passport so I could get back to the UK,' I lied. I didn't want to complicate things by telling him what really happened.

'I coloured my hair and changed the style to match Lisa's passport photo. And here I am.'

'I'm glad you came back. You're bloody lucky to have met Lisa.'

'You know I'm always lucky. Now I want to get rid of Mike, but need your help.'

Gary screwed up his face. 'Are you serious?'

I shouted, 'Of course, I'm serious.' Gary shook his head.

Before he could say anything, I shrieked, 'Mike tried to bloody kill me! I'm convinced he murdered his first wife and got away with it. He deserves everything he's got coming to him, the shit. Don't you agree?'

'You're crazy! You'll never get away with it.'

'Listen, Gary. I've got a plan. If it works, think about what's in it for you. With Mike out of the way, I'll revert to being Mandy, get a new passport and return Lisa's. If you help me, we can live together in the house on the River Hamble. We'll be together all the time. We'll fuck our brains out every night. What do you think?'

Gary sat still, saying nothing but staring at me as if I was an alien.

I lost patience. 'Look, if you don't want to help me, I'll find someone else. There's plenty of takers. For starters, there's a fit Latino guy who works on reception at my hotel. He'd be a pushover. He flirts with me every time I see him. *He'd* help me if I asked him.'

Gary sneered. 'You can be such a bitch sometimes, Mandy.'

'Are you thick or something? I've told you my name's Lisa until I've dealt with Mike. If that's what you think of me, I'll get dressed and go.' I stood up and flounced to the bathroom.

Before I'd reached the door, Gary said, 'OK. OK. What's your plan?'

I turned back to face him. 'I'll tell you but first, I need to know; are you in or out?'

I untied the belt of my dressing gown, opened it and shrugged it off. It landed in a crumpled heap on the floor. I posed provocatively in the doorway, showing Gary what he could be missing. I'll never forget the look of lust in his eyes. 'I'm in,' he said.

CHAPTER SEVENTEEN

The following day, Monty called Flood at his office. 'I've got news. Doctor Rogers called me from the hospital. He said he's signed off Gemma's transfer to prison.'

Flood groaned. 'I'm not sure she'll cope. It took her enough time to adjust to life in the psychiatric unit.'

'We don't have a choice, Andy. Doctor Rogers calls the shots. There's nothing we can do. He's making arrangements for the transfer to Send Women's Prison in Woking, the day after tomorrow. You can visit Gemma before she leaves. As she's on remand, she'll be able to wear her clothes in prison. You might want to take something appropriate. You can have a chat with the good doctor while you're there.'

Later, Flood googled the prison website. Categorised as a 'closed' female prison, it housed high-risk offenders, a quarter of them serving life sentences. The blurb said, 'Escape needs to be made very difficult'. He scoffed when he read that. He couldn't imagine Gemma setting up an escape committee.

Three two-hour visits a week were allowed for prisoners on remand. Each had their own cell with toilet and shower facilities. Gemma's future home could have been worse.

Seconds after he hung up, his mobile rang again. He recognised the American number; Detective Chuck North.

'Hi, Flood. Thought I'd bring you up to speed on the Lisa Black situation. We visited Lisa's condo and spoke to Pete, the caretaker. He confirms that he last saw her around the end of February, over three weeks ago. Following your visit, he said he cleaned up the room, packed her belongings into bags and put them in a storeroom. We're checking out the room and the store right now.'

Flood said, 'When I visited the condo, I spotted a stain on the living room carpet which I assumed to be food. You might want to run a Luminol test on the carpets, see if there are traces of Lisa's blood, that could suggest a crime scene.'

'Will do.'

'What did you make of Pete?'

'He's a bit weird, but his background checks came back clean. We don't think he's a suspect. We also had a chat with Mario, the bar manager. He confirmed that Lisa had texted him to say that she and Mandy were packing up their jobs to go travelling. And he told us about Lisa's boyfriend, Douglas Moreno. Said they regularly met up at the Yen Karaoke bar. We spoke to the manager there. This is where it gets interesting. He witnessed a furious argument between Mandy and Lisa outside the bar. Lisa ran off in the direction of her condo, a few minutes away. He says Mandy ran after her and he's not seen either of them since.'

'Have you interviewed Moreno?'

'Yeah. We carried out background checks on him. All clear. He said the reason for the argument was that Lisa accused Mandy of flirting with him. He denied it. Said they were only having fun. We checked his movements for the rest of that evening. Several witnesses reported seeing him back at the karaoke bar. He stayed until 1 a.m. and was seen taking a girl back to his place. We interviewed her and she made a statement saying that they were together until the following morning. It's looking likely that Mandy was the last person to see Lisa alive. She'd definitely be a person of interest if she was still alive.'

Flood's brain worked overtime trying to connect the dots. A thought flashed into his mind. He asked, 'Did Lisa have a car?'

'Yeah. Pete, the caretaker gave up the make, model and registration number. We ran the plates and confirmed that a 2008 Toyota Camry is registered to her. It's not at her condo. We've filed it on our Missing Vehicles list.'

'You said the last sighting of Mandy in the US is outside the karaoke bar near Lisa's apartment. The next is when she's in my office impersonating Lisa. So it's fair to assume she used Lisa's car to get to Miami airport to catch a flight to the UK via the Everglades. You could try to locate it in one of the parking lots. They'll have a record if it's there. Maybe the car will reveal forensic evidence explaining Lisa's disappearance. It could also point to Mandy being responsible for Lisa's death.'

North paused, thinking through the points, then said, 'OK. Sure thing. I'll let you know if we find the Toyota.'

***

That evening, Laura cooked Flood's favourite meal as they'd planned a quiet evening in.

'You do the best roasts in the county,' Flood said, wiping his mouth with a napkin.

'Thank you, kind sir,' Laura replied. 'Coffee?'

'I wouldn't say no. I'll top up the wood burner.'

When Laura returned, they both snuggled down on the sofa watching the flames licking the logs.

'Do you miss being a detective?' Flood asked, staring into the fire.

'No, I don't. I love my job at the forensics lab.'

'What are you working on?'

Laura's face lit up. 'We're developing a mixture of compounds and chemicals to lift latent fingerprints on specific fabrics like nylon and silk. The current technology is less than forty per cent effective. We're so close to getting a result.'

The ringing of Flood's mobile interrupted their conversation. He glanced at the caller's name and said to Laura, 'Do you mind if I get this?'

'No, go ahead,' she said, picking up Flood's empty cup and waving it at him, silently mouthing, *another one?* Flood nodded.

By the time Laura returned, he'd finished the call. 'Who was that?' she asked.

Flood smiled. 'Ashford. He says DI Wells from Hertfordshire Police wants to come down to Southampton Police Station at two o'clock tomorrow to discuss his findings on the Angela Bradshaw murder case in person.'

'Why in person do you think?'

'I hope it's because he's got something positive to say.'

***

The following day, Flood was directed to a Murder Incident Room at the police station. He hadn't been in one since leaving the Met twenty years ago.

Ashford and Wells were already seated next to each other at a long table at the front of the room. A heap of files with different coloured Post-It notes sticking out of them lay on top.

Ashford stood and greeted Flood with a handshake firmer than usual.

'You'll recognise DI Keith Wells from your FaceTime chat,' he said.

'Yes. Of course.'

The Hertfordshire DI stood and shook Flood's hand before motioning him to sit opposite. 'Thanks for coming in,' Wells said. 'I've followed up your potential leads in the Angela Bradshaw murder case. Thought I'd share my findings so far with you and DI Ashford, face to face.

'DI Cunningham, the Senior Investigating Officer, put a lot of effort into getting Wharton's conviction. However, you asked me to look into three aspects of the case: checking the rucksack for Bradshaw's dabs, reviewing the webcam film taken by a passing motorist close to the crime scene, and talking to Barry Bradshaw about his alibi for his brother, Michael on the night Angela was murdered.'

Flood approved Wells' approach. *Matter of fact, down to earth.*

'Regarding the fingerprints on the rucksack; you'll be pleased to know that I've got the authorisation. It'll take a while but we should get an answer in the next two to three days.

'You were right about the dashcam recording as Wharton drove from the crime scene. It showed that Wharton wasn't wearing gloves.' Wells opened his palms in a gesture of apology. 'We cocked up. It should have been spotted.'

Taking a deep breath, he added, 'We know from the original investigation that Wharton's prints were found on the front door handle. As you said, that's odd for someone about to burgle a house.'

Flood, trying hard to contain his excitement, said, 'That's what I thought.'

'We've spoken to Barry Bradshaw. We intimated that, since the trial, we'd learnt a great deal more about the circumstances surrounding Angela Bradshaw's murder. We warned him about the seriousness of withholding important information. He came across a bit jittery, nervous.

'We challenged him to think carefully about the alibi he'd given for his brother's whereabouts at the time of the murder. Despite that, he still maintains his brother spent the whole evening with him watching a soccer match.'

Disappointed, but not surprised, Flood turned to Ashford who sat quietly observing the conversation. 'What about Mandy's death? If Bradshaw did murder his first wife, it makes him a candidate, doesn't it? Where are you on that?'

Ashford glanced at Wells, then Flood before saying, 'We need to find, then question him. I'll step up the alerts to every police station in the UK, and organise a check with the ports and airports. I've sent a team over to Bradshaw's house in Hamble to conduct a thorough search of the premises. That might give us a clue as to his whereabouts.'

Flood, pleased that Ashford had finally snapped into gear, stopped himself from saying, *about bloody time.*

Instead, he asked Ashford, 'Did you discover the registration number of the white van seen leaving Bradshaw's house on 7th March? The daughter of an eyewitness, Mrs Crompton, made a note of it but didn't report it.'

'Yes we traced ownership to a local van hire company. All hire companies these days operate a tracking device for their vehicles. We're going through their records as we speak.'

'Good. And me? What can I do?'

124

Ashford stood and offered his hand to Flood with a supercilious expression on his face. 'You can leave finding Michael Bradshaw to us now. Thanks for your help. I'll call you if there are further developments.'

Flood, feeling the muscles in his neck twitching, stood up and ignored Ashford's outstretched hand. He hissed, 'So that's the thanks I get for getting both of you off the hook.' He jabbed a finger towards Wells. 'For a start, it's looking like Hertfordshire Force could have banged up the wrong man. Talk about a miscarriage of justice.'

Turning to Ashford, he jabbed the same finger in his direction. 'And you misinformed the American Embassy, saying *Lisa Black* had died in a fall from a hotel balcony in Southampton.'

Flood headed for the door, stopped halfway and turned to face both DIs. 'Call yourselves detectives. Aren't they meant to detect?' He stormed out of the room slamming the door shut behind him.

CHAPTER EIGHTEEN

As Flood made his way back to the car park, smouldering with anger, his mobile rang. He yanked it from his pocket, put it to his ear without looking at the screen and barked, 'Andy Flood.'

'How are things hanging on the other side of the pond?' He recognised Detective North's Floridian drawl.

'Fine. How are things with you?'

'Pretty good. We've made headway in the Lisa Black case. We've found her automobile in one of the long-stay car parks at Miami Airport.'

Flood's mood immediately improved. 'Fantastic,' he said, pleased that North had followed up his suggestion.

'We've examined it thoroughly. Found blood stains and a bloody towel in the trunk. The Medical Examiner checked the DNA with Lisa's. It's a match. We also found fingerprints other than Lisa's on a torch in the glove box and on the steering wheel. When we searched Lisa's condo, we found the same prints. Be keen to check those against Mandy's, for the record.'

'I'd put money on them being the same.'

'So would I. Can you get a set sent over to us?'

'I don't have access, I'm afraid.' Flood assumed North had forgotten he was a private investigator and not a police detective. 'I'll speak to the officer in charge of the case and ask him to get the pathologist to send them to you.'

'Awesome! Following your tip off, we checked the stains on the carpet. They were dried blood and a DNA check proved it was Lisa's.'

North continued, 'So ... it's looking like this: we know Mandy had a bust-up with Lisa over a boyfriend. Seems it carried over into Lisa's condo. Mandy almost certainly killed her there, put her body in the trunk of Lisa's car, drove to the Everglades and dumped it. Then she drove on to the airport.'

'Did you check the flights to the UK around the same time Lisa went missing?' Flood asked.

'We did. A 'Lisa Black' caught a British Airways flight at 7.45 p.m. on February 26th. That's the day after the bust up. We confirmed your info about Lisa and Mandy looking hellishly alike after speaking to eyewitnesses at the café and the karaoke bar. We still haven't found Lisa's purse which we assume held her passport. We believe that Mandy flew back to the UK using it.'

'That sounds plausible. Has Lisa's mobile turned up yet?'

'You mean her cell phone? No, it hasn't. It wasn't at her condo. We searched the area around her remains. No luck. Could be anywhere.'

Flood put two and two together. Mandy had given him a US number as her contact. 'I think Mandy brought Lisa's mobile to the UK. It's not turned up yet. What's your next move?' he asked.

'We've passed the file, including the results of the autopsy, to the DA. The Medical Examiner's Report indicated that Lisa had received a blunt force trauma to the front of what was left of her face. We haven't discovered a weapon, but the DA believes that Mandy Bradshaw murdered Lisa for her passport. We'll not be looking for anyone else in this case. Apart from getting the pathologist's report on Mandy's prints, that wraps things up our end.'

'OK. Thanks for updating me.'

Flood found it difficult to imagine the bright, attractive young woman who'd come to his office six weeks earlier, being capable of murder. Except his police experience told him never to doubt the capacity of ordinary people to do extraordinary things if it meant so much to them.

***

Flood and Laura visited Gemma at the hospital psychiatric unit for the last time before her transfer to the prison.

Doctor Rogers welcomed them, smiled and in his best bedside manner, said, 'Gemma's done well. She's not a danger to herself anymore. My only concern is that she believes she should be punished for what she did and deserves to be sent to prison.'

Flood replied, 'She has no idea what it will be like. I'm not sure she could handle it.'

'I can understand that, but I know the people in the therapy unit at the prison. They'll continue her treatment for her borderline personality disorder. That should help her grow out of thinking she's not worthy of being loved.'

Laura placed a palm on the table and leant forward. 'She is. We love her.'

'I'm sure you do. Your support is vital. I'll be sending a detailed report to the prison therapy unit asking them to follow through on our work. Unless you have any other questions, I'll take you through to see your daughter.'

Gemma, sitting at a table looking out of a window, looked up as Flood and Laura entered the room. Flood smiled, delighted to see her looking marginally better. Her cheeks showed more colour, and she'd regained a little weight. She slowly got to her feet and Flood and Laura took turns in hugging her. Gemma's hugs in return were still less than enthusiastic.

They sat around a table and Laura said, 'You'll be able to wear your own clothes while you're on remand. We've brought some for you. Hope they're OK.' Gemma shrugged, indicating that it wasn't important.

Flood tried to lighten the mood. 'Doctor Rogers says you've made great strides.' Gemma turned, looked at her father then at Laura, a defiant expression on her face.

'Look. I've killed Simon. I deserve to go to prison for a long time. And I don't want you visiting me. I couldn't stand it. It's too demeaning.'

Flood snorted, 'Don't be ridiculous! Of course we'll visit. We *want* to see you. Make sure you're OK.'

Gemma's eyes blazed at Flood. 'Why the sudden interest? Still feeling guilty, are you?'

Flood shot a glance at Laura before saying, 'For God's sake, Gemma! When will you realise we care deeply about you? You can't cut us off.'

Gemma's lips tightened. 'If you'd spent more time with Pippa and me when we were kids, I wouldn't be in here. You preferred pulling baddies out of their beds in the middle of the night. You missed most of our school sports days, concerts and even parents' evenings because you were too busy with your investigations. We *needed* you. Especially after what happened to me and Pippa.'

Flood felt a rush of blood to his head. 'What kind of man would I be if I didn't want to hunt down the gang who murdered your mother? I couldn't live with myself if I didn't bring them to justice, more so after the Met gave up on the case.'

'But even after you'd got the convictions, your job *always* came first. You're obsessed with it.'

Flood couldn't think of a suitable rebuttal. He glanced at Laura again, and opened his arms as if to say; *what can I do?*

Laura reached over the table and held Gemma's hand. 'I *know* your father cares about you. A day doesn't go by without him telling me how worried he is. You've been through a great deal. You'll need him more than ever now.'

Gemma bowed her head, looking down at the floor. Flood wanted to scream at her, shake some sense into her troubled mind.

He stood and walked around to her side of the table. 'I can see that you're not in the right frame of mind to talk about it now, Gemma. Another time, maybe.' He bent down and kissed the back of her head.

Laura stood, placed her hands on either side of Gemma's face and gently forced her to look up at her. 'We do love you, you know. We always will.' Gemma didn't respond.

***

For the first five minutes of the drive home, Flood and Laura didn't speak, each occupied with their own thoughts. Eventually, Flood said, 'I don't think I was cut out for parenting. I've screwed up Gemma's life.'

Laura, sitting in the passenger seat clutched his elbow. 'Oh, Andy. That's not right. Given all that's happened to your family, you've done everything you could. No one outside the Force understands the pressures of being a senior police officer. It's the people closest to you who suffer the most. You need the focus of solving crimes. It's what you do. And don't forget, in the early days, *you* were grieving, too.'

Flood's thoughts flashed back to the day of his first wife's funeral at the crematorium. Seeing the coffin disappearing behind the curtains with Pippa and Gemma in tears remained a snapshot etched in his mind.

Laura added, 'Your obsession with justice is your way of dealing with what happened to your family. All you can do now is to make up for the lost time and sort out your relationship with Gemma. I know it's important to you. Which reminds me. Have you heard from Pippa?'

'No, I haven't. I'll try again this evening.'

CHAPTER NINETEEN

MANDY
THREE WEEKS EARLIER

The following morning, Gary and I woke up late, not unsurprising given my Oscar-winning performance the previous night. I pulled back the heavy curtains. A shaft of weak sunlight bled into the room. Gary blinked as he struggled to sit up in bed. I ordered a continental breakfast from room service.

I showered and dressed and when I emerged, pulling a brush through my damp, blonde hair, I felt fresh and invigorated. Our breakfasts had been delivered. Gary got up, pulled on a dressing gown and poured the coffees. 'How are you feeling this morning?' I asked.

'Great. You OK?' He picked up a croissant from the tray and ripped off one of the knob-ends with his teeth.

'Fine. You haven't changed your mind about helping me?'

He finished chewing and put the croissant down on the plate. 'You know I'll do anything for you.' Gary picked up his cup of coffee and slugged it back in one gulp before replacing it in the saucer. 'I don't know what you saw in that wanker. You should have married me.'

'I should,' I lied. 'Listen, once we've dealt with Mike, I'll tell everyone that he and I separated and that he'd agreed to leave me the house and the boat. He'd keep our savings and investments. We'll live like royalty, be the King and Queen of Hamble. How does that sound?'

He didn't need to reply. His ear-to-ear grin told me it sounded damn good. The combination of living in 'River Landing' on the Hamble River and the prospect of a glorious sex life proved irresistible.

'Have you ever skippered a cabin cruiser?' I asked.

'Of course. Owners at the boatyard often ask me to crew their boat. Haven't got a Boat Master's Licence, nothing like that. But I know the drill.' He blabbed on about tides, currents and navigation aids, trying to impress me. Gary could bullshit for England. I wasn't sure whether to believe him, but he sounded authoritative. I gave him the benefit of the doubt.

Whenever I'd sailed with Mike on his boat, the *only* thing he'd let me do was steer the bloody thing in a straight line when we were miles out at sea. He didn't like me playing with his toys. Talk about a control freak.

Gary asked, 'What do you want me to do, exactly?'

I explained my plan, and added, 'You'll need to hire a van. One with no external markings. You'll also need to buy ropes, masking tape and a couple of bags of large pebbles, plus something like a mallet.'

'When are we going to do it? I'll need to check tides and stuff.'

'Before he finds out I survived. If we don't get to him first, he'll come after me. Finish me off. So let's do it tomorrow night.'

'OK. I'll look up the tides later today when I get back to Ocean Village. I'll call you on your mobile if it's doable.'

'Good. I'll need to make sure Mike will be at home. I'll call him on his landline before you pick me up. You're sure you can handle a *Sunseeker* cabin cruiser in the Solent at night?'

''Course I bloody can.' If he lied, he covered it well.

'There's a couple of other things, Gary. Wear gloves and turn off your mobile before you leave home, but bring it with you. I'll do the same.'

Gary nodded. 'OK. Good idea.' Over several more cups of coffee, we ran through the plan in detail once more to make sure we'd covered every eventuality. A ripple of euphoria surged through my body at the prospect of having Mike out of my life forever. And we hadn't even begun.

'OK, Gary. If the tides are OK, pick me up from the Sturridge Hotel around seven tomorrow night.' I wagged a finger at him. 'And don't be late.'

***

That night, I lay awake wrestling with the problem of what to tell Mike's brother, Barry, after we'd done the deed. Although they weren't close, he was Mike's only living relative. I didn't want him looking too closely into his brother's disappearance.

I'd only met him twice, once at my wedding and again when their mother died. Mike always described Barry as a loser with a drink problem. A *functional alcoholic* Mike called him. Even at the funeral, Barry had too much to drink. Mike was furious, putting him down and ridiculing him at every opportunity.

I considered calling Barry after we'd got rid of Mike, tell him I'd returned from the US and that we'd split up and he'd left Hamble to seek a fresh start. But I had no way of knowing what Mike may have already told him. I decided not to call.

CHAPTER TWENTY

Flood and Laura rarely missed the late-night news bulletin from ITV's Southern News. It became a ritual. He switched on just in time to hear the newsreader state that a badly decomposed male body had been found washed up on the beach at Lee-on-the-Solent.

A camera panned the grey waves rolling on to the overcast shoreline as he said, in a sombre voice, 'The body had masking tape wrapped around the torso and arms. A frayed rope was attached to his legs. The police are therefore treating the case as murder. I spoke earlier to Doctor Lesley Butler, an expert forensic anthropologist. Here's what she had to say.'

A dark-haired, middle-aged woman, wearing black-rimmed glasses looked straight into the camera. 'We estimate the body spent three weeks or more in the seawater. Given the amount of decomposition, it is proving difficult to identify the body. We cannot rely on DNA and fingerprint analysis. We are checking dental records but this will take time.

'The victim had a pacemaker fitted which is still intact. We hope to identify the body by the make, model and serial number contained in medical records. That could take several days.'

Doctor Butler paused before continuing. 'We discovered a tattoo on the back of the right hand. We hope a member of the public may recognise it.' The camera cut to a photo of a faded image. The newsreader's voice-over thanked the doctor before asking viewers to call Southampton Police Station or 101 if they could provide any information to help identify the body.

Flood paused the screen with his remote and leant forward, peering at the tattoo, thinking it looked vaguely familiar. He could just make out two initial Ms inside a pair of entwined hearts. He racked his brains, trying to recall where he'd seen it.

Suddenly, he stood and pointed to the screen, his voice crackling with excitement. 'Laura, look! That tattoo is the same as Mandy's. That's bloody Bradshaw!'

'Are you certain?'

'I'm positive. I'll visit DI Ashford first thing tomorrow.'

***

'What crackpot theories have you come up with now?' Ashford's cynicism couldn't be mistaken for anything else.

'I know what happened to Michael Bradshaw.'

Ashford smirked. 'Do you? Pray tell.'

'I assume you are aware of a body being washed up in the Solent yesterday?'

'Of course. One of my colleagues is on the case.'

'You'll remember that the pathologist confirmed that Mandy Bradshaw had a tattoo on the back of her right hand. It's identical to the one found on the washed-up body. Mandy and Michael Bradshaw probably had them done when they got married.'

Ashford's smirk disappeared. He immediately picked up his phone and urged DS Bridges in the outer office to join them.

Bobby put his head around the door. 'Yes, Guv?'

'Come in, sit down. That body washed up in the Solent yesterday; Mr Flood, here, believes it's Michael Bradshaw; says he had an identical tattoo in the same place as the woman who fell from the balcony at the Sturridge Hotel. Can you get photos of both from forensics and the pathologist? I'd like to compare them.'

Bobby stood. 'I'll get on to it right away.'

Ashford said, 'before you go, tell Mr Flood what you discovered when you searched Bradshaw's house yesterday and spoke to the neighbours.'

'We found no male clothing of any sort. And no personal effects, laptop, mobile, nothing. His car's missing, too. It looks like he's moved out except his boat's moored on the jetty.'

135

Flood gasped in frustration and shot back, 'I know all this. I told you I went there, *remember*?'

'You did, but there's something you didn't discover. Tell him.' Ashford nodded at Bridges.

'When we checked the CCTV, the hard drive from the recorder had been removed and the mains electricity turned off. We also searched the boat. We found a thread of clothing which had snagged on a side rail. It could be Bradshaw's of course, except we can't check, because, as I said, his clothes are missing.

'We also found traces of semen on the main deck and three blonde hair fibres on the back of a seat in the cockpit area. We're particularly keen to see if the blonde hairs match Mandy's dyed hair. The forensics team are analysing them as a matter of urgency.'

Flood's admiration for Bridges grew with everything he did and said. *That's proper policing. He's more competent than Ashford, despite the difference in rank.*

Bobby added, 'We asked the neighbours if they'd seen any unusual movements of the boat. One said he saw it leaving the mooring at around ten o'clock on the night of the seventh of March. He wasn't sure whether it was Bradshaw at the helm. It was back on the mooring the following morning. The neighbour went to bed so couldn't say what time it returned.'

Flood did some mental arithmetic. 'If Michael Bradshaw hasn't been seen since, that's what? Nearly three weeks ago?'

'Sounds about right,' Ashford conceded.

Flood asked, 'Did the boat have GPS tracking fitted?'

DS Bridges flicked through his notebook. 'It's one of the first things we checked. The boat was built in 2013. GPS wasn't fitted as standard until the 2016 models.' *Another point to Bobby Bridges.*

'That's a shame,' Flood said, adding, 'It would be good to know the exact time of Bradshaw's death.'

Bridges replied, 'The forensic anthropologist's report has been given top priority. Should be here tomorrow morning.'

As Flood drove back to his office, his thoughts drifted to Barry Bradshaw's alibi for his brother's movements on the evening Angela was murdered. It concerned him that it hadn't been independently verified. And when he and Laura had spoken to Barry, they both felt uneasy with his demeanour. DI Wells, too, had mentioned Barry's nervousness when questioning him.

Flood was certain that the body washed up in the Solent was Mike Bradshaw. He decided take a chance and visit Barry at his home, tell him about his brother's death and judge his reaction.

He used his laptop to get Barry's address via the Electoral Roll which showed that he lived alone. Waiting until Barry had returned from work, he drove through drizzling rain, arriving at the house in Hemel Hempstead shortly after 6.00 p.m. A shiny BMW demonstrator parked in the driveway of a 1960s bungalow confirmed Barry's presence.

When Barry saw Flood on his doorstep, his expression gave away his disdain at seeing him. 'What do you want?' he mumbled.

'I have some news about your brother.'

'What news?'

'It's better if I tell you inside. It's important.'

Barry paused before answering, obviously intrigued. 'OK. You'd better come in.'

He ushered Flood through a hallway into a scruffy, gloomy living room with flower-patterned wallpaper. Two shabby sofas covered in dull, ruby-coloured velour sat either side of a table with a bottle of Jack Daniel's and a half-full tumbler on it. Flood frowned. Either BMW sales weren't going well or Barry had terrible taste.

Noticing the look on Flood's face, Barry said, 'None of this is my choice. This used to be my mother's house. I lost a load of money in a messy divorce, so moved in here after she passed away a couple of years ago. Haven't got round to sorting it out yet.'

Flood gave him an understanding nod. Barry motioned him to sit on one of the sofas as he sat opposite him. 'What's this about my brother?'

'I'm sorry to tell you he's been found dead in suspicious circumstances.' Flood waited for a reaction.

Barry put both hands to his mouth and collapsed back in the sofa, his face creasing with disbelief. 'What? How? When?'

Flood explained how Mike had been found on the beach at Lee-on-the-Solent. Barry took his hands away from his mouth and sat forward. 'That's awful. You're sure it's Michael?'

'I'm certain. Tell me again, when did you last have contact with your brother?'

Barry paused before replying, his mind processing what he'd heard. 'It must have been about a year ago. I'd sold him a new BMW. He had a problem with it, so he called me, accused me of selling him a dud. I got it sorted out but never got a thank you, though. Typical.'

'You told me when we last met that he'd mentioned Mandy leaving him. But she told me it happened less than a month ago. So how would you know if your brother hadn't told you?'

Barry stammered, 'Oh, yes. I'd ... I'd forgotten. He did call me, thought I should know. To be honest, I couldn't give a fuck.' He snorted. 'My brother's not exactly the easiest person in the world to get along with. Look, are you sure it's my brother's body they found?'

'I'm afraid so. Tell me, in what way was your brother difficult?'

Barry grunted. 'He always had to have his own way and could get people to do whatever he wanted. Including me, right from when we were kids. If I didn't cooperate, he'd drag me to the garden shed when our parents were out, put his hands around my neck and throttle me until I couldn't breathe. Then he'd lock me inside until our parents came home.'

Flood, sensing Barry wanted to talk, let him continue.

'Another time, when I was eleven and Mike was fifteen, he bullied me to into going shoplifting with him. I wanted to show him that I was as good as him, so I went along with it. He told me to pinch the stuff while he'd keep a lookout and tip me off if someone spotted me. But when the owner caught me in the act, he ran off, laughing. He had no intention of warning me. Classic Michael.' Barry couldn't disguise the bitterness in his voice.

'For as long as I can remember, we always argued. The last time was over Mum's will. He persuaded her to leave most of her inheritance to him, insinuating that I'd piss it up against the wall. All I got was this place.' He waved an arm around the room. 'All Mum's investments, left to her by my dad, went to him.'

Barry looked down at the floor and shook his head. 'I can't believe he's dead. He thought he was indestructible.'

'I'm sorry for your loss, Barry, and having to ask these questions. I'm trying to find out what happened to Mandy. She told me before she died that Michael had let slip that he'd killed before. If he did, it's possible he killed her.'

Barry didn't react so Flood pressed on. 'The alibi you gave your brother at Sam Wharton's murder trial was crucial. You claimed you both spent the night watching a soccer match on TV. Is that true?'

Barry raised his head. 'It is. That's what I told the police.' Flood noticed Barry's leg twitching again, as it did previously when Flood and Laura met Barry at the BMW showroom.

Flood played his trump card. 'Then you may have a problem. I understand the police believe that they're close to obtaining evidence suggesting that Michael murdered Angela and framed Sam Wharton. They're rechecking the rucksack containing her jewellery and the tools used to break into the house. If Michael's fingerprints are present, it will prove your brother is guilty.'

Barry's already pale complexion turned the colour of chalk. Flood added, 'If that's the case, you can expect another visit from the police to question you about the alibi. It proves that you lied. The maximum term for perverting the course of justice in a murder case is life imprisonment.'

In the hush that followed, Flood tried maintaining eye contact with Barry. He looked everywhere except at Flood who broke the silence. 'Anything you tell me, I promise I won't pass on. I'm only interested in what happened to Mandy.'

Barry's hands shook as he reached for the tumbler of whiskey on the table, drained it, and threw his head against the back of the sofa, looking up at the ceiling. Flood recognised Barry's reactions. Other witnesses he'd interviewed had wanted to get something off their chest, too.

Thirty seconds later, Barry faced Flood and blew out a deep breath.

'I've been carrying this load of shit for the past four years. I don't know why I bloody-well covered for Mike. He bullied me into it. He told me that he'd found out about Sam Wharton coming to the house after he and Angela split up. It drove him crazy to think of her having sex with another man. He said he planned to smother her to death and that she deserved it. He asked me to cover for him. I said I would, thinking that he'd treat me better afterwards. Fat chance. He still treated me like a wanker.'

Flood leant forward, getting so close to Barry, he could smell the whiskey on his breath. He spoke softly, like a priest in a confessional box. 'What exactly happened during the evening Angela was murdered?'

'Mike left my house around mid-afternoon and caught the bus to St Albans Railway Station. Then he told me he'd walked the forty-five minutes to his house in Marshalswick, suffocated Angela and walked back into town to catch the bus back, arriving home at about 8.30 in the evening. He never told me anything about getting a taxi ride and framing Wharton. By the time I found out, I was in too deep.'

Barry reached for the whiskey bottle on the table, poured himself a large glass and took another glug. 'You don't have to tell the police any of this, do you?'

'No. I won't.'

On the drive home, Flood felt pleased with himself; his hypothesis had proven accurate.

***

Most Friday nights, Flood and Laura went out for a meal in one of Winchester's pubs. They chose the Wykeham Arms, an old-fashioned inn complete with hundreds of pewter tankards hanging from the beams and Victorian school desks, complete with inkwells, used as tables.

Over their first drink, Flood asked Laura about the new fingerprint research project she was working on at the forensics lab. She smiled and nodded. 'You know how it is – some days we make progress, then the next, we find ourselves up a blind alley. It's my job to find a way through. We're not far off getting a solution.'

She smiled at Flood. 'Anyway, you look a bit smug, if I may say so. What's your news?'

Flood smiled back, nodded and took a sip of his beer. 'I've made a breakthrough in the Bradshaw case.' He told her about Barry confessing to providing a false alibi for his brother.

'How did you get him to admit it?'

'You know me, Mister Persistent. In a way, I feel sorry for him. He was totally under Michael's influence, had been since they were kids. He'd bottled everything up, couldn't wait to tell someone about it. I'm confident Michael Bradshaw was responsible for Angela's murder.'

Laura gave Flood a quizzical look. 'You'll need more than Barry's confession to prove it; like forensic evidence.'

'That's why I've asked DI Wells to follow up my leads.'

'Are you going to inform Ashford and Wells about him lying?'

Flood stroked the side of his cheek. 'I can't. I promised Barry that whatever he told me was in confidence. He wouldn't have owned up otherwise.' He took another sip of his beer and placed the glass back on the table.

Laura frowned. 'In the absence of forensic evidence and you not informing the police about Barry lying, where does that leave Wharton?'

'So you want me to break my promise to Barry?'

'I don't think you've got a choice. If Barry's telling the truth about his brother's alibi, an innocent man is serving twenty years for a murder he didn't commit. You're the one always banging on about justice.'

Laura picked up the pub menu and made a point of studying it. 'Anyway, what are you going to have to eat?'

CHAPTER TWENTY-ONE

Gemma's decision not to want to see him at the prison ate away at Flood like flesh-eating bacteria. Powerless to help her, he tried relaxing at home with Laura the following evening, gazing vacantly at the TV screen, his mind miles away in a whirlpool of guilty emotions. He'd called Pippa three times and left messages. She'd not called back.

Laura flapped a newspaper in front of his face to get his attention following his latest bout of introspection. 'Cooeee! 'Where's Andy Flood? Remember me?'

Flood put a hand to his forehead and rubbed it gently. 'Sorry, Laura. I was miles away.'

'You've been a pain in the arse lately. It's Gemma, isn't it?'

'I don't get why she won't see us. She needs us now more than ever.'

'Why don't you write her a letter? Explain how you feel. Be therapeutic for you.'

'You think so? I haven't written a letter to anyone for ages.'

'Go on. Do it now.'

Flood disappeared to his study and emerged back in the living room half-an-hour later. Sitting down next to Laura, he said, 'What do you think of this? I've had a few goes at it.' He read it out.

Darling Gemma, it's breaking my heart to think of you cooped up in your prison cell. Whatever's gone on before, I want to make it up to you. I know I wasn't the best parent in the world. I want to visit, make up for lost time. So does Laura. We want to support you through what is going to be a tough time ahead.

There's so much we need to chat about. We plan to come next Thursday, the 24th. Please say yes.

We love you.
Dad.

'What do you think?'

Laura placed her hand on Flood's arm and said, 'It's perfect.'

'I've kept it short, hoping she'll respond.' He kissed the letter before carefully placing it inside the envelope, noticing Laura's smile. Slightly embarrassed, he added, 'I'll drop it in the post box tomorrow on my way to the office.'

***

At home the following morning, Flood received a call from Ashford. 'I've been thinking about your special insights into Mandy's death. How would you like to act as a consultant, reporting to me?'

Despite thinking that Ashford's offer sounded suspicious, Flood couldn't resist. 'Are you sure?'

'I've spoken to my Superintendent. I told him everything you've brought to this case. He's impressed. Says it's highly unusual, but, subject to the usual background checks, he's agreed. Can you come to the station later? DS Bridges and I would like to share some information with you.' He sounded upbeat.

'I'll be with you in an hour.'

On the way to the police station, Flood agonised whether to tell Ashford about Barry's confession. Laura's comment about Wharton being banged up for a crime he didn't commit hung over him like a black cloud.

DS Bridges came to collect him from the front desk. On the way to Ashford's office, Flood asked, 'How long have you been in the Force, Bobby?'

'Coming up fifteen years. I went to police college straight from school. My dad was an officer. He made it to DI working out of Portsmouth. Unfortunately, he got killed on a raid. The villains had no chance of escape, just wanted to go down in a blaze of glory. One of the bastards shot Dad with a pistol. He died instantly.'

'That's dreadful. How old were you?'

'Still in short trousers. Even since then, joining the Force was all I ever wanted to do as a mark of respect. My mum wasn't too pleased.'

'I bet.'

When they reached Ashford's office, Bridges tapped the door, opened it and said, 'Andy Flood's here.'

Ashford invited them both to sit at his desk. 'Welcome to the Force, Mr Flood. DI Wells called me late last night. He's received the forensics report from the lab regarding the prints on the rucksack. You'll be pleased to know they found traces of Michael Bradshaw's fingerprints on it.'

Flood's body simmered with satisfaction. A wave of relief washed over him, too. He didn't want to break the promise he'd made to Barry. Now, he didn't need to. The police could prove that Barry lied and he'd have to face the consequences.

Ashford continued, 'DI Wells agrees with you that the most likely explanation is that Bradshaw wasn't wearing gloves when he bought the rucksack. Or stupid enough not to wear any when he filled it with Angela's jewellery and the tools. This proves Bradshaw murdered Angela and set up Sam Wharton.' As if reading Flood's mind, he added, 'DI Wells is going to question Barry about the alibi he gave his brother.'

Forcing himself not to sound too self-righteous, Flood said, 'But the question remains; did Michael Bradshaw murder Mandy as well?

'That's a possibility. I agree.' Ashford sounded more authoritative than Flood could remember. He continued, 'Yesterday, I asked Bobby to follow up Mrs Crompton, the neighbour who told you about the white Transit van seen leaving Bradshaw's house in a hurry on the night of 7th of March. The hire company's tracking device showed it stopping at a lock-up close to Southampton docks shortly after it left Hamble. We sent a team there and broke in. They found men's clothes, personal items, golf clubs and a BMW registered to Michael Bradshaw.'

Bridges added, 'A Gary Fleming hired the van. He's now a person of interest. We'll be visiting him later today.'

Pleased for once, that Ashford had followed up his leads, Flood nodded and said, 'So it's possible Bradshaw discovered Mandy had survived, sought her out and pushed her off the sixth-floor balcony of the Sturridge Hotel, making it look like an accident. The only caveat for this theory is timescales. We need to find out precisely when Bradshaw died. Is that imminent?'

Ashford nodded at him. 'I'm expecting a report from the forensic anthropologist any minute.'

'What are you going to do about Sam Wharton? He's already served four years.'

'We'll submit a file to the Criminal Cases Review Commission. If they accept the new evidence, and there's no reason not to, they can order an appeal.'

Before Flood could reply, a DC knocked at Ashford's office door brandishing a document. Ashford looked up. 'This might be what we're waiting for.' He waved in the officer who handed over a folder.

'Sorry to interrupt, Guv. You asked me to let you know as soon as the anthropologist's report came through. The summary's on the front.'

'Thanks, Jack.' As the DC left, Ashford spent twenty seconds reading the preliminary conclusions.

Flood couldn't contain his impatience. 'Well?'

Ashford stopped reading and looked up. 'They've analysed Bradshaw's pacemaker. It stopped working at 9.16 p.m. on Saturday 7th March.'

Flood realised the importance of the date before Ashford. He blurted out, 'Mandy's time of death is estimated to be in the early hours of the following morning, the 8th. That means Bradshaw couldn't have killed Mandy.'

'Shit!' Bridges cursed, as Ashford took a sharp intake of breath, flung the report on his desk and slumped in his chair.

●▲●

CHAPTER TWENTY-TWO

MANDY

Gary called the next afternoon to say the tides would be in our favour. He'd hired the van and bought everything I'd asked. Shortly before 7.00 p.m., the headlights of a plain white Transit van swung into the Sturridge Hotel car park, lighting up the entrance where I stood waiting for him. I wheeled out an empty suitcase I'd bought earlier in the day. I'd also purchased two battery-operated head torches, the sort used by night-time joggers, which I'd popped in my bag.

Gary jumped out of the driver's seat, rushed round to the rear doors and opened them. He looked menacing, dressed in a black zipped-up hoodie, trousers and baseball cap. He greeted me with, 'So this is how Bonnie and Clyde must have felt!'

'I wouldn't know,' I replied, giving him a scathing look. I wanted him to be serious, not flippant. And besides, Bonnie and Clyde died in a hail of bullets. Not the ending I envisaged.

He threw the suitcase inside the van and joined me in the front. As he started the van, I said, 'Mike's at home. I rang him earlier and hung up as he answered. Did you get everything?'

'Yep. No problem.'

We headed east on the M27 to my house in Hamble, around twenty-five minutes away. He drove fast and frequently changed lanes. 'Please slow down, Gary. You're not driving a bloody fire engine. Are you on something?'

Turning to me, he winked, brushed a speck of white powder from his nose and replied, 'Just a quick confidence builder.'

Typical. The last thing I wanted was a prick for a partner. I needed an extra pair of hands, that's all. If I'd had enough time, I could have trained a gorilla to help me. But Gary's ability to handle a boat was crucial to achieving my plan. I was stuck with him ... for now.

I told Gary to park in a little-used side road fifty yards from the house where the sparse street lights gave off a Dickensian half-light. We walked round to the back of the van, opened the doors and clambered inside. We tipped the bag of pebbles into the suitcase, zipped it up and together, lifted the heavy load on to the road.

Gary locked the van, pulled his bag onto his shoulder and dragged the suitcase behind him towards my house. We melted into the gloom with our hoodies pulled up over our heads.

The front gates to River Landing were closed, as I expected, but I recalled the code, hoping Mike hadn't changed it. My luck held. They slowly opened with a mechanical hum. Mike's BMW was parked on the driveway. As we walked up to the front door, we tripped the outside lights which lit up the entrance. Gary stood out of sight behind a pillar next to the porch.

I rang the doorbell. I'd forgotten how much I loved the sound of those chimes. Thought I'd never hear them again. Mike opened the door. His large frame stood, silhouetted by the lighting from the hallway.

'Hello,' I said, offering my sweetest of smiles and flicked back my hood. He stepped out onto the porch to get a closer look at me. I'd have given anything to have photographed the expression of astonishment on his face.

'What the fuck …' he said. Before he could finish the sentence, Gary stepped in between us and hammered Mike in the head with the mallet he'd taken from his shoulder bag. Blood spurted from his wounds. I shuddered at the force Gary used. As Mike fell, Gary carried on hitting him until he lost consciousness.

'That's enough, Gary! Let's get him inside,' I shouted. He smashed the mallet onto Mike's head one more time as he lay in the porch. We dragged him and the heavy suitcase into the hall and closed the door.

Gary removed a roll of masking tape from his bag and began wrapping it around Mike's torso, trapping his arms down by his side. His face looked as if he'd gone ten rounds with Mike Tyson. I stared at him, wishing he'd come round; I wanted to tell him what an arsehole he is.

I hoped he wasn't dead. Rushing to the medicine kit in the kitchen, I returned with wads of cotton wool, which I held tightly against Mike's wounds to stop the bleeding. I had other plans for him.

Once the bleeding stopped, I reached into my bag and pulled out the head torches and threw one in Gary's direction as I fixed mine to my head. 'Turn it on now. I'm going to the utility room to switch off the mains and take out the hard drive from the CCTV recorder.'

The previous night, I wondered how we could gain entry without being recognised. Technology wasn't my strong point, so I googled how to remove the hard drive. A YouTube video showed how simple it is: undo four screws, detach the leads and take it out. It took me less than three minutes. When I'd finished, I dropped the hard drive in my bag and made my way to the fuse box in the kitchen. The room plunged into darkness as I flicked off the mains switch.

Next, I headed for the back door, my head torch lighting the way, needing to confirm that Mike's boat was tied up to the mooring. I rushed part-way down the jetty and inwardly cheered as *Providence* gently bobbed on the docile River Hamble. I never doubted it not being there; sailing's Mike's passion and he loved that boat.

Retracing my steps to Mike's office, I immediately found what I wanted. Mike's mobile sat on his desk. I switched it off and placed it in my bag. I knew Mike kept the boat keys in the left-hand drawer of his desk. I slid them into my jeans pocket.

By the time I returned to the hallway, Gary had finished wrapping the masking tape around Mike's entire body, including his ankles and mouth, and stood over him. The beams of light from our head torches created eerie, shifting shadows dancing on the walls. Mike gave out muffled groans as he came round. He stared at me with a look of confusion, his eyes bulging, not with fear as I'd expected, but anger.

Taking the boat keys from my pocket, I dangled them in front of his face. 'Shall we go for a little boat ride? You like to go sailing, don't you?'

He tried to say something, but Gary had done an excellent job with the tape. Mike could only muster a gurgling sound.

He weighed around a hundred kilos, twenty more than Gary. So with some difficulty, he and I pulled Mike to his feet and half-dragged, half-carried him from the hallway through the back door and down the jetty to the boat. Once we got him aboard via the swim platform at the stern, we dumped him in a sitting position on a seat in the cockpit next to the helm station. I switched on the lights which highlighted the sumptuous, parchment-coloured leather seating and the deck's teak panelling. Gary looked from bow to stern and back again. The expression on his face reminded me of the first time he saw me naked.

'Wow! Nice bit of kit. Must be worth at least half-a-million quid.' I could tell he'd already dreamt about motoring down the River Hamble on a sunny summer's day as the captain of *his* ship.

I interrupted his reverie. 'Gary, go back. Bring the suitcase. Come on. Let's get going.'

Moments later, he returned, dragging the suitcase behind him. As he lugged it onto the boat's deck, I noticed Mike's body twitching. He'd probably guessed his fate.

Gary unhooked the hawsers from the bow and stern bollards, threw them onto the deck and, as the boat drifted away, sprung back on board. We turned off our head torches and Gary started the engines which spluttered into life with an urgency matching our exhilarated state of minds. He checked the navigation console to ensure everything was ready to go. I panicked; what if we didn't have enough fuel? I hadn't thought of it until now. I asked Gary.

'Yeah. We're fine,' he said, as the boat slowly edged away from the jetty.

I asked Gary, 'Have you been on this river before?'

'No, I haven't, but don't worry. The rules are the same everywhere. See those channel marker buoys over there with green and red coloured lights? They mark the shipping lanes. We need to stay well clear of those. I know what I'm doing.'

I looked across the river towards Fawley on the opposite bank. The lights from the oil refinery reflected on the shimmering sea, reminding me of the lights on the coast of the Gulf of Mexico where Mike had dumped me.

How apt. Surely, nothing could stop me getting my revenge now.

***

Gary did a great job steering the boat down the River Hamble heading for the Solent. Just as well. Two massive black hulls of container ships, their navigation lights piercing the darkness, stealthily appeared in the shipping lane to our starboard side within ten minutes of each other, causing our boat to pitch and roll in it's the wake. Gary skilfully rode the wash.

Mike sat slumped, trussed up on the cockpit seat, his bulging, fearful eyes darting between Gary and me. He continued to gurgle through the tightly wrapped tape around his mouth.

After half-an-hour's sailing, Gary said. 'I've checked the depth finder. We're deep enough. This'll do.' He cut the engines and dropped anchor. The flickering lights of East Cowes on the Isle of Wight on the starboard side told me we were seven or eight miles from Hamble.

I'd thought a lot about what else I could do to make Mike suffer. Dumping him at sea wasn't enough. As Gary sat at the wheel, I stood next to him and began fondling his crotch and whispered, 'Before we dump the bastard, I've got one more thing I'd like to do.' Leaning my body close to his, I snogged him, stopping occasionally to grin at Mike.

As Gary grew harder, I dragged him off his helm seat and pushed him down on the couch opposite Mike. I unzipped his trousers, pulled down my black, skinny jeans and guided him into me as I rode him like a rodeo rider.

Gary groaned with pleasure. He'd have sex, anytime, anywhere. I grinned at pathetic Mike again. 'See what you're missing?' I said. He squeezed shut his swollen eyes, not bearing to watch. He could hear everything, though. I gave, arguably, the best audible sexual performance of my life. Mike couldn't possibly have mistaken it for anything but the best orgasm any woman had achieved. Ever.

When we'd finished, Gary said, 'That was so good!' I got the impression he liked performing in front of an audience. I had to admit, I did too.

As we pulled up our clothes, I said to Gary, 'OK. Let's dump him now.' We dragged Mike to his feet, as his gurgling grew louder. Gary tied the suitcase full of pebbles to Mike's ankles. I watched his body tremble as the finality of his fate dawned on him.

Holding him upright against the side of the boat, Mike looked at each of us in turn again, his eyes pleading for mercy. His gurgling grew even more frenetic. Pushing my face close to his, I spat out, 'Now you know *exactly* how I felt when you dumped me in the sea leaving me to drown.'

I nodded to Gary, who grabbed Mike under the armpits. I held his legs. As I counted, 'One, two, three,' we lifted him up and over the side rail and left him hanging there, the heavy suitcase attached to his feet acting as a counterweight on the deck. Gary heaved it over the side rails with a grunt.

'Good riddance,' I yelled as Mike and the makeshift millstone splashed into the water before disappearing from view in frothy foam. We silently stared at the water long enough to make sure we'd achieved our goal. I closed my eyes and exhaled.

I turned to Gary who couldn't take his eyes off the spot where Mike had sunk. I asked, 'Did you remember to switch off your mobile before you left home?'

'Yeah.'

'Good. We don't want anything to connect us. Throw it overboard. I'll throw Lisa's, too. And Mike's. There's no way they'll be discovered from the seabed.'

Reaching into my bag, I pulled them out and flung them into the Solent. I did the same with the CCTV hard drive. At last, I could get my life back and revert to being Mandy.

Gary weighed anchor and we motored back to Hamble. As we got closer to the house, we donned our head torches and switched them on. I told Gary to turn off the engine and lights, moor the boat and fetch the van round to the front of the house. I gave him the code for the gates.

As he left, I entered the house by the back door and pulled several black plastic sacks from Gary's shoulder bag, which he'd left in the hallway. I went upstairs, cleared out Mike's wardrobe and his washing and shaving gear from the bathroom, stuffing everything into the sacks. Then I went to Mike's office and filled more sacks with his laptop, printer and business files.

When Gary returned, we stashed the plastic bags in the back of the van. 'There's more stuff in the garage,' I said. We carried Mike's golf clubs, bike and toolbox to the van through the side gate I'd unlocked, and threw them into the back, too.

'Right, that's everything,' I said, gratified that the Transit proved big enough to take all Mike's possessions. 'You drive the van, Gary. I'll follow in Mike's BMW.' I picked up the car keys hanging on the wall just inside the front door which I pulled shut. Switching off my head torch, I dropped it into my bag, slid into the BMW and followed Gary out of the gates.

He revved up the Transit van as if he was on the Formula One starting grid. Shooting out of the gates, the fierce blast of a horn made me jump as the van almost collided with another car. As Gary slammed on his brakes, I nearly rammed him from behind. When I challenged him later, he played it down. 'It wasn't my fault. Some stupid bitch was driving on the wrong side of the road.'

Earlier that day, I'd cashed some of Scottie's dollars into pounds and paid three months' rent in advance for a lockup garage close to the docks in Southampton. I'd given Gary the satnav details and followed him, cursing the idiot for driving so fast. The last thing we needed was the cops pulling us over.

When we reached the lockup, it took us twenty minutes to unload the contents of the van and stack everything inside. I left the BMW there too. I'd deal with it later.

We arrived back at the hotel around 11.15 p.m. Before I'd undone my seatbelt to get out of the van, Gary turned to me, a lascivious look on his face. 'I want to stay with you tonight.'

'It's probably best if you don't, Gary.'

'Don't mess me about, Mandy,' he wailed. 'I can call you that now, can't I?' I undid my seatbelt and tried to open the door, but he reached out, seized my right arm and gripped it so tightly, I couldn't move away.

'I need you, Mandy. Now.'

I slapped his cheek with my free hand, taking him by surprise. 'Let me go, Gary,' I yelled, wrenching my arm away from his grasp. I opened the door and ran towards the hotel entrance. Once inside, I glanced back through the windows and watched Gary get out of the van, lean against the side and light a spiff as he stared in my direction.

He'd served my purpose, and now I wanted him out of my life.

CHAPTER TWENTY-THREE

Ashford, Bridges and Flood sat still, stunned by the latest forensics information. Flood broke the silence. 'Everything pointed to Bradshaw. But it's obvious that someone abducted him, took the boat out and dumped him in the Solent. That someone has to be Mandy. She had a motive. She told me Bradshaw would go after her if he found out she'd survived. I'd put money on the dyed hairs found on the boat matching Mandy's. But she couldn't have done it on her own. What about the guy who hired the van, Gary Fleming?'

'He's got to be our number one suspect. I want to question him as soon as possible,' Ashford said.

'Good. Have you found the mobile Mandy was using?'

'No, we haven't.'

'That's vital now. We need to know if there was contact between them before she died.' As Flood finished the sentence, he fished out his notebook, flipped through it and stopped at a particular page. 'When Mandy came to see me, posing as Lisa, she gave me her mobile number. It's registered in the US. She told me her rescuer, Scottie, got it for her. Maybe he didn't. What if it's Lisa's and Mandy stole it?'

Flood added, as he tapped a forefinger on Ashford's desk. 'You should get your team to check with my contact in Florida, guy called Chuck North, a detective with Naples Police Department. I'll give you his details. You can ask him to check the number with the main mobile providers in the US. Whoever it is, they'll have tied up a deal with a British provider who can download every number called in the UK. From the log, they can provide names and addresses; see if Gary Fleming's name turns up. If you stress the urgency, it's pretty quick.'

'You've done this before, haven't you?' Ashford said.

'I've used a couple of websites which provide this service. RPNL they call it – Reverse Phone Number Lookup. It's a bit hit and miss on the internet. It's better to go through official police channels because the providers *have* to cooperate by law.'

'And why would North assist us?'

'I helped him account for Lisa Black's death and her link to Mandy. He owes me a favour. Do you want me to contact him?'

'No. We'll handle it. Give DS Bridges the number.'

The DS noted it down and headed for the door. 'I'll follow this up right away, Guv.'

***

As soon as Flood left the police station, he called Detective North in Naples and told him to expect a call from Bridges. North assured him he'd give it top priority.

Another idea struck Flood as he spoke. 'There's something else you could do for me, Chuck. Can you get background information on a Scottie McPherson? Find out if he has any UK contacts, for example? He was a big-shot lawyer working out of New York before he retired. He's living in downtown Naples. I can give you an address. It's only a long-shot, but he may know something about Mandy's death.'

'Sure thing.'

***

As Flood shaved the following morning, he heard the familiar clang of his letterbox. Wiping off the remains of the cream from his face, he sprinted, barefoot, down the stairs wearing only his boxer shorts. A formal buff-coloured envelope stood out on the doormat among the usual gaudy-coloured junk mail. He instantly guessed the source of the letter.

He bent down, picked everything up and went to his study. After dumping the mailshots in the bin, he sat at his desk and slit open the envelope, removed the folded sheet of formal prison notepaper and opened it.

He read:

Dear Dad, I thought long and hard about what you said in your letter. I wanted to call you, but there are always long queues for the payphone, and anyway, probably better to write to clarify what I wanted to say. I'm sorry if I upset you when we last met. You were right about prison life. Being locked up in a cell every night is driving me mad. Although the officers are OK, I'm struggling to cope with the other inmates. I'd love you to visit next Thursday. Give me something to look forward to.
Lots of love to you and Laura,
Gemma. XXX

Flood leaned back in his chair, a wave of relief washing over him. Clutching the letter, he rushed upstairs to the bedroom to show Laura. She was sitting at her dressing table brushing her hair. Flood placed the letter in front of her. 'Look at this!'

Laura read it and smiled up at him. 'I'm so pleased, Andy. It's a start. Do you want me to come with you?'

'I'd love you to.'

'Well, you'd better finish shaving. You don't want going to the prison looking like a vagrant.'

Ever since the police had charged Gemma with murder, a growing feeling of despair and guilt had lodged in the pit of Flood's stomach. Her attitude towards him hadn't helped. Now the feeling wasn't as intense.

***

The following afternoon, they drove to the prison. After passing through strict security, similar to that experienced by Flood when he visited Sam Wharton in Pentonville, they arrived at the reception area of the Block A visiting hall. Around fifty other visitors sat on benches against the walls chatting amongst themselves as noisy children enjoyed themselves in a play area.

The youngsters' shrill voices grew louder in anticipation of the opening of the doors to the prisoners' hall. Everyone surged through when they did, anxious to make the most of every available second. Some of the younger children whooped as they rushed towards their mothers, throwing themselves into their arms.

Female guards wearing white tunics, black skirts and beetle-crusher shoes patrolled the hall, several sporting severe haircuts. Flood and Laura spotted Gemma three rows from the front, wearing a red sash, like her fellow prisoners, to differentiate them from the visitors. Her hands fiddled with the sash and her expression was edgy and insecure.

She offered a feeble smile when she noticed them, stood and briefly hugged them both. Anything more was a breach of the rules. At the hospital, she'd been defiant, accepting her fate, like a martyr facing her punishment. Not now.

'How's the food, Gemma?' Laura asked.

'It's OK. But I don't trust it.'

'Why not?'

'I'm sure the inmates working in the kitchen are messing about with my meals. Most of them are seriously screwed up. A lot think I'm posh, too good for the likes of them. That doesn't help.'

She glanced around the room again and fidgeted in her chair. Flood fought the urge to hold her hand across the table, but even that breached the rules.

'And your accommodation?' Laura didn't like to use the term *cell*.

'It's tiny, but at least, I'm on my own. I couldn't bear to share with anyone. You know I can't stand being confined in a small space. As soon as the door closes, I break out in a sweat, can hardly breathe. Some of the inmates told me I'd get used to it, but I *know* I won't.'

Flood asked, 'Have you had any therapy sessions yet? Doctor Rogers rates the psychiatrist.'

'I've only had one introducing me to prison life. They say they'll start counselling next week.'

Gemma paused, looked at Laura, then at her dad. Wiping away the beginnings of a tear with the back of her hand, she said, 'There's no way I could serve a long term in this place. It's awful.'

Flood recognised the doleful expression on her face. The same one she'd often used as a youngster. She'd look at him with sheep's eyes and speak in a whiny voice if she didn't get her way. It usually worked. This time though, Flood could tell she wasn't putting it on.

He said, 'Gemma, you need to think hard about the charges against you. I know you believe you should go to jail for what you did, serve whatever sentence the judge might throw at you, but now you're getting an idea of what time inside entails. It's going to be tough.'

Laura nodded her support. Flood added, 'We know you're not a murderer, but unless we can prove that you didn't *plan* to kill Simon, or he provoked you, that's how it's going to look to a jury. You could spend fourteen years in here, maybe more.'

'Oh, God, don't say that!'

'You told us you'd split with Simon because he made unreasonable demands on you. Can you elaborate? Was he abusive?' Gemma looked around the room, saying nothing.

Some of the younger children had grown bored and started bickering between themselves.

Flood had to raise his voice. 'Answer me, Gemma. This is important.'

'This is so embarrassing.'

Flood and Laura remained silent. Eventually, Gemma said, 'Straight after we got married, he wanted to do things to me sexually that I didn't like. He said it was normal.' She looked at Flood and Laura in turn before continuing. 'He grew impatient with me, frustrated, I suppose. That's when he got physically abusive if I didn't cooperate.'

Laura, sounding more cross than she intended, said, 'Why didn't you tell us at the time?'

'I didn't tell *anyone*. Not even the police. I felt too ashamed.'

'How long had it been going on?' Flood said.

'It happened almost every night in the month before we split up.'

Flood desperately wanted to hug her again. 'Oh, Gemma. You must tell Monty. He'll ask the police to amend your statement. Are you certain you didn't see anyone who may have witnessed Simon provoking you?'

She threw her head backwards and closed her eyes as she relived the incident. Eventually, Gemma turned to face her father. 'Simon came out of the gents as I went to the loo in the same area. He cornered me, pushed his face close to mine, saying horrible things. I told him to back off, but his hands were everywhere. He wouldn't stop. Then he tried to touch me.' She lowered her voice. 'Down there. That's what triggered my reaction. That's when I saw another man coming out of the loos. He must have seen what was going on, but glanced at us, and then walked away in the opposite direction, like he didn't want to get involved.'

'What did he look like?'

'It's hard to say.'

Flood demanded, 'Think, Gemma.'

Another short silence ensued until she shook her head, saying, 'To be honest, he was gone in a flash. I'm not sure I'd recognise him if I saw him again.'

'Did you mention this to the police?'

'About seeing someone witnessing the incident? No, I didn't. I was a total mess at the time.'

'If we can find him and he confirms what you said, it'll make a huge difference to your sentence.'

'I hope so.' Gemma closed her eyes and stared down at the floor.

***

Driving home, Flood felt more positive about Gemma's predicament. At last, he had something to work on, now she'd realised the seriousness of her position and offered an explanation for what she did.

At home that evening, Flood turned to Laura. 'I've been thinking about what Gemma said. Do you think she's telling the truth about Simon abusing her that night?'

'Of course. Why would she lie about it?'

'She's desperate. When we saw her at the mental hospital, she believed that doing time was her penance. Now she's experienced the reality of what life inside is like and the possibility of serving a long stretch, it's spooked her, made her think of ways of reducing her sentence.'

'However desperate she is, I'm sure she's telling the truth.'

Flood leant forward, picked up a wine bottle and filled Laura's glass. 'There's only one way to find out. I'm going to find the eyewitness.'

'You're wasting your time. The police have made several appeals and no one's come forward.'

'Maybe they missed something.'

Laura groaned. 'Didn't you tell me that the SIO didn't want you to get involved?'

'So what? Do they expect me to stand by and see my daughter spend the best years of her life in prison?'

'You think you can do better than the police?'

'I can't sit on my hands and do nothing, can I?'

Laura fired back, 'The trouble with you is that you think you're above the law. You can't ignore it just because it suits you. You've got to promise me you won't do anything silly. Otherwise, you won't get any support from me.'

'Don't be like that, Laura.'

She stood and picked up her glass. 'I'm serious, Andy. Think about it. Anyway, I need an early night. I'm part of the team presenting the results of our research into that improved method of testing fingerprints on fabrics to the Head of Forensics. I told you about it.'

'Yes, I remember. Good luck,' Flood said, trying to recover the situation.

After Laura went to bed, Flood went to his study. He thought he'd try to make contact with Pippa again. He looked at his watch which showed 10.30 p.m., 7.30 a.m. the next day in Sydney.

To his great surprise, she picked up. 'Hi Pippa. I've been trying to speak to you for ages. Are you OK?'

'We're doing fine here. You?' She sounded bored.

'Laura and I are good. Listen, I'm calling you about Gemma. I left you a message. She's been charged with murdering her husband. I thought you should know.'

Following a moment's silence, she replied, 'Yes. I got it. What do you expect me to do about it?'

'She's your bloody sister, Pippa.'

'You know we never got on. Let's not pretend we were ever a close family. You always favoured her, anyway, not that you spent that much time with us, as I recall.' Flood rode the metaphorical punch in the head.

'This is serious, Pippa – I thought you'd want to give her some support. She's having a tough time.'

'Look, Dad. I've built a good life here. I've got a great job, a loving husband and loads of new friends. Life is good. This is my life. I don't want anything to do with what's left of my family.'

'Is there nothing I can say to change your mind?'

'No. I must go, I'm late for work.' She hung up.

Flood sat still for several minutes, the phone still in his hand, wrestling with his feelings of failure. Eventually, with a heavy heart, he made his way up to bed.

***

The following morning, Flood called Monty and explained what Gemma had told him.

'Why didn't she mention this before?'

'She's been in a fragile state ever since it happened. Now she's had time to think about it, she recalls seeing a man who may have witnessed seeing Simon harassing her.'

'Don't you think the police have heard that one before, Andy? Why didn't this mystery man try to save her? Or call 999?'

'I don't know, but I believe my daughter, Monty. If someone did come forward, it would help Gemma's case immeasurably.'

'As far as I can see, the police have done everything by the book: trawled through the CCTV at the entrance to the pub, spoken to the staff and customers and produced flyers. They also appealed for witnesses at their last press conference which made the local papers. I'm not sure how much more you expect them to do,' Monty replied.

'Look, Monty, my daughter is on a murder charge. Can you call the SIO? Tell him Gemma remembers seeing someone. Who's dealing with the case?'

'A DI Austin.'

'If he doesn't respond, I'll visit the pub, talk to the bar staff myself and hope one of them will be able to identify the man.'

'Are you sure that's wise? That's guaranteed to piss off the police.'

'I don't give a shit about that! We're talking about my daughter.'

'What does Laura think?'

'She doesn't approve.'

Flood heard Monty sigh. 'OK, I'll inform DI Austin, ask him to take another statement from Gemma.'

'Thanks, Monty.'

'I've just heard from the court. They've accepted Gemma's plea of not guilty of murder, but guilty of manslaughter, loss of control. So that's something. The date of the trial is Monday, October 22nd at Winchester Crown Court. The judge has allowed three weeks.'

●▲●

163

CHAPTER TWENTY-FOUR

MANDY
EARLY HOURS OF 8TH MARCH

Carlos, the reception manager and Latino admirer, greeted me with a smarmy smile. In his exaggerated Latino accent, he asked, 'Everything OK, lady? Hope you had a great evening.' If only he knew.

'Yes. Fine. By the way, I'll be checking out in the morning. Can you organise a taxi for 10 a.m.?' I couldn't wait to go back to living in my lovely Hamble home. Reboot my life ... without men. For a while, at least.

'I'll do it right away,' he said. As I turned away from Carlos, I felt a tug on my arm. Gary had followed me into the hotel.

'Gary, I told you it's best if you didn't stay tonight,' I hissed. 'What don't you understand about that?'

'I promise I won't stay long, right? Just a nightcap to celebrate, chat about our future.'

'The answer's "no", Gary.' I turned away from him and headed towards the lift. He grabbed my shoulder, pulled it backwards, forcing me to face him.

He put his head close to mine. 'C'mon on Mandy. You know you want me.'

I tugged my arm away from his grip and shouted, 'Get off me!' People in the nearby crowded bar looked up. Carlos, who'd presumably seen everything, opened the flap of the reception counter and headed towards us.

'Is everything OK?' he asked, looking directly at me.

Gary glared at him. For a moment, I worried about him swinging a punch. I moved between them in case he did. 'Yes. We're fine,' I replied, not wanting Gary to cause a scene. Dragging him away from Carlos's earshot, I spat out, 'You're *not* coming to my room. I mean it,' and strode towards the lift.

He uttered, 'bitch' under his breath as I got into the lift and went to my room. I took off my coat and poured myself a glass of red wine, knocking most of it back before going to the bathroom and slipping into my fuchsia pink, silk pyjamas. I lay on the bed, going over the evening's events, revelling in the thought that I'm free from Michael Bradshaw at last.

Fifteen minutes later, I heard a tapping at the door. Fearing it was Gary and that he might start hammering the door down or making a scene, I opened it. He stood in front of me with a contrite expression. 'Sorry, Mandy. I need to talk, that's all. You know I can't get enough of you,' he whined. I reluctantly let him in.

He helped himself to a glass of the red wine on the table and topped up mine. He handed it to me and I sat on the foot of the bed.

He settled in a bedside chair. 'Before we talk about us being King and Queen of Hamble, I need some Charlie. Don't suppose you've got some?'

'Haven't you had enough already?'

'Obviously not.'

With Gary in this unpredictable mood, I thought it best to humour him. Just one more night wouldn't hurt, would it? Except, the last thing I wanted to talk about was our 'Royal' status. The more he spoke about our future together, the more difficult it might be to dump him. He wasn't exactly my idea of a long-term partner.

'There's some gear in the safe inside the wardrobe. I'll get it.' Gary prepared four lines on the glass coffee table. As soon as he'd finished, my resistance collapsed like a pricked balloon. We snorted two lines each. As I sat back down on the edge of the bed, Gary stood over me and chattered on incessantly, saying how much he looked forward to living a life of luxury in my beautiful house on the River Hamble with the sexiest woman he'd ever met.

After half-an-hour, I'd had enough. 'Gary. We've had a hell of a night. I don't want to talk about this anymore. Maybe tomorrow, OK?'

He slugged back his wine leaving the glass empty and slammed it on the table. He jumped up, came towards me and pushed me down onto the mattress.

Standing over me, he snarled, 'Are you trying to fob me off? I'm not having it. You *owe* me.' He leant forward, grabbed my neck with both hands and squeezed so hard, I couldn't swallow.

I tried to stand, but he held me down. His eyes bulged like a raging bulldog as I felt my face turning crimson. *Oh, my God, this is Michael Bradshaw all over again.*

From somewhere deep inside, I found the strength to thrust my knee into his groin. He groaned in agony and his grip on my throat loosened enough for me to escape from under him. Coughing and spluttering, I staggered to the bathroom. He followed, but by the time he reached the door, I'd closed and locked it. I gulped down a glass of water.

I couldn't believe Gary would *ever* treat me like this. He yelled 'bitch' again, and, seconds later, I heard the door slam as he left. I squeezed my eyes shut and grabbed the sink with both hands, worrying about what he'd do next.

Returning to the room, I slumped down on the bed, feeling shitty. A few minutes later, as I lay there, my head swimming, I heard another knock at the door. I yelled, 'Fuck off, Gary. I don't want to see you anymore.' I watched as the door opened.

CHAPTER TWENTY-FIVE

The following morning, Flood called Monty from home. 'What did DI Austin have to say about Gemma seeing an eyewitness?'

'Sorry, Andy, he didn't want to know. Says his team have all the evidence they needed to persuade the CPS to support charging Gemma with murder.'

'Prick!' Flood said. 'Give me his number. *I'll* talk to him.'

'It won't do any good, Andy.'

'Maybe. But I want to try.'

Flood called Austin, whose first words were, 'I wondered how long you could resist getting involved. Before you go any further, let me make something crystal clear. I don't want you prejudicing my investigation. I'm not having it.'

'At least, re-interview her; hear what she's got to say.'

Austin responded in a monotone voice. 'We've put out a string of appeals for eyewitnesses. No one's come forward. As I told Gemma's solicitor, the CPS have decided that there's a realistic prospect of a murder conviction. That's good enough for me. I understand that must be tough for you to accept.'

Trying not to whinge, Flood said, 'But my daughter's not mentioned an eyewitness before, she's been too traumatised. She wants to add to her statement. Surely that should be enough for you to put more resources into finding this man.'

'Look, I'd like to help. I can't imagine what you're going through, but the fact is, I can't spare any more officers to investigate this case. We're pretty stretched.'

Flood took an extra deep breath, conscious of saying something he'd later regret. Before he had a chance to formulate the words, Austin said, 'I'll tell you what I'll do. I'll put out one more plea for eyewitnesses.'

'I appreciate that, but you also need to double-check every line of enquiry – re-interview the pub customers, for example.'

'Don't push your luck, Mr Flood. What I've offered is better than nothing. And don't forget what I said about you stirring things up. It's not going to help.'

Flood switched off his mobile and thrust it back into his pocket so hard, he almost ripped the lining.

***

Still seething at Austin's attitude, Flood drove to the Blue Anchor pub, a stone's throw from the Sturridge Hotel where Mandy met her death.

Flood entered the deserted bar and approached the counter, trying to imagine exactly what happened on the night that Gemma stabbed Simon. He asked for a pint from a lean, bright-eyed student type.

Handing over a ten-pound note, he asked the barman if he'd like a drink. 'Yeah. I'll have a half. Thanks.' The barman handed back the change, poured out the beer and took a sip.

'Cheers,' Flood said, raising his glass.

The barman started washing and drying glasses as Flood asked, 'I understand a serious incident occurred here a couple of weeks ago?'

'Yeah. It did.' The student's eyes lit up, clearly keen to be seen as something of an expert on the shocking event that made the local press. 'I was working that night. One of our regulars got stabbed to death.'

'Did you see what happened?'

'No. I didn't, but I learnt later that it was his wife who stabbed him up there, outside the loos.' He jabbed a hand holding a towel inside a pint glass towards the back of the pub. 'The landlord told us they'd broken up two weeks previously.'

'Was the landlord working that night?' Flood asked.

'No. It was his night off. He lives upstairs. As soon as he heard the commotion, he came down to see what happened.' The barman appeared happy to continue chatting, which suited Flood. 'By the time he realised the seriousness of the situation, most of the customers had left the premises. When the police and paramedics arrived, no one still here was allowed to leave, especially the staff. Detectives interviewed all of us. I didn't get home 'til after two.'

'Did you know the victim?'

'You're asking a lot of questions. Are you the police?'

Flood trotted out his usual response. 'I'm a private investigator working for the family. They want to ensure the police haven't missed anything.'

Satisfied, the barman continued, 'Simon's been coming here for a while. He brought his wife in a few times, too. Both seemed nice enough.'

Flood had an idea. 'Before they married, did he bring anyone else here?'

The barman thought for a moment. 'Not as far as I know, but I've only been here a few months. You need to ask the landlord.'

'Is he around?'

'He's changing the barrels in the cellar. I'll give him a shout.'

'Before you do, who else worked behind the bar that night?'

'Only Phil and Donna.'

'Did they see anything?'

'It happened next to the loos. You can't see them from the bar. We've got CCTV at the entrance and in the bars but none covering that area. Phil said another of our regulars, Charlie Dobson, had told him that when he went for a pee, he saw Simon, slumped outside the loos with blood oozing out all over his clothes and onto the floor. Said he was barely conscious. Charlie works as an orderly at the General, so knew what to do. He called 999, took off his coat and jumper and pressed them hard against the wounds trying to stem the flow.'

'What happened to Simon's wife?'

'Charlie said she sat on the floor, covered in blood and in a state of shock. One of her friends comforted her until the police and paramedics arrived.' Flood tried to imagine what was going through Gemma's mind in those moments.

The barman continued, 'Although it's a rough and ready pub, the landlord told us that he'd never experienced anything like this. No one expects to get stabbed on a night out, do they? Business has picked up a bit now, though. People's memories are short.'

'So, as far as you know, no one saw the actual stabbing?'

'If they did, no one's told me. Two detectives visited the bar for a few nights afterwards and chatted to our regulars, asking if they were drinking here that night. Oh, and the police gave us several printed notices asking for anyone who may have witnessed the incident to contact them. They asked us to display them in the pub. To be honest, the landlord took them down after a week. He didn't want customers to be reminded of what happened.'

A grey-haired, wiry man emerged from the cellar. The barman turned to him. 'John, this is a private investigator. He's looking into that stabbing incident a while back. He wants to talk to you.'

The landlord closed the hatch to the cellar with a thump. 'Does he?' He leant on the bar to face Flood. 'What do you want to know?'

'How well did you know the victim?'

'Pretty well. Simon's been a regular here for the last five years. Usually came in with a pretty woman in tow.'

'What women?'

The landlord laughed. 'Bit of a lady's man, Simon. Before he got married, he brought a different girl to the pub every few months.'

'Did you know any of them?'

'Only the one immediately before Simon wed. Young girl, quiet type but a real beauty. They came in here a few times. She only lasted a month or so.'

'Do you know her name?'

'Zara.'

'Last name?'

'I don't know. Only ever knew her as Zara.'

'Do you know where she lived?'

'No. But I know they worked for the same firm just outside Southampton. That's where they met.'

Flood recalled his background search on Simon Saltus before he married Gemma. He worked as a director for an advertising firm, Davies & Co. Flood thanked the landlord, finished his pint and walked back to his car, turning up the collar on his coat to protect him from the ever-strengthening breeze.

***

On his way back to the office, Flood rang Ashford. 'Did Bridges get the info about Mandy's call history?'

For once, Ashford sounded enthusiastic, taking Flood by surprise. 'I was about to get in touch. I've got the mobile data report in front of me. There are thirty-five calls to and from the same number in the week immediately before Bradshaw's death. Nothing since. Too much of a coincidence, I'd say.'

'Sounds like it. Did you get the contact details from the phone provider?'

'The mobile's registered to a Gary Fleming. The billing address is in Ocean Village in Southampton. I'm going to pay him a visit this evening, have a little chat.'

'Haven't you got enough to arrest him and take him down to the station for questioning?'

'We have, but I'm hoping Fleming will reveal more information by having a friendly conversation in his home surroundings. If he's in a police interview room, *lawyered-up* and had the caution read to him, he'll most likely go "no comment" on us.'

Flood recognised Ashford's approach. What suspects didn't know is that whatever's said in a voluntary interview can be used in evidence if the case proceeds to court. He'd used the strategy to good effect when he was a police officer, although it was frowned upon by the top brass.

Flood tried his luck. 'Can I come?'

'If you want to. It's against the rules, but it's only a preliminary chat. I won't say anything if you don't. I'll meet you in the marina car park at about half six. It's close to Gary's flat.' Flood looked at his watch. He'd have plenty of time to get there.

CHAPTER TWENTY-SIX

Flood drove to the recently refurbished marina development, parked and got out. Shielding his eyes from the last rites of the setting sun, he looked across at hundreds of boats on their moorings as they bobbed in the glossy water. Spotting Ashford sitting in his car, he walked towards it. Ashford leant across and opened the passenger door. Flood slid in next to him as they nodded an acknowledgement to each other.

Ashford said, 'You'll be pleased to know that before I left, I got confirmation that the dyed blonde hairs found on Bradshaw's boat were Mandy's.'

'So it looks like Mandy and Gary Fleming were in cahoots.'

'Correct. Gary lives on the second floor of that apartment block over there.' Ashford pointed in the direction of a five-storey,1960s run-down block. The contrast between the smart new buildings making up the marina complex and the apartments couldn't have been starker. The block showed its age; much of the exterior grey cladding had turned dirty brown, matching the rusting balcony railings. Graffiti covered the metal up-and-over doors to the garages adjacent to the apartments.

Ashford continued. 'Fleming works in one of the boatyards here. He should be finishing work now and making his way home.'

'I've been thinking about his possible involvement,' Flood said. 'Did you check his background?'

'Yes, we did. There's nothing in our files.'

'It could be that the guy who rescued Mandy from the Gulf of Mexico in Florida, Scottie McPherson, is involved. When I interviewed him, it became apparent that he'd taken a shine to her. He reminded her of his daughter who was murdered by her husband so he lent her money and set her up in an apartment before she returned to the UK.'

'What are you thinking?'

'I'm thinking that maybe Scottie hired Gary Fleming as a hit man to help Mandy take revenge on her husband. I've asked Chuck North, my police contact in Florida, to check whether there's a connection. I should hear something soon.'

Ashford nudged Flood's arm and nodded towards the Ocean Village Marina. 'Look, I reckon that's him. What do you think?' He pulled a photo of Fleming, taken from his Facebook page, from an inside pocket and showed Flood.

He looked at the image, then the man. 'You're right.' Gary, dressed in a black anorak and dark trousers, carried a rucksack on his shoulder as he headed for the apartment block.

Ashford said, 'We'll give him ten minutes to settle. Once we get inside, leave the interviewing to me. Only chip in if you think I've missed something.' Flood nodded, thinking, *I'll say what I want if it's important.*

Ten minutes later, they got out of the car, made their way to the building and climbed the steps to the second floor. Ashford led, as they strode along the walkway to Fleming's flat.

He rang the doorbell. The door opened and Ashford asked, 'Gary Fleming?'

'Yes. Who wants to know?'

Ashford flashed his warrant card in Gary's face saying, 'DI Ashford, Hampshire Police. This is my colleague, Andy Flood. We want to chat with you about your relationship with Michael and Mandy Bradshaw. May we come in?'

Gary's face contorted into a mixture of alarm and fear.

'Er ... yes. Come in. Excuse the mess.'

They entered the flat straight into a living room with beige-painted walls matching a worn, oatmeal carpet. The smell of curry, presumably last night's takeaway, permeated the flat.

Gary removed several crumpled shirts and a jumper spread out over a brown leather sofa. He brushed crumbs from the coffee table onto the floor. 'Take a seat,' he said, indicating the couch positioned against the wall furthest away from the front door. Gary sat in a chair opposite them.

Ashford said, 'Rather than drag you down to the police station, we'd like to chat to you informally. We think you can help us clear up a case we're working on. Is that OK?' Gary nodded.

Ashford produced his notebook and rested it on his lap, often referring to it. 'Let's first talk about your relationship with Michael Bradshaw. How do you know him?'

'Who? I've never met him.'

'Have you ever been to his house in Hamble?'

'No.' Gary scratched his neck.

'What about *Mandy* Bradshaw? How do you know her?'

Gary fidgeted in his chair. 'I've known her for years, on and off. We dated for a while until she got married.'

'Have you been in contact with her or seen her since then?'

The fidget became a squirm. Following a short silence, he said, 'Sometimes we chatted on the phone.'

'Can you clarify when you last spoke to her?'

'I can't remember.'

'It's important, Gary.'

'I dunno. Maybe a few months ago.'

'Could you be more precise?'

Gary snapped back, 'No. I can't.'

'That's odd because we have evidence suggesting that you recently had a great deal of contact with the Bradshaws.' Ashford flicked through his notebook, stopping at a particular page.

'We know you hired a Transit van for two days on the seventh and eighth of March this year. The hire company uses telematics data to track the movements of all their vehicles. So we also know that on the evening of the seventh, it travelled from the Sturridge Hotel in Southampton, where Mandy Bradshaw was staying, to the Bradshaw's marital home in Hamble. CCTV in the hotel car park clearly shows you picking her up.

'Two hours later, the van was tracked to a lock-up garage in Woolston, near the bridge, where we found Michael

Bradshaw's clothes and other belongings, including his BMW. Can you explain that?'

Flood was impressed with Ashford's competence in the interview. *Why hadn't he been like this when Flood first contacted him about Mandy's death?*

Gary remained silent, looking down at the floor. Ashford pressed on. 'In that two-hour window, a neighbour saw Michael's motorboat sailing away from its mooring. He noticed it had returned by the following morning. You work at Ocean Village as a boatyard assistant, don't you, so you'd know how to sail? Did you take his boat out to sea?'

Looking up, Gary blurted, 'Of course I didn't. I'm sorry, but I'm not happy with what you're implying. I want to call a solicitor.'

'You're perfectly entitled to do so. But you're not telling us the truth, are you?'

'I've got nothing to hide!' Gary fell back into his chair and crossed his arms.

'Michael Bradshaw is dead, Gary. His body has recently been discovered, washed up on a beach in the Solent. You might have seen it on the local news. Do you know anything about that?'

'I'm not saying anything else.'

Having skewered his suspect, Ashford didn't let up.

'Our forensic team are analysing recent DNA traces from semen found on the boat. If we check it with your DNA, will it match?'

Gary glowered at Ashford.

'I think we both know the answer, don't we?' No response.

'Now what about Mandy? Phone records show that you contacted each other thirty-five times in the week leading up to your visit to Hamble. Do you still maintain that you haven't spoken to her recently?'

Flood studied Gary's face as he remained slumped in his chair, pursing his lips as if to stop saying anything that might incriminate himself. His unblinking eyes revealed the turmoil going on in his brain, trying to think of an explanation for his involvement. It became clear that he didn't have one.

Ashford continued. 'We know Mandy had recently dyed her hair blonde. We found strands of it on the boat. Did you and Mandy conspire to kill Michael Bradshaw?'

Yet another silence ensued from Gary, who stared out of the window. Ashford persevered. 'At 11.35 a.m. on the seventh of March, CCTV recorded someone looking remarkably like you following Mandy into the Sturridge Hotel entrance after you dropped her off. Did you go to her room?'

Gary sat upright as if Ashford had prodded him with a red-hot poker and yelled, 'I don't know where you're getting this information from. I told you I haven't seen Mandy for months.'

Remaining calm, Ashford persisted, 'Our forensics team took DNA traces and sets of fingerprints from a wine glass in Mandy's hotel room. Will they match yours, Gary?'

Again, he didn't respond. Ten seconds passed. Then twenty. All the time Ashford stared at Gary who looked everywhere except at Ashford. Flood broke the silence.

'Does the name, Scottie McPherson, mean anything to you?'

'What? Who the hell's Scottie McPherson?'

'What about the name, Lisa Black?'

'Never heard of her.'

Ashford picked up the reins. 'Mandy Bradshaw used that name as an alias. We believe somebody pushed her off the balcony on the sixth floor of the Sturridge Hotel. Did you do it?'

'No!'

'What was it? A lover's tiff?'

Gary stood and hollered, 'That's fucking nonsense.'

'We don't think so,' Ashford said, as he got to his feet. 'Gary Fleming, I'm arresting you on suspicion of the murders of Michael and Mandy Bradshaw.' As Ashford finished the caution, he unclipped a set of handcuffs from his coat pocket. Before he could put them on, Gary leapt out of his chair and charged towards the door, taking Flood and Ashford by surprise.

He yanked the door open and fled, slamming it behind him so hard, the frosted glass panel rattled in its frame.

They glimpsed Gary dashing past the living room window along the walkway towards the stairs. Flood, being closest to the door, pulled it open and ran after him in the gathering dusk. Ashford, twenty years younger than Flood, overtook him and led the chase. They both reached the ground floor in time to see Gary racing away from the apartment block towards a busy road.

Flood had a perfect view of what was about to happen. As Ashford closed the gap, Gary sprinted across the road without looking. The headlights from a speeding car picked him out as if he was on centre stage. The 4x4 hit him full-on taking his legs from underneath him.

The car's tyres squealed as the wheels locked up. Flood watched in horror as Gary's body, arms and legs flailing, flew onto the roof of the vehicle and bounced on to unforgiving tarmac. The cars behind swerved to avoid him and several crashed into each other, filling the air with the sound of gashing metal.

One of the cars left the road and careered onto the pavement, clipping Ashford, leaving him lying on the ground, groaning and clutching his knee. Flood reached for his mobile and called the emergency services before running towards Gary's mangled body. The side of his skull had hit the road first. Dark patches of blood began pooling around his head.

Flood thought Gary was probably past help, but he tried anyway. He ripped off his coat and pressed it firmly against the wound. Gary tried saying something. Flood put his ear close to his mouth as Gary whispered in a stuttering, hoarse voice, 'I didn't kill Mandy.'

They were to be his last words. Sam Wharton had uttered similar words about Angela Bradshaw when Flood interviewed him in prison after being set up by Bradshaw. *And they proved to be true.*

CHAPTER TWENTY-SEVEN

Once Gary's body had been taken away and Ashford's knee had been sorted out by the paramedics, he and Flood were interviewed separately at Southampton Police Station by officers from Professional Standards.

They had no jurisdiction over Flood. He'd done nothing wrong. Still, they'd need his testimony to establish whether there was a case for charging Ashford with misconduct. He should have followed the police's code of practice in interviewing Gary under caution at the station.

Flood explained precisely what had happened and left the police station around midnight. When he reached home, he was surprised to see the lights still on downstairs. He'd called Laura earlier to say he'd be home late and not to worry.

Laura, wearing a dressing gown and with her hair tied tightly back, sat at the kitchen worktop surrounded by files, her laptop and a half-full mug of coffee.

He leaned in and kissed her neck. 'What are you doing still up?' She took off her reading glasses and rubbed her eyes with the knuckle of both index fingers.

'I needed to mug up on the results of my research into that new forensic technique for obtaining fingerprints I told you about. I'm presenting my report to the top brass soon, hope to get it accepted as normal practice.'

'Are the results positive?' Flood asked, as he retrieved a can of beer from the fridge, snapped it open and took a long slug before slumping down on a kitchen stool opposite her at the table.

'They're excellent. It's a major step forward.' She closed her laptop and looked at him. 'You look dreadful. Is everything OK?'

Flood recounted the interview with Gary. Laura put a hand to her mouth when he told her about the fatal consequences.

'You witnessed the whole thing? That must have been horrible.' She slid off her stool and walked round to Flood. She put her arms around his shoulders and rubbed her cheek against his. Stepping back, she said, 'Do you think Gary was responsible for the deaths of Michael Bradshaw and Mandy?'

'Bradshaw, probably it's a yes. Mandy, I'm not so sure. I'm hoping we'll know more after the police search Gary's flat. I'll call DS Bridges first thing tomorrow, get an update.'

***

'I thought it might be you.' Bobby Bridges sounded upbeat, confident.

Flood asked, 'Did you find anything useful at Gary's flat?'

'I'd say. There's damning evidence pointing to his direct involvement in Bradshaw's death. The most convincing is a pair of his trousers matching the cotton thread found on the motorboat. We also discovered masking tape and rope in a cupboard. The forensics team are checking to see if they match those found on Bradshaw's body. We even found the invoice for the van hire in his wallet. There's no doubt he and Mandy abducted Bradshaw, took him out to sea and dumped him. It all fits.'

'What about Mandy? What have you got putting Gary in the frame?'

'Not as much as we'd like. We've matched his DNA and prints to a wine bottle and glass in her hotel room. The hotel's CCTV footage shows a man approaching Mandy in the lobby less than an hour before her death. DI Ashford identified him as Gary Fleming. The problem is, we can't pinpoint what time he left the hotel, despite checking the CCTV many times. There was a big party in the bar that night and everyone left at about the same time. That means we can't be one hundred per cent sure it was Gary who pushed her off the balcony.'

'What about a motive?'

'The calls between them prior to Bradshaw's death show they were in some kind of relationship. Could be they had a falling out. Maybe they had a financial arrangement, and Mandy didn't want to pay him for his part in the murder. It's all conjecture on our part. We've nothing to back it up.'

'What about Ashford?'

'Professional Standards ordered the Super to put him on restrictive duties at a different station while he's under investigation. Ashford's not best pleased.'

'Is the Mandy Bradshaw case closed now?'

'In the absence of any hard evidence against Fleming for Mandy's death, and ruling out Michael Bradshaw, it's looking more than likely that she accidentally fell after taking drugs and drinking alcohol. The Super's appointed me as Acting SIO to wrap things up. He thinks I'm ready to take the inspector's exams soon, so this is good experience.'

Flood couldn't help thinking; *something doesn't sound right.*

***

On Flood's next visit to see Gemma, he told her about his chat with DI Austin who'd promised to make another appeal for an eyewitness to come forward.

'I hope someone does,' she said, her eyes reflecting a dullness Flood hadn't seen before. 'It's bloody hard in here.'

'Have you mentioned how you feel to your therapist?'

'Yes. I have. She says I'll get used to it. That's all everyone says. I know I won't.' She shook her head. 'You've no idea what it's like cooped up in here with these people.'

'You've got no choice, Gemma. You're going to have to tough it out to survive. I suggest you stay away from drugs and don't get in debt. That'll make life worse, believe me. Look me in the eye. Promise?'

Gemma gave a deep sigh and replied, 'Promise.'

'Good. I'm working on something which might help. I visited the Blue Anchor pub a couple of days ago, made some enquiries. Did Simon ever mention a previous girlfriend, called Zara? They worked together at the same firm.'

Gemma frowned. 'How's that going to help?'

'I'm digging into Simon's background, looking for evidence about the way he treated other women. The police won't have checked that because you didn't tell them he'd been abusing you and provoked you on *that* night. It could throw up something to support your case. The problem is. I've only got the name. Zara.'

'Sorry, Dad. He never mentioned her.'

***

Keen not to give up on this lead, Flood visited Davies & Co, the company where Simon and Zara worked. It was located in a business park on the outskirts of Southampton.

He entered the spacious, open-plan ground floor, full of light reflecting off the white marble floor and headed for the reception area. A smartly dressed, young woman with a plummy English accent, asked, 'My name's Jennifer. How may I help you today?'

Flood handed over his card, saying, 'I'm trying to trace one of your employees, a young woman. She's not in any trouble or anything like that. It's to do with a possible inheritance issue.'

Jennifer smiled. 'Lucky for some. What's her name?'

'That's part of my problem. I've only got her first name. Zara. I believe she had a relationship some months ago with one of your directors, Simon Saltus.'

The receptionist's jaw dropped open. 'Simon? Oh, that's Zara Warwick. Poor Simon. I assume you know what happened to him?'

Flood played dumb. 'No. I'm only interested in tracing Zara. What happened?'

Jennifer lowered her voice. 'It was all over the newspapers. Simon and Zara had a relationship but then stopped seeing each other. Simon met someone else and got married. Would you believe, two months later, his wife stabbed him to death in a pub. The whole company was in deep shock for weeks.

182

Simon was very popular. He always had time for people.' Jennifer looked close to tears.

Flood stopped himself from wanting to put Gemma's side of the story. Instead, he replied, 'I'm sorry to hear that.'

Jennifer recovered her composure and asked, 'Simon's relationship with Zara has nothing to do with what happened to him, has it?'

'No. No. I need to speak to Zara about something else entirely. Is she in work today?'

Jennifer shook her head. 'No, she left shortly after they broke up. It's rumoured that they decided working together in the same company wasn't a good idea.'

'Can you give me Zara's address?'

Jennifer shook her head. 'No. Sorry. It's more than my job's worth. The company has strict rules about data.' It wasn't a big deal for Flood, except it would save him time. Now he had her surname, he'd be able to find her address from the Electoral Roll or through social media.

On the way home, Flood received a call from Chuck North, his police contact in Florida. 'We've done a background check on Scottie Macpherson. Sorry, Flood. There's nothing to suggest he's involved in anything sinister. He's cleaner than a freshly laundered shirt.'

***

That evening over dinner, Flood told Laura about his visit to the advertising company on the outskirts of Southampton. 'I found out the name of a previous girlfriend of Simon's. It's a long shot, but she might be able to tell us more about him. You know, how he treated women.'

'Now that *is* a long shot.'

'I'll find out where she lives and visit her tomorrow.'

'Have you heard anything more about the Mandy Bradshaw case?'

'DS Bridges told me the police have closed the file. They don't have enough proof to put Gary Fleming in the frame, and there are no other suspects. They believe she died accidentally.'

'And you don't?'

'No. I don't.'

'You're obsessed with her. Why can't you let it go?'

'If the case is closed, no one else will care what happened to her. It's unfinished business as far as I'm concerned.'

Laura smiled. 'Actually, I like that about you. You never give up on your commitment to justice. It makes you the man you are.' She leaned across the table and kissed him on the cheek.

After dinner, Flood retired to his office. Within ten minutes he found Zara Warwick's address from the Electoral Roll and discovered the only other occupant was a Joanne Warwick.

From the online Births, Marriages and Deaths Register, he discovered that Zara was twenty-three and Joanne fifty-nine. Flood presumed she was Zara's mother. When he checked Zara's social media, he drew a blank. It was as if she'd never existed.

CHAPTER TWENTY-EIGHT

MANDY
EARLY HOURS OF 8TH MARCH

As I lay on the bed, fearing it might be Gary again, Carlos walked in, holding the key card he'd used to open the door. I leapt off the bed and yelled, 'What the fuck are you doing here? Get out!'

Carlos gave me a sickening smile. 'I wanted to see if you're OK. Your friend left looking angry. Did you have argument?'

I shrieked and waved my hands at him, shooing him away. 'No. Everything's OK. I need to sleep now. Please leave.'

He leered at me with a supposedly charming, *I've-come-to rescue-you* smile. 'Maybe you need someone like me?'

My stomach churned. 'What's that supposed to mean?'

'You seem like a young woman who likes a good time.'

I didn't like the way this was going. I tried a gentler approach. 'Look, Carlos, I want you to leave.' I staggered towards him, ushering him closer to the door. Bad mistake.

As I got closer, he gripped both my wrists and pulled me towards him. Our noses almost touched. His tone grew more menacing. 'I give you drugs. You know what I want.'

'I never promised you anything.'

I tried pulling my arms away from his grip, but he was too strong. He then pushed me hard against a wall. I smelt mint on his breath as he tried kissing me on the lips. I twisted my head from side to side, making it impossible.

Now my hands were free, I tried shoving him away, but Carlos pressed his weight against my body, touching my breasts through my pyjama top.

Summoning every ounce of energy, I heaved him off me and rushed towards the main door but he blocked my path. My only other escape route was out onto the balcony. From there, I'd be able to shout for help.

I rushed to the balcony door, gripped the handle and yanked it open, just wide enough for me to squeeze through the gap. A rush of damp, cold air brushed my face as I slid the heavy glass door closed behind me with both hands. Carlos put a hand in the way trying to keep it open. He screamed with pain as the door slammed into the door jamb, trapping his hand. I stood next to the balcony railings and yelled, 'Help! Help!'

Carlos slid the door open with his good hand and stepped outside, cursing me in Spanish. I'll never forget the look of hatred on his face. 'You are just a fucking prick-teaser. I give you drugs; you give me nothing.'

I turned my back on him and yelled into the darkness, 'Somebody, please help me!' Then I felt his hands picking me up and lifting me over the balcony rail.

CHAPTER TWENTY-NINE

Early the following evening, Flood visited the Warwick's house located in a row of neat, red-brick terraced houses in Fair Oak in the outskirts of Southampton. He rang the bell and noticed a curtain in the front window twitching. Seconds later, the door opened.

A large woman, with cropped, mousy hair who didn't look particularly well to Flood, said accusingly, 'You're not a politician, are you? Because if you are, you can push off.'

'No, I'm not. I'm looking for Zara Warwick. I understand she lives here.'

'Zara? No, she left ages ago. What do you want with her?' she scowled.

Flood handed her his card. 'I'm a private investigator. I assume you're her mother, Joanne?'

She took a step backwards, a puzzled look on her face. 'I'm Joanne, yes.'

'I'm investigating a gentleman who had a relationship with your daughter. You may be able to help me.'

Joanne inspected Flood's card then waved her head towards the hallway. 'You'd better come through,' she said. He followed her down the hall and into the living room. The decor suggested a younger person's taste: contemporary paintings, modern furniture and a state-of-the-art Smart TV sat in the corner of the room. Half-a-dozen photos of a young girl at various ages vied for prominence on one of the walls.

As they sat opposite each other, Flood asked, 'Can you tell me where Zara is? It's important.'

'She told me she doesn't want to be contacted. She's travelling around Europe, has been for the past six or seven months. It's somewhere different every time she calls me.'

'Is she on an extended holiday?'

'No. All she told me was that she wanted to get away for a while. She said she wanted to find herself, whatever that means. I'm guessing it's something to do with a man. Anyway, she packed in her job and took off. I've no idea when she'll be back.'

'When she calls you next, would you ask her to call me? My number is on the card.'

'I can ask, but don't hold your breath.'

'Tell her it's very important.' He paused before asking, 'What's your daughter like?'

'She's a bright kid. Left school at seventeen and started working as a graphic designer. She's always been good at drawing and stuff. She got a job working for a local advertising company. She earned well, too. Paid for all this.' Joanne waved an arm at the furniture and decor.

'Did she have any boyfriends?'

'Not really. Zara was too much into her work, and she's quite shy. Although before she pushed off, she told me she had met someone at work who she quite fancied. I asked her to bring him home to meet me. She said she wouldn't do that until she was sure he'd be the *one*.'

Joanne suddenly stopped talking and put a hand to her mouth. 'I've just thought of something. One of the directors of the company Zara worked for was stabbed by his wife. It was all over the papers a few months back. You coming here is nothing to do with that, is it?'

Flood shook his head. 'No. No. No,' he lied. 'How often does Zara call you?'

'Once a month. I made her promise to call to let me know she was OK. That's it. Not much to ask, is it?'

'No. It isn't.'

'And after all I'd done for her, bringing her up on my own.' Joanne's voice betrayed a note of bitterness.

●▲●

CHAPTER THIRTY

Not accepting that Mandy had died accidentally, Flood visited Carlos, the receptionist at the Sturridge Hotel. He wanted to talk to him about the other guests staying in the hotel that night. The police had carried out room to room interviews with the occupants closest to the crime scene, but he hoped they'd missed something. It wouldn't be the first time.

Susan, the young girl who'd stood in for Carlos when he'd shown Flood Mandy's room, smiled a look of recognition as he approached the desk.

'Is Carlos around?' Flood asked.

'No. He doesn't start until four o'clock today. Can I help?'

'I hope so.' Flood gained the impression that Susan thought he was part of the police investigation. He didn't correct her. 'We're still investigating the young woman's death but we're having difficulty in tracing the people staying in the rooms closest to hers. Can you let me have the names and addresses of the occupants of those rooms again? We need to make sure they're correct.'

'Yes, of course. Give me a few minutes and I'll run them off. If you'd like to wait in the bar, I'll bring them over.'

Flood ordered a cup of tea from the barman, and as he sat at a table in the window, his mobile rang. Laura's breathless voice told him something wasn't right.

'I don't want you to get upset, but I just got a call from the prison. Gemma's had an altercation with another inmate. They've taken her to St Peter's Hospital A&E department in Chertsey.'

Flood's heart caught in his chest, He tried to remain calm. 'What the hell happened?'

'She needs stitches to a head wound. The prison thought we should know. They wouldn't go into detail on the phone. They said her injury isn't life-threatening but needs urgent attention. They're confident she'll be back in prison later this evening, and will allow her to call us between six and seven. Gemma can explain what happened then.'

'Bugger that! I'll go to the hospital now.'

'There's no point, Andy. They won't let you see her. You'll have to wait until she calls. We're visiting her the day after next, anyway.'

Flood sagged further down into his chair. 'OK. I'll be home soon.'

As he waited for Susan to reappear, he took a sip of his tea and recalled everything that had happened to his 'little princess'. *She'd been through a lot. And now this.* He placed the teacup back on the table and thumped the table with a clenched fist. A couple sitting two tables away peered at him. Flood glared at them until they looked away, embarrassed.

Susan returned and he switched back into professional mode. She handed over a list of four names and addresses. 'As you can see, married couples occupied the rooms both sides and opposite 621 but the room immediately underneath was occupied by a single person, a Mr Stuart Golding.'

'Thanks, Susan. Were you working that night?'

'Yes, but only until nine o'clock. Once everyone had checked in, Carlos told me I could have the rest of the evening off.'

'Do you know anything about these guests? Have any of them stayed before?'

Susan frowned and hesitated before saying, 'I'm not sure I can tell you. I don't want to lose my job.'

Flood spoke in a grave tone. 'A young woman is dead, Susan. If you know anything which helps us establish how and why she died, you should tell me.'

She looked up to the ceiling and took a deep breath. 'I don't know anything about the couples. They were all first timers. The guest in the room immediately below visited the hotel regularly over the last six months. I got the impression he's a big-shot businessman.' Flood looked at the list. Stuart Golding had given an address in Wimbledon.

Susan lowered her voice, 'On every visit, he meets the same woman in the bar. On that particular night, after they'd eaten and had drinks, I watched them walk arm in arm to the lift, presumably going to his room. I'm sure she's an escort.'

'Did you mention this to anyone?'

'I told Carlos. He said I shouldn't make assumptions. She might have been his girlfriend. Anyway, it would be difficult to prove that she's a call girl without causing a problem. He told me to ignore it.' Flood scribbled a note next to Stuart Golding's name.

'Do you think this is important?' Susan asked.

'Could be. Did you tell my police colleagues about your suspicions?'

'No. Carlos told me the owner wouldn't like it. He didn't want to get the hotel a bad reputation.'

'Do you know the name of the escort?'

Susan screwed up her face as she tried to remember. 'Katya, I think that's what he called her. Possibly Polish from her accent. There are lots of them in Southampton.'

'Can you describe her?'

'She looks to be in her mid-twenties, petite with jet-black hair and heavy makeup.'

'Thanks, Susan.' Placing the list in his top pocket, Flood stood. 'You've been very helpful.'

***

Flood arrived home early, desperate not to miss Gemma's call. Laura sat in her usual place when she worked from home – the kitchen worktop. She got off the stool and hugged Flood close to her and kissed him on the cheek.

As they parted, he asked, 'Have you heard anything more about Gemma?'

'I haven't. She'll be calling soon. There's nothing you can do. Why don't you have a hot shower, then try to relax?'

He took Laura's advice and afterwards changed into a T-shirt and jeans. Laura offered to cook him something, but he didn't feel hungry. He sat in the living room and tried to concentrate on watching the TV, drinking tea and glancing at his watch every few minutes, willing it to speed up. Despite expecting the landline to ring, it startled him when it did. Flood switched off the TV.

He expected to hear Gemma's voice. Instead, Monty's boomed over the line. 'Good news, Andy. DI Austin, the SIO on Gemma's case, called me a few minutes ago. He told me that following their latest appeal, a male eyewitness has come forward and he's confirmed Gemma's version of events. He saw her being provoked and her retaliation. Austin's sending me a copy of his statement.'

Flood closed his eyes and tilted his head upwards in silent thanks to an unseen power.

'That's fantastic,' he said. 'Why didn't he intervene or call 999?'

'I asked the same question. The eyewitness told Austin he didn't want to get involved and left the pub immediately. Austin suspects he's a drug dealer who probably had some gear on him. The Blue Anchor's got a reputation for dealing. He said the eyewitness changed his mind after he read in the press that the victim had died and the police had charged Gemma with murder. He didn't think it right; felt he had to come forward. His conscience got the better of him.'

Flood let out an audible sigh of relief. 'Thank goodness for consciences. Listen, Monty, thanks for the news, but I'm expecting a call from Gemma any minute. I'll call you later.'

A minute after putting the phone down, it rang again. 'Dad? It's Gemma.' Flood walked into the kitchen to join Laura and turned on the speaker so she could hear the conversation.

'Are you alright? We've been worried about you.'

'Sort of.'

'What the hell happened?'

Gemma's tone changed from crushed to incensed. 'Another prisoner head-butted me while we were working in the kitchen. Split my forehead open and broke my nose. Blood everywhere. They took me to A&E.'

'That's what we heard. How bad is the wound?'

'It's about three inches long. My nose is swollen and bent. The bruises are coming out under my eyes. I'll look like a panda in the morning. My face is a mess.' Flood looked across at Laura and shook his head as they heard Gemma stifle a tear.

'Why did she do it?' Laura asked.

Gemma took a moment to reply. 'As she struck me, she said, "that's for being an ex-copper's daughter!"'

Flood asked, 'How did she know that?'

She spat out, 'Everyone knows everything in here. You have to be careful about what you say. I reckon one of the screws told her to wind her up.'

'That's terrible, Gemma. How were you treated in the hospital?'

'The whole thing was a nightmare, Dad. Because I'm on a murder charge, two prison officers handcuffed themselves to me, one each side, when they took me to A&E. They didn't even take them off when the doctor patched me up. When I had to go to the loo, they put me on an extended chain so I could go in private. If you can call that private. It's bloody humiliating.'

Hearing her starting to sob, Flood struggled to find anything positive to say before Gemma, snivelling between taking gulps of air, said, 'I don't know if I can survive in here. I don't trust anyone. That includes the screws. The only place I feel safe is in my cell. It's so claustrophobic, but it's better than being attacked.'

Flood wanted to hug her close to him, to protect her, as Gemma's sobbing increased. He glanced at Laura again. She appeared close to tears, too.

He tried to lighten the mood. 'I have some good news, Gemma. A man who witnessed the attack has come forward and made a statement confirming that Simon provoked you. It's vital testimony. Means that, hopefully, the jury will convict you of manslaughter, not murder. It'll reduce your sentence significantly.'

Gemma whispered in a voice so quiet that Flood strained to hear her. 'God, I hope you're right.'

'I'm going to talk to the Governor,' Flood said. 'This is shocking. The prison has to protect you.'

'Dad, please don't do that!' Gemma pleaded. 'It will only make things worse for me if you make a fuss.'

'The prison *has* to do something. You're not safe.'

'I know, but if you complain, the other prisoners will make my life hell. Please, Dad?'

'OK. OK. I understand, but I'm not happy. Let's talk about it when we come and see you on Thursday.'

'Alright. I've got to go. I'm only allowed five minutes on the phone.' Laura joined Flood in saying, 'We love you,' before she hung up.

He turned to Laura. 'What do you make of that?'

'She's probably right about you not making a fuss. Let the Governor deal with it.'

***

Flood went to his study and googled 'escort agencies in Southampton'. He found seventeen online, all showing photos of young, attractive models posing provocatively in sexy underwear. Most of the sites had been designed so that once the punter expressed an interest in one of the girls, he'd be asked to input a name and contact number. The models would call back to talk about the services they offered and their rates. If the punter agreed, they'd arrange a meeting.

He looked for a young woman called Katya matching Susan's description. On the tenth website, he discovered her. Through gritted teeth, he shouted, 'Yes!' He completed the agency's online form with his name and his mobile number and sent it.

Within fifteen minutes, Katya called back. Flood told her he was lonely, having lost his wife recently and wanted to spend time in the company of an attractive lady over drinks and dinner, maybe more. He agreed the fees and arranged to meet her the following evening at a trendy bar in the city.

Flood returned to the sitting room. Laura switched off the TV, turned to him and said, 'How are you feeling now?'

He told her he'd arranged to meet a girl from an escort agency.

Laura sat bolt upright. 'You've done what?'

'Don't worry. I'm not going to avail myself of her services.'

'I should hope not.'

Flood told her about his conversation with Susan at the hotel. 'She said she didn't tell the police about an escort being there, so they haven't questioned her. I want to know whether she or her punter, Stuart Golding, saw or heard something that'll drive this investigation forward.'

Laura gave him a reproachful look and then smiled. 'As long as that's *all* you want to talk to her about.' Her tone changed. 'Why the hell don't you let the police do their job? You're not a DCI in the Met anymore.'

***

The following evening, as dusk turned to darkness, Flood arrived at the Bunch of Grapes gastropub, a hundred yards away from the Sturridge Hotel, a few minutes before the planned rendezvous with Katya. The bar had recently had a significant makeover. Art deco lighting flared down every wall, and the smell of newly-painted woodwork flooded the room. Smooth, mellow music played in the background.

Flood had dealt with many escorts when he was in the Force and as a private investigator. He'd learnt that most of them, provided they were rewarded handsomely, would offer up information.

It wasn't the sort of place that served draft beer, so Flood opted for the cocktail of the night, a pina colada, served by a bow-tied barman. He took his drink to a table with a good view of the entrance. Ten minutes later, a petite, dark-haired woman with high cheekbones, thick mascara and dressed in a black, suede, leather jacket and short skirt entered. A red bow in her hair matched her lipstick and high heels. She looked around confidently. Flood stood and walked towards her.

'Katya?'

Her chestnut-brown eyes took in Flood from top to toe. She smiled, revealing teeth looking so even and white, she could make a living appearing in toothpaste ads.

'Yes. I am Katya. You are Andy?' Her accent confirmed her Polish origin.

'That's right. Come and sit down. What would you like to drink? The house cocktail is good.'

'I'll have a vodka and tonic, please.'

Flood returned to the table with her drink and after a brief, mindless conversation, he said, 'Katya, I'll come clean with you. I'm a private detective investigating a case which you might be able to help me solve.'

She glared at Flood, stood, picked up her vodka and tonic, took a gulp and slammed the glass back on the table. 'That's not what I thought you wanted me for.' She headed for the door.

Flood stood and reached out a hand catching her arm. 'This is nothing to do with your job. I'm happy to pay you what we agreed.'

She turned back and faced him. Flood said, 'Please sit down, Katya. Listen to what I have to say. All I need is some information.'

She spat back, 'And if I don't give it to you?'

'It's not a problem.' Flood reached into his pocket and pulled out five crisp twenty-pound notes he'd collected from the ATM earlier and surreptitiously squeezed them into the palm of her hand.

Katya drained her drink, leaving the rim of the glass smeared with lipstick. 'I need more vodka.' She thrust the empty glass in his direction.

'I'll get you one.'

Flood returned and placed the glass on the table, pulled his chair closer and leant forward.

'I know you were at the Sturridge Hotel with a client, Stuart Golding, on the evening of the seventh of March.'

Katya's eyes opened wide at the mention of Golding's name.

Flood said, 'He's a regular, isn't he?'

'I've got lots of regulars.'

'In the early hours of the following morning, a young woman fell to her death from the top floor. You were in room 521 directly underneath hers. I want to know whether you or your client saw or heard anything which might help me to understand what happened.'

Katya remained silent and started rubbing both sides of her glass with her palms. Flood played the silent game too, but maintained eye contact. The music continued to play in the background.

She took a sip of vodka before placing the glass back on the table. 'Yes. I was there with Stuart. He'd paid to spend the night with me.' She closed her eyes momentarily, thinking through what happened.

'We had dinner then drinks at the bar and went to his room. We had more drinks and went to bed. Must have been after midnight when Stuart went to the balcony to smoke a cigarette. I stayed in bed.

'He surprised me by rushing back into the room, said he'd heard a violent argument between a man and a woman on the balcony above. Then he said that he'd seen a woman's body falling past him and hitting the ground. I didn't hear anything. The windows must be thick, yes? I could see it upset him. He asked me to leave. He said if police came to investigate, he didn't want them to know he was with me. He's married with kids. I dressed and left the hotel as soon as I could.'

'Did he say anything else?'

'No. Stuart just wanted me out of the way.'

'Have you spoken to him or seen him since?'

'No. I haven't. I read about it in the papers. Poor girl. The police say she must have been drinking or on drugs. Not a nice way to end your life, is it?'

'No. It's not. Thanks, Katya.'

CHAPTER THIRTY-ONE

As soon as he arrived home, armed with Katya's and Susan's information, Flood browsed the internet and looked up Stuart Golding on social media. Susan was right about him being a big shot. He headed a stock exchange-quoted pharmaceutical company based near his home in Wimbledon. It boasted several large contracts, one with the NHS.

Aged forty, Golding married Amelia five years ago and had two children aged two and three. His Facebook page showed recent photos depicting a smiley, happy, family. *No wonder he didn't want his meetings with Katya to become public knowledge.*

Flood visited the happy family home the following morning, a Saturday. The satnav led him to a broad, leafy avenue not far from Wimbledon tennis courts. High railings protected mini-mansions as big as boutique hotels, with sweeping, tree-lined drives, some with daffodils nodding gracefully in the spring sunshine.

Flood found a parking spot not far away and strode back towards the entrance to Golding's house. He pressed the button on the security pad, and seconds later, heard a male with an upper-class accent, say, 'Can I help you?'

'Mr Golding?'

'Yes.'

'I'm Andy Flood, a private investigator investigating the death of a young woman who fell from a sixth-floor balcony of a hotel in Southampton. Can you spare me a few minutes?'

Following a slight hesitation, Golding replied. 'I've been interviewed by the police and given them a witness statement. That's all I have to say on the matter. Goodbye.'

Flood interjected quickly, realising he only had a second or two to put Golding on the back foot. 'I've had a long chat with Katya.'

'Katya?'

'Yes. Katya, the escort you spent the night with at the hotel the same night the young woman died. I don't want to get you into any trouble. I just need a few minutes of your time.'

Golding hesitated again before replying, 'You'd better come inside.' Flood heard a click and watched as the gates slowly opened.

Flood walked up the drive and the front door opened as he climbed the steps. A grim-faced Stuart Golding, wearing a polo shirt, jeans and loafers, stepped out. Without offering a hand, he said, 'You've got five minutes to tell me what you want.'

'I'm not interested in your extra-marital activities, Mr Golding. I simply want to talk to you about what happened. Here's my card.'

Golding glanced at it before sliding it into his back pocket. He ushered Flood into a room off the hallway and closed the door behind them. A heavily-laden bookshelf took up one wall and family photos dominated the top half of another. A laptop and files lay on a desk.

'We can talk in here. My wife's out with the children, due back soon.' Golding motioned to Flood to sit opposite him at his desk. 'I've told the police all I know, which wasn't much.'

'But you didn't tell them you had a woman in your room, did you?'

'I don't see what that's got to do with it. I saw and heard nothing.'

'That's not what Katya told me.'

'What *did* she tell you?'

'That you know much more than you admitted to the police.'

'So you believe a hooker?' he snorted.

'The police would be highly interested to know that you had a girl in your room and you didn't tell them. She could be a key witness. They could charge you with perverting the cause of justice. That's a custodial sentence for sure in a potential murder case.'

Golding looked up to the ceiling and ran his fingers through his mop of curly dark brown hair. 'I can't believe this,' he muttered under his breath.

Flood made a point of looking up at the pictures on the wall behind Golding. 'You've got a lovely wife and family. It would be a shame for them to know what you got up to in a Southampton hotel.'

Golding, his eyes squinting, leant forward. 'Are you trying to blackmail me?'

'No, I'm not. I don't have to tell the police or your wife anything. I'm a free agent. I only want to know what you saw and heard that night when a young woman fell to her death in suspicious circumstances.'

Golding bit his lip. 'If I tell you what I saw, you've got to promise me it won't get out. It would ruin me.'

'I can't promise a hundred per cent, but I'll do my best to keep your name out of this. And I can't speak for Katya. You'd have to talk to her. Now, did you see or hear anything which would help my investigation?'

Golding stared at Flood and drummed the fingers of one of his hands on his desk. Eventually, he said, 'It must have been just after midnight. I went out on the balcony for a cigarette. I heard a hell of a commotion above me, an argument between a man and a woman. It got louder and louder, the man especially so. I couldn't understand a lot of what he was yelling – part English, part Spanish, I'd say.'

'Spanish? Are you sure?'

'I own a holiday home on the Costa Brava, so I've picked up some of the language. Something to do with not paying for drugs.'

'Did you hear her say anything?'

'She screamed out for help repeatedly. To be honest, I'm surprised no one else heard her. I looked up but couldn't see what was happening from my balcony. The next thing I know, her body's hurtling down past me. I heard a sickening "thud" as she hit the ground. Oh, my God, it was awful.' Golding put his head in his hands. 'I'll never forget it.'

'Did you call 999?'

Golding looked up. 'I know I should have, but I didn't want anyone to know I had Katya in the room. I panicked, told her to get dressed and leave the hotel as soon as possible.'

'So you told the police that you saw and heard nothing?'

'Look, I'm not proud of that. Any married man with a family would have done the same in similar circumstances. I knew that if I told the police the truth, I'd have to make a statement and appear in court as a witness. Everyone would know that I'd spent the night with Katya. It would ruin my marriage and my career.'

Flood frowned. 'But a woman died.'

Golding bowed his head. 'I know. That's something I'll have to live with for the rest of my life.'

Quite right, too, Flood thought. *He should suffer. Not coming forward was despicable.* Leaving the words hanging in the air, Flood eventually said, 'OK. Thanks for telling me what you witnessed.'

Golding stood and leaned forward. 'You've got to make sure this conversation doesn't go any further.'

Flood made his way towards the door. Turning back to face Golding, he said, 'I'll try.'

***

On the journey home, Flood called Carlos's assistant, Susan, at the Sturridge Hotel. 'I need your help again with a couple of points. Can you talk?'

'Yes. It's quiet here.'

'This is a bit delicate. Is Carlos there with you?'

'No. It's his day off. He usually spends them at the pub up the road.'

'Good. Can you tell me anything about his relationship with the woman who fell from room 621? Were they friendly? Did he chat to her, for example?'

Flood heard Susan snort. 'Carlos thinks he's God's gift to women. He flirts with them all the time.' She paused before saying, 'I did see him hand over a small envelope to her once. He's done that with a few regulars as he passes over their room card. He thought I wouldn't notice.'

'Could they have been drugs, do you think?'

'I'm pretty sure they were. It was all a bit furtive. You won't tell Carlos I told you about this, will you?'

'Of course not. You have my word. But there is something else you can do for me. I need to speak to the owner of the hotel. Can you give me his contact details?'

'I have it here, somewhere. Give me a moment.' She came back on the phone and gave him a mobile number, email address and the name, Gus Martin. He thanked her, hung up and immediately dialled the number.

'Mr Martin, my name's Andrew Flood, a private investigator. You'll remember I asked Carlos to speak to you on the phone a while back following the accidental death of one of your guests.'

Martin's clipped tone resonated over the phone. 'Yes. I do remember. Very unfortunate. Why are you calling me?'

'I'm tying up a few loose ends. I'd like to know more about Carlos Ramirez's background. He's your reception manager at the hotel. What can you tell me?'

'Can't you ask him yourself?'

'I'd rather hear what you have to say.'

Martin paused before saying, 'He's family, my wife's brother. They're Costa Rican. I sponsored him on a six-month visitor's visa.'

'So why did he work for you?'

'This is a little embarrassing. I know the rules say he can't work while in the UK, but I didn't think it would harm anyone if he helped out. He speaks excellent English and he's a great hit with my customers. I thought the experience would help him get a job back home to support his wife and two kids who still live in Costa Rica.'

'What's the main language there?'

'Mostly Spanish. You're not going to report me, are you?'

'No. That's fine. Thanks for your help.'

***

Flood called DS Bridges next. 'Did you find a match on the database for any prints other than Mandy's in her hotel room?'

'Yes. One set on a wine glass matched Gary's. But we found a different set on the balcony door frame. We haven't got a match for them. They could have belonged to anyone.'

Flood visualised Mandy being pushed over the balcony railings. 'What about Mandy's pyjamas?'

'They were checked too. Nothing showed up. Why do you ask?'

'Which lab did they use?'

'Same as usual. The one in Abingdon.'

Flood inwardly cheered. It's where Laura worked. 'Where are Mandy's clothes now?'

'We'd have sent them from the mortuary directly to the lab. I assume they're still there. I'll check the chain of evidence document. Why the interest?'

'I'm following up a line of enquiry involving the head receptionist at the hotel, Carlos Ramirez. When I've got more information, I'll let you know.'

***

That evening, Flood arrived home to a smiling Laura who greeted him with a warm hug and kiss. 'You're in a good mood,' he said.

'I've every reason to be. You remember that new fingerprinting test for fabrics I've been working on? We've proved that it works especially well on high thread-count fabrics like silk, nylon and polyester. It's been signed off!'

'Congratulations!' Flood said, and raised his glass. 'I know how hard you've worked on that. You must be delighted.'

'All we need now is a live case. That's the real test. It will have to stand up to examination by the experts in court. Anyway, what sort of day did you have?'

Flood told Laura about Carlos's involvement with Mandy. As he spoke, an idea sparked in across his mind.

'What about testing this new forensic technique on Mandy's pyjamas? They'll be in your forensics store. I need to prove if Carlos pushed Mandy over the balcony railings.'

Laura shook her head. 'It's not as simple as that. Previous tests may have compromised the fabric.'

'Worth a try, though?'

'Yes. It is. I'll talk to my director. See what he thinks.'

'Tomorrow?'

Laura sighed. 'Never stop, do you? I'll do my best. OK?'

***

When Flood visited Gemma at the prison the following day, he frowned and tut-tutted at the sight of the stitched-up wound on her forehead, swollen nose, and bruises under her eyes. He hugged her close for no more than the few seconds allowed under the watchful eyes of the prison officers.

Looking sorry for herself, she said, 'They took the dressing off today. The medics think it will heal better if the stitches are exposed to air.' Gemma ran a finger lightly over them as she spoke.

'What happened to the perpetrator?' Flood asked.

'The Governor's transferred her to another block, thank God. Mind you, everyone in here now knows I'm an ex-copper's daughter. They remind me all the time, think I'm fair game.'

'You should request a transfer.'

'I don't see what difference it would make. Prisoners smell anything to do with coppers a hundred yards away. I spend most of the day in my cell. It's pissing me off, but it's the only way I can cope. There's no way I can handle being cooped up in here for years.'

'Having an eyewitness will make a huge difference to your sentence. Thank goodness he came forward.' Gemma smiled for the first time he could remember since she was charged.

Laura called his mobile as Flood drove back from the prison. 'How is Gemma?'

'She's feeling sorry for herself. Who could blame her? She's finding prison tough.'

'Poor girl. I'm sorry I couldn't come with you today. I'm up to my neck in work. Listen, I've got good news. I told my boss about your case, and he's discussed it with the Superintendent at Southampton nick.'

'And?'

'They've agreed to use the new test. We'll be doing it later today. I'm staying on this evening to analyse the results. I'll call you then.'

'That's fantastic, Laura. What would I do without you?'

'Probably, not much. Must go. Love you.'

When Flood arrived home, he finished the remains of a pizza Laura had left in the fridge and washed it down with a glass of red wine as he caught up with the newspapers. His mind drifted back to Laura working on Mandy's pyjamas at the lab. He wondered how long it would take to get the results. If it showed nothing, that would scupper his theory.

Three hours later, his mobile rang. Laura's voice shook with excitement. 'It worked! We've lifted clear palm prints and a full set of fingerprints. From their position, our initial conclusion is that they're conducive with Mandy being shoved from behind. My boss is chuffed to bits. He's pretty confident it will satisfy the experts.'

Flood punched the air with his free hand. 'Excellent!'

'Well, it's not like Professor Sir Alec Jeffreys' mapping of DNA, but this new test fills a gap in our fingerprinting armoury.'

'I'll meet up with Bridges first thing tomorrow; get him to check the prints against Carlos's. Thanks, Laura.'

***

DS Bridges looked entirely at home sitting in DI Ashford's former office. Flood told him about Laura's research project and his suspicions about Carlos.

Flood also told Bridges about Golding witnessing Mandy falling from the sixth-floor of the hotel after hearing an argument. 'He heard a male speaking Spanish. Carlos is Costa Rican.' Flood paused to let the connection sink in.

Bridges whistled and said, 'That puts Carlos at the scene at the time of her death.'

'There's enough information here to arrest him and compare his fingerprints with those on Mandy's pyjamas.'

Bridges nodded. 'I agree.'

'Can I also suggest you carry out background checks on Gus Martin, the owner of the hotel? Carlos is his brother-in-law. Martin sponsored him on a six-month visitors' visa and employed him to work in the hotel.'

Bridges looked up. 'You've been busy! I'll set that up. You've met Carlos and know what he looks like, so why don't you come with me now to pull him in?'

'That's fine with me.'

'OK. Let's get cracking.'

●▲●

CHAPTER THIRTY-TWO

Flood followed Bridges out of the room and down to the carpool in the underground garage. As the DS clicked his remote to open the car doors, he said, 'How's your daughter's case progressing? She's been charged with murder, hasn't she? I hope you don't mind me asking.'

As they sat in the car and buckled up, Flood replied, 'Not at all. We're pinning our hopes on a male eyewitness who saw Gemma being provoked. He's a regular at the pub where it happened. We hope it'll reduce the charge from murder to manslaughter. She can't deny stabbing her ex. I'm not sure I'll ever come to terms with that.'

'I don't think I would. How reliable is the witness?'

'Our solicitor thinks he's OK.'

'Would you like me to run a check on him? Discreetly, of course. Sometimes the lawyers don't always know where to look.'

'Yeah, that would be good.'

'What's his name?'

Flood hadn't thought to ask Monty. The eyewitness was just a guy in a pub. 'I can find out.' Flood drew his mobile from his pocket and speed-dialled his pal. Flood asked the question.

'It was a Carlos Ramirez who made the statement. He works at the Sturridge Hotel.'

Flood, his jaw gaping, glanced across at Bridges. 'Are you sure? Carlos Ramirez?'

Bridges stared back and let out a low whistle.

'Yes,' Monty replied.

'You won't believe this. I'm in a police car with a detective. We're on our way to question him in connection with the murder of Mandy Bradshaw. It's a case I've been working on for the last month. You must have read about it; the young woman who fell from a sixth-floor balcony of the Sturridge Hotel.'

'Bloody hell!'

'I'll call you later.' Flood hung up and turned to Bridges. 'Christ! What do you make of that?'

Before Bridges could reply, a streak of lightning blazed across the sky followed by a booming clap of thunder as he drove out onto the road.

'This is the same Carlos?' Bridges asked.

'It must be.'

Flood kicked himself as he remembered that Susan at the hotel had told him Carlos spent his days off at the 'pub up the road' where Gemma had stabbed her husband. *Could it have been the Blue Anchor?*

'You've met him, right? So how come he didn't connect your surname with your daughter when you spoke to him?' asked Bridges.

Flood recalled giving Carlos his card before replying, 'Gemma was charged in her married name, Saltus.'

Torrential rain bounced off the roof and the bonnet of the car, forcing Bridges to turn on the wipers to maximum speed. They made little difference except to increase the noise level inside the car.

Bridges shouted above the din, 'He's in for a shock when he discovers who you are.'

They reached Carlos's modern apartment block, less than a mile from the Sturridge Hotel, and Bridges parked the unmarked police car in the closest parking spot he could find. They raced to the covered entrance with rain pelting in their faces. After taking the lift to the fourth floor, they ran along the balcony towards Carlos's flat. Bridges rang the doorbell several times to no avail. As Flood peered in the windows, Bridges shouted through the letterbox, 'Police. Police. Please open up.' No answer.

'Shall we break in?' asked Flood.

'We can only do that if we suspect there's a danger to life.'

'That only applies to the police. I can do it. Charge me with breaking and entering if you like.'

Bridges nodded. Flood smashed his elbow against the windowpane set in the centre of the door with such force, it shattered into pieces. He put his arm through the gap, turned the lock on the inside, pushed the door open and they both entered. It didn't take them long to realise that Carlos wasn't there.

Flood turned to Bridges. 'Check with the neighbours, see if they know when he left or if they have any idea where he might be. I'll have a poke around; see if I can find anything interesting.'

He went straight to the kitchenette and touched the coffee machine. It felt warm. Next, he searched each room starting in the bedroom. A few clothes hung limply from wire hangers in the wardrobe. There was no sign of a passport in any of the drawers.

A breathless DI Bridges dashed back into the flat. 'A neighbour saw Carlos get into a cab twenty minutes ago, carrying a large shoulder bag. She noticed the cab's name, Colin's Taxis. I called them. They say he's headed for the railway station. It's not that far away. Let's go.'

They retraced their steps and ran back along the balcony to the lift. Bridges pushed the ground-floor button and cursed as it stopped at every floor to let in more people before reaching ground level. 'We'd have been quicker if we'd taken the bloody stairs,' Flood shouted, as they ran towards the car.

Bridges turned on the blue lights set inside the car's front grille and sped to the station. The rain had stopped by the time they arrived. A crowd of noisy football supporters wearing blue and white scarves and yelling moronic chants, swarmed out from the platforms.

'Shit!' Bridges shouted. 'I'd forgotten. Saints are playing Chelsea at St Mary's. We'll never find Carlos in there. Where do you think he's headed?'

'There's no sign of his passport. My guess is Heathrow or Gatwick to catch a plane back to Costa Rica. I'll check the flight schedule.'

Bridges parked outside the station and turned off the blue lights. A wag dressed in Chelsea's blue kit shouted out, 'Keep your blues going, mate. We need your support.' Other fans cheered.

Flood googled *flights from London to Costa Rica* on his mobile. A couple of minutes later, he turned to Bridges and groaned. 'There are twenty-three flights a day to Costa Rica via Miami and two early morning direct flights from the UK. He could have made a booking on any of them.'

'Let's go back to the nick. I'll get the team to check it out and arrange a forensic search of the apartment, including fingerprints. There's no point in you coming back to the station. I'll call you as soon as I have any more information. By the way, I've decided not to arrest you for breaking and entering. I didn't see anything.'

Flood drove home, and shortly after he arrived, called Monty to update him. When he finished, Monty said, 'It's essential you find him, Andy. There's no extradition treaty in place between the UK and Costa Rica. If he makes it home, we'll not be able to get him back to testify at Gemma's trial.'

'But we've got his statement. That should suffice, shouldn't it?'

'Not necessarily. The prosecution will argue that they won't have had the opportunity to question him and test his credibility. The judge would advise the jury to that effect. That would considerably weaken Gemma's case.'

Flood slammed a fist on the desk in front of him and yelled, 'Bugger!'

***

That evening, Flood sat with Laura watching television, his mind constantly drifting to Carlos Ramirez being Gemma's eyewitness and the ramifications if he wasn't found soon. His mobile rang. Flood recognised Bridge's number. He nodded across at Laura, walked into the hallway to take the call.

'We got a break. We checked the direct flights first. British Airways confirmed that earlier today, at 2.33 p.m. to be precise, a Carlos Ramirez booked a seat online on the 8.05 flight leaving Heathrow tomorrow. They've sent me a copy of the boarding pass.'

'Good work. It sounds like he made the booking on the train. Did the search of the apartment reveal anything?'

'The CSIs took fingerprints from the usual sources: cups, glasses, TV remote, etc. All of them are identical, so we're as sure as we can be they belong to Carlos. We've sent the samples to the lab as you suggested to see if there's a match to those on Mandy's pyjamas. They're pulling out all the stops. We should hear something within the next twenty-four hours.'

'We also found a stash of cocaine, about two hundred two-gram wraps packed in cellophane and hidden away behind an air vent. If it's good gear, it's worth around forty to fifty grand on the streets. It's a lot to leave behind.'

'He could hardly take them with him to the airport,' Flood replied. 'He may have asked another dealer to collect them if he's part of a gang but we got there first.'

'There's something else. The wraps match those found in Mandy's hotel room.'

'How do you know that?'

'The cellophane packets have a scorpion logo inscribed in one corner, like a brand. Our drugs intelligence people say there's a lot of bad gear going around where the cocaine's mixed with dangerous chemicals to make it go further. Can be lethal. The suppliers have latched on to the fact that if they brand the good stuff, the shit giving the greatest highs, they can get better prices.'

'We need to find out who's involved in the supply chain.'

'I agree. I've asked the team to talk to their contacts, get some answers. About tomorrow; I've arranged for Carlos to be intercepted at the departure gate by the Border Force. Then I'll arrest him, bring him back here for questioning. As you're the only person who can positively identify him, can you come with me?'

'I'd love to.'

'Good I'll text you the arrangements.'

CHAPTER THIRTY-THREE

Flood was dressed and ready to go as a car arrived outside his house at 5.00 a.m. as planned. He pulled on his jacket and quietly closed the front door behind him, not wanting to wake Laura. The heavy rain of the previous day had petered out to a steady drizzle in the darkness. He slid next to Bobby Bridges sitting in a rear passenger seat of the police car as the driver nodded an acknowledgement.

'Did you manage to get any sleep?' Bridges asked.

'Not a lot. How about you?'

'A couple of hours. Before I got my head down, I called the head of security at Heathrow and informed him that I'd put Carlos on the Watch List on the Police National Computer. That should flag up his entry through the security gates at Terminal Three. I need you to identify him before we can make the arrest.'

'Good,' Flood replied. 'Sounds like a plan.'

The driver turned on the blue lights as darkness turned to misty dawn and the traffic increased around the airport perimeter road. He parked in the drop-off zone, Bridges and Flood jumped out and made their way through the main doors to the concourse.

Picking their way through hundreds of travellers wheeling their multi-coloured cases towards the check-in desks and bag drop areas, they headed for the security gates patrolled by several Armed Response Officers. Bridges flashed his warrant card at one of them and asked to speak to the Head of Airport Security. The officer scrutinised it and nodded.

'He's in the Control Centre. Follow me.'

He led the way up a flight of stairs and pressed the intercom next to a heavy door marked, AUTHORISED PERSONNEL ONLY.

The officer said, 'I've got two officers here from Hampshire Police. They've arranged to see the Head of

Security.' After a short delay, the door opened and Flood and Bridges entered. The vast room reminded Flood of the TV pictures of Mission Control during the moon landing. Giant CCTV monitors covered every wall. Around twenty-five staff sat or stood at their work stations, either intently peering at the screens or fiddling with their keyboards.

A slim man with close-cut, silver hair approached them. His self-assured body language implied supreme confidence. He offered his hand. 'Hi, I'm Phillip Woodman. We've been expecting you. Please follow me.'

Woodman led the way towards the monitors at the furthest end of the room. 'We've done this drill many times.' He waved his arm in a theatrical gesture towards the screens. 'Cameras cover every automatic security gate and boarding gate. As your target is on the Watch List, he'll be denied automatic entry. The Border Force will detain him and you can make the arrest. I've got back-up standing by if we need it.'

He tapped the shoulder of a young, dark-haired woman surveying the screens and introduced her. 'Tricia, here, is the supervisor in charge today. If you need her to zoom in on anything or anyone, just ask. I'll be around if you need me.'

Tricia looked up, smiled and said, 'Please make yourselves comfortable.' She nodded at a pair of vacant chairs next to hers. Both men took off their coats and hung them on the backs before sitting down. Tricia pointed at the monitors on the wall directly in front of her. 'These cover the entry points to all the automatic security gates. If the Watch List system works, we'll see your man being denied entry. Just to be on the safe side, though, I suggest you concentrate on the screens; see if you can spot him. If you do, we'll get the border guards to detain him. Which flight are you interested in?'

Bridges replied, 'It's British Airways, flight number 226, direct to San José, Costa Rica, scheduled to depart at 8.05.'

Tricia replied, 'That means boarding will start at 7.15 and close at 7.45.' She looked at her watch. 'It's now 6.45.'

Flood, frequently checking his watch, peered closely at the screens which showed a constant wave of passengers milling through each automatic gate leading to the security check area. No one resembled Carlos.

With ten minutes remaining for the final boarding time, he focused on the screens even harder before turning to Tricia. 'Suppose Carlos somehow got through security. Is there any way we can see if he's arrived at the departure gate or boarded the plane?'

'What's the boarding gate and seat number?'

Bridges pulled a copy of Carlos's boarding card from his inside pocket and read, 'Boarding Gate 74, Seat C3.' He placed it on her desk, next to her keyboard.

Tricia hit the keys. The desk at Gate 74 appeared on the screen showing no one queuing. She picked up her phone and called the attendant standing at the gate. 'You should have a passenger on your list, Carlos Ramirez. Do you know if he's boarded?'

'No. We've put out two calls already. I'll make a final call now. He's one of two passengers we're waiting for. They're cutting it fine. We're about to close the gates.'

'OK. We've got you on camera. Please detain if he turns up.'

Flood rubbed his sore eyes, willing Carlos to appear. He gripped the back of Tricia's chair as a man rushed up to the gate, carrying a holdall in one hand, his boarding card and passport in the other, offering profuse apologies. It wasn't Carlos.

As they watched the attendants close the gate, Tricia turned to Flood and Bridges. 'It looks like your man's a no show.'

Flood blurted out, 'How many passengers buy a ticket, check-in and don't board the plane?'

'It's rare,' she said. 'But sometimes, people have a last-minute change of plans.'

'Is there *any* way our target could have boarded the plane?'

Tricia shook her head. 'I don't think so. Even if he got through security, he'd have to be checked-in as a passenger at the departure gate. You could ask the boss to speak to Air Traffic Control. It's beyond my responsibility, I'm afraid. He can call the pilot, ask him to get one of the crew to check to see if the seat is occupied.'

'Let's go to his office,' Bridges said, as he picked up the copy of Carlos's boarding card from Tricia's desk.

Woodman waved them in. Placing the copy on his desk, Bridges said, 'It's vital we know if our target is on this flight. Can you check with the pilot?'

'I'll call Flight Control now.' Woodman grabbed his phone, hit the digits and explained the problem. He put the phone down and said, 'It's all set up. The aircraft's in a queue on the runway. We'll have to wait a few minutes.'

Flood wasn't the superstitious type, but he crossed his fingers anyway. It reminded him of the countless times he'd waited for a jury's verdict.

After what seemed an age sitting in silence, Woodman's phone bleeped. He snatched at it, listened and said, 'Thanks,' before putting it down. He looked up at Flood and Bridges. 'The seat's empty and the aircraft has been cleared for takeoff.'

***

Flood and Bridges found a quiet spot in the Control Centre staff room to debrief. 'There has to be a reason why Carlos didn't board the plane,' Flood said. 'Someone must have tipped him off.'

'You may be right. But who?'

'What about members of your team? They're the only people who would know about us going to Carlos's apartment and the airport.'

Bridges shook his head. 'You can't be serious? I've worked with these guys for a couple of years. I know them well. I can't think of anyone.'

'What about the owner of the hotel? Gus Martin? He sponsored Carlos. Maybe he's involved?'

'How would he know our plans?'

'I don't know. You could question him. You have every reason to. We're talking about someone who sponsored a visitors' visa for a guy who is suspected of murder.'

'I'll follow that up when we get back to the nick. What do you think Carlos will do now?'

'He's trapped. He can't go back to the hotel or his apartment. He's also left his stash of gear behind. Once his cash runs out, he's stuffed.'

Bridges nodded in agreement. 'He could try another flight, another day?'

'That's what worries me. If Carlos gets through security another time, he could travel anywhere in Europe using his visa. There must be hundreds of daily flights from there to Miami. Then he could catch a connecting flight to Costa Rica.'

'So where does that leave us?'

'My guess is he'll contact Martin. Remember, he's his brother-in-law. He's the only person Carlos can rely upon to get back home.'

The harsh tone of Bridge's mobile interrupted their conversation. As he listened, a grim expression crossed his face. 'Thanks for letting me know.'

He turned to Flood. 'That was the forensics lab. The fingerprints taken from Carlos's flat match those on Mandy's pyjamas and the balcony door handle. It looks like he's responsible for pushing her over the railings.'

CHAPTER THIRTY-FOUR

The following morning, as he sat in a barber's chair having a grade four trim, Flood's mind drifted back to Zara Warwick, Simon Saltus's previous girlfriend. Her name hung over him like a brooding black cloud. *Could she tell him something about the way he treated women?*

He prided himself on being able to find anyone, anywhere, anytime. But despite spending hours trying to trace her via social media, he drew a blank. He called her mother, Joanne, once a week to the point when, on his last call, she'd said, 'Stop bothering us. Zara wants to be left alone,' and cut him off.

Another problem hovered into his mind; how to break the news to Gemma that the eyewitness she depended on to reduce her sentence had gone missing? At least he knew who he was. *Did Gemma know him?* He'd ask Monty to call the prison and ask Gemma to call her father as soon as possible.

As soon as he left the barbers, he checked his texts. The latest from DS Bridges, read, *I've got news on Gus Martin. Call when u can.* Flood rang back immediately.

Bridges said, 'You're not going to believe this. Gus Martin's on the Police National Computer file. Three months ago, one of the banks filed a Suspicious Activity Report with the National Crime Agency. They suspect him of being involved in money laundering. The NCA believes he's set up a dozen or so drug dealers to sell gear brought in from Colombia. He finances the purchase and takes a share of the sale proceeds.'

'That means Carlos is one of his dealers.'

'There's something else. As well as the hotel and the apartment block where Carlos lives, Martin owns several fish and chip shops and betting offices on the south coast – all cash generators, the perfect cover for the operation. The hotel is a respectable front.'

218

'How far are they into the investigation?'

'Martin's been under surveillance for the past two weeks. They've bugged his Mercedes with a listening device and fitted a tracker. The Financial Investigation Unit, part of the NCA, is keen to get into Martin's businesses and look at the books. They've applied for a warrant to search his house and are waiting for authorisation.'

Flood groaned. 'Shit! If the police shut down his operation and take Martin into custody, Carlos will go to ground. Who's dealing with the case?'

'A DCI Samuels. He's the coordinator between the NCA and the Force.'

'Could you persuade him to delay for a week? Tell him we're dealing with a murder suspect and we've enough evidence to convict.'

'I've already called him and put him in the picture. He's agreed to delay for forty-eight hours.'

'I suppose it's better than nothing. Thanks, Bobby,' Flood said, impressed by Bridge's competence.

Bridges continued, 'I asked if the name Carlos Ramirez had come up in their enquiries so far. He checked and said their Intelligence Unit says no. I've asked him to let me know if Carlos gets in touch with Martin. There's not much more we can do. We'll have to wait.'

Flood thought, *You may be happy to wait, but I'm not.*

***

Later that evening, Flood and Laura enjoyed a drink at another of their favourite pubs. Flood updated Laura about Gus Martin's alleged money-laundering activities and his connection to Carlos.

He added, 'In less than two days' time, Martin will be out of circulation. There goes our bait and we'll have no idea where Carlos is.'

'Do you think he's still in the country?' Laura asked.

'I don't know. He'll need a fake passport to get through the security gates. Maybe Gus Martin has already got him one? Carlos could already be in Costa Rica. If he is, Monty told me he can't be extradited. Just what we needed,' Flood scowled.

'What are you going to do next?'

'I thought about staking out Martin's house; see if Carlos was holed up there.'

He immediately knew he'd said the wrong thing, judging by Laura's icy stare. 'Is that necessary? You said the NCA have him under observation, bugged his car and tracking its movements.'

Flood dug a deeper hole, ignoring Laura's plea. 'I need to do something, Laura. I'll drive around Martin's neighbourhood first thing in the morning, check out his house. You never know, I might spot something.'

Laura shook her head. 'You don't care about upsetting anyone, do you? Even the NCA.'

'Not if there's a chance of getting Carlos to testify at Gemma's trial and paying the price for murdering Mandy.'

She looked him squarely in the face. 'You could prejudice the whole operation. It's not worth the risk, Andy.'

***

The following day dragged like no other for Flood. As he sat in his office, he wrung every last ounce of his brainpower going over his investigation into Carlos, seeking clues to his whereabouts. He thought about investigating the possibility of discovering other eyewitnesses to the incident, despite the police having made numerous appeals.

At that very moment, he received a call from Gemma. 'How are you feeling?' he asked.

'Fine. Just want to get the trial over. Monty's been great at telling me what to expect.'

'That's good. Laura and I will be there at the courtroom every day. Listen, Gemma, there's something I wanted to ask you. The name of the eyewitness who came forward was

Carlos Ramirez. It looks like he's a drug dealer. He only came forward and made his statement when he learned that Simon had died and that you were being charged with murder. Did you know him?'

Gemma hesitated for a moment. 'No. I didn't.'

'You're sure?'

'Yes. I'm sure.'

Flood said, 'OK. That's all I wanted to know.' He didn't burden her with the fact that he was missing.

***

Flood trawled the internet to find Gus Martin's address and discovered that he lived on the edge of Romsey, a bustling market town, fourteen miles south-west of Winchester. It would be easy to drive there, have a look around, but Laura's words of reason resonated in his mind. She was right. He'd leave it for now.

DS Bridges called at lunchtime. 'I thought you'd be interested to know that I checked with Interpol to see if they had anything on Carlos Ramirez. He has a criminal record in Costa Rica: two serious assaults and drug dealing. It doesn't help if we don't find him, but it goes some way to explain what kind of man we're dealing with.'

'How come the Border Force didn't pick up his record when he came to the UK?'

'They don't require a criminal record certificate for tourists coming to the UK on a visa. They just have to make a declaration.'

'Wonderful! Are there any developments?'

'That's the main reason I'm calling. DCI Samuels confirmed that they're raiding Martin's home at 6.00 a.m. tomorrow. Intelligence is concerned if they leave it any longer, he could get wind of the operation and scarper. The plan is to arrest him, search the house, seize his computers and impound his car. Simultaneous raids are planned for all his business

221

locations. I'll update you tomorrow; let you know if they find Carlos.'

At home later that evening, a restless Flood spent time surfing the internet and catching up on the news. He tried watching TV, got bored and aimlessly walked around his garden until it got too dark. All the while, he imagined the early morning raids. He'd been in charge of numerous operations when he worked for the Met and missed the anticipation, excitement and threat of danger.

Laura, sitting at the table going over research notes she'd brought home, recognised his symptoms. She put her pen down. 'Why don't you go down the pub? You're driving me bloody crazy.'

'What do you mean?'

'You're like a caged tiger. There's nothing you can do until Bridges calls you tomorrow.'

'I have to know whether Carlos is at Martin's place or holed up in one of his business premises.'

'You'd better prepare yourself if he isn't.'

'In which case, what do I tell Gemma?'

'You'll have to tell her the truth. I'll tell you what you *can* do. Make yourself useful. Get me a coffee.'

Flood, grateful of something to do, emerged from the kitchen with two cups and a plate of chocolate biscuits. 'Anything else you'd like me to do?'

'Yes. If you don't want to go to the pub, sit in the sitting room, play some of your music and try to relax. I've got work to do.'

***

Following an uneasy night's sleep, Flood breakfasted on coffee and a bowl of muesli. Laura had left to go to work in the lab. As he took a final spoonful, his mobile rang. Snatching at it, he noticed the caller was Bridges. Flood took a deep breath and swiped the screen. 'How did it go?'

'Good and bad. The NCA have arrested Martin. The techies have begun their investigation into the accounts.'

'Any sign of Carlos at any of the premises?'

'I'm sorry, Andy, no. Samuels told me that he asked Martin if he knew where he was. He said he had no idea.'

'Do you think Carlos is still in the country?'

'It's looking less and less likely. I've asked Interpol to add him to their Most Wanted list.'

'What about Martin's bugged car? Do the tapes tell us anything?'

Bridges sounded weary. 'Give 'em a break, Andy. It's only been a few hours since the raid. I'm sure the team are going through them as a matter of urgency. I'll call you if anything interesting comes up, OK?'

Flood had put his other cases on hold for the past few weeks. But one required his urgent attention, a messy divorce case where he'd proved that the husband had stashed funds away in overseas properties and not admitted it in court. The hearing was next week, so he spent the day in his office writing up a report for the lawyers.

Laura had called to say she'd be working late, so on the way home, he picked up a Chinese takeaway. He'd set it out on a plate and opened a can of beer when his mobile buzzed.

'It's Bobby Bridges. I've heard from a member of Samuels' team monitoring the taped conversations from Martin's car. They say there's one which will interest us. They sent me a copy which I've just listened to. It's dynamite! Can you get down here now?'

'I'm on my way.' Flood slid his mobile back in his pocket, gulped down a mouthful of noodles, and covered the plate with Clingfilm. He'd microwave it later. He took a swig of beer from the can and poured the rest down the sink. Picking up his car keys, he headed out of the door and reached Southampton Police Station in record time.

DS Bridges stood to greet him. 'Have a seat and listen to this,' he said, as he loaded a tape into a cassette player on his desk and pressed 'play'.

Flood heard a car door slamming shut and a voice saying, *'the police are on to me. I need a fake passport; I can't leave the country using mine.'* Flood immediately recognised the speaker. He stopped himself high-fiving Bridges. Instead, he grinned and gave him a double thumbs up. He'd recognise Carlos's distinctive accent anywhere.

Martin: *I can get you one from a contact, but it'll take a few days.*

Carlos: *What you mean, a few days? I've got to get back to Costa. If the police find me, I'm finished.*

Martin: *And whose fault is that?*

Carlos: *You blame me?*

Martin: *We have a nice operation going on here. You earn well; I earn well. You should have stuck to dealing, not shoving clients off sixth-floor balconies, you bloody idiot.*

Carlos: *The bitch came on to me, offered sex instead of money. Then she said no to sex and didn't want to pay me either. She deserved it.*

Flood glanced at Bridges and nodded.

Martin: *I can't believe you said that! You've dropped me right in the shit. It's not good publicity for my hotel, and the last thing I need is coppers crawling all over my businesses. I've spent a shitload of money on paying off a police contact. Not to mention the cost of the drugs you left behind in the apartment which, incidentally, I never got paid for.*

Carlos: *I couldn't take them with me, could I? I was going to call you to get someone to pick them up.*

Martin: *You've let me down big-time. If you weren't my brother-in-law, I'd leave you to stew in your own vomit.*

Carlos: *If you get me a passport and plane ticket to Costa Rica, you'll never see me again. When can you get it?*

Martin: *You can't buy them off the shelf these days. They're bloody sophisticated works of art. Give me your passport. I need the photo.*

A muffled sound followed.

Carlos: *Here it is. So when?*

Martin: *I'll try to get it in the next twenty-four hours. Meet me here tomorrow afternoon at three. Then you can piss off back home.*

Carlos didn't reply. The next sound Flood heard was a car door slamming shut.

Bridges switched off the cassette player and sat back in his chair with a smug expression on his face. 'Now we know.'

'We do. Where was the car was parked?'

'The tracking device gives the location as a secluded parking area on Southampton Common.'

Flood's brain revved into overdrive. 'I've got an idea how to trap Carlos, assuming he's unaware of Martin's car's being impounded.' He explained his plan. 'What do you think?'

Bridges nodded. 'I'd been thinking along the same lines. I'll put it to the Super.'

'I suggest you keep the operation covert. The reason Carlos is still at large is that someone tipped him off the last time we tried to arrest him.'

Bridges nodded. 'You're right. I'll look into it once I've set up the trap. Would you like to be there?'

'Try and stop me.'

'After the work you've put into this case, you deserve it.'

***

At 2.30 p.m. on the following sunny but chilly day, Flood and Bridges sat on separate benches twenty yards away from each other, close to the meeting point on Southampton Common. Flood made himself look occupied by appearing to use his mobile while Bridges pretended to read a newspaper. An unmarked police car with two plain-clothed officers sitting inside had already parked in a car park twenty yards away.

Flood counted down the minutes, continually looking at the time on his mobile until an identical car to Martin's, a Mercedes G-Wagon with tinted windows, pulled into the parking area five minutes before the assignation. He'd suggested to Bridges that the police hired the same colour, same model car, fit it with Martin's number plates and have an experienced undercover officer drive it to the meeting point.

Assuming Carlos would arrive on foot, Flood kept an eye on the common and spotted a squat, dark male figure striding down the path from the direction of the boating lake carrying a bag on his shoulder. As he got closer, the man quickened his pace towards the snare.

The minute Carlos opened the passenger door to the replica Mercedes, the officers jumped out of their car and surrounded him. One held him in an arm lock. Simultaneously, Bridges leapt from the bench, rushed towards Carlos, handcuffed and cautioned him before making the arrest for the murder of Mandy Bradshaw. Flood stood and watched the entire operation and allowed himself a smile of satisfaction.

Before the officers bundled Carlos into the rear seats of the unmarked police car, he spotted Flood. His angry expression morphed into one of puzzlement.

***

Flood relished the idea of questioning Carlos. If only he could. He'd enjoy making him squirm as he presented the mountain of damning evidence against him. Instead, he had to wait for DS Bridges to call, which he did, twenty-four hours after the arrest.

'Great news, Andy. Carlos has confessed. We've charged him with possession, supplying Class A drugs and the murder of Mandy Bradshaw.'

Flood punched the air, letting out the frustrations of missing Carlos at his flat and the airport. 'How did you get him to confess? He didn't strike me as the confessing type.'

'His lawyer must have told him that the tape recordings of his conversation with Martin in his car amounted to a confession anyway. At the interview, Carlos tried to make out that Mandy's death was an accident. He said he tripped over the balcony door's threshold, put his arms out to break his fall but hit Mandy, pushing her over the balcony railings. But the more we presented our evidence, the more agitated the duty solicitor became. He called for several breaks to confer with his client. I'm sure he advised Carlos that if he confessed and pleaded guilty at the earliest opportunity, the judge would have the power to reduce his sentence by a third.'

Flood scoffed. 'I never agreed with that ruling. What he did to Mandy was shocking. People need protection from the likes of him.'

'I'm with you. What bothered Carlos most is serving his sentence in the UK before being deported. He's got a wife and kids back in Costa Rica.'

'He should have thought of that. Did Carlos give any more details about the incident?'

'Carlos told Samuels that Mandy had come on to him big time, promising him the greatest sex of his life in return for the drugs, but reneged on the deal. She didn't want to pay for them either. Carlos said he lost his temper. Especially after she'd mangled his fingers between the door and the frame as he followed her out on to the balcony.'

'That fits with Golding's version of events. Did Carlos show any remorse?'

'No. He's too wrapped up in what's going to happen to him.'

'What about Gus Martin?'

'DCI Samuels told me that the money-laundering investigation is going to take ages. It's a bigger operation than they realised.'

'Has Martin been charged with anything yet?'

'Yes. When Samuels' team arrested him, he had a passport in his pocket showing Carlos's photo, but with a different name. They charged him with aiding and abetting the forgery and denied him bail because of the threat of using his counterfeiting contacts to leave the country. The sting worked well, eh? We'll have to recruit you back into the Force.'

'You don't want a dinosaur like me getting in the way'.

Flood called Monty to tell him Carlos had confessed and that the police had charged him with murder and possession of drugs.

'That's good, Andy, but if he's convicted before Gemma's trial, which looks likely, the prosecution will ask the judge to have the conviction declared to the jury. That puts Carlos's credibility on the line.'

'But he's our only witness.'

'Is Carlos aware of your relationship to Gemma?'

'I doubt it. He knows my name because I gave him one of my cards when I visited him at the hotel. As you know, the police charged Gemma in her married name. Why do you ask?'

'It occurs to me that if he knew you were largely responsible for his arrest, it might affect his testimony.'

'He can't alter or withdraw his statement, can he? Our legal team would want to know why.'

'To be on the safe side, I think it's best if he doesn't know. It's a complication we could do without.'

CHAPTER THIRTY-SIX

FOUR-AND-A-HALF MONTHS LATER

Flood spent the time waiting for Gemma's trial catching up on his backlog of cases and visiting her at the prison every week without fail. Laura joined him when she could get time off work from the lab.

He updated Gemma on the trial preparations, trying to keep her spirits up. She picked his brains as she recalled her childhood memories for her writing project. As she was just five years old when her mother was murdered in a hit and run by a vengeful gang, she wanted to know more about her. Flood found it hard to talk about it, despite happening over twenty years ago. Yet he always felt better afterwards. Neither discussed the abduction. Still too painful to recall, even after all these years.

***

Although Flood and Bobby Bridges had spoken several times on the phone. Progress on the Gus Martin case had been slow until Flood received an early morning call from him.

'There have been some developments, at last. Let's meet away from the station. I'll update you.' They settled for a lunchtime visit to a pub, half-way between Winchester and Southampton. As the country enjoyed an August heat wave, they agreed to meet in the pub garden.

Bridges ordered two pints of shandy and joined Flood sitting under a parasol. 'So, is DCI Samuels getting somewhere at last?' Flood asked as Bridges sat down.

Taking a sip from his glass first, Bridges said, 'Following the raid on Martin's house, analysts found an encrypted spreadsheet on his computer. The techies have finally hacked their way into the coding and mined it for information. The agency likened it to cracking the Enigma code. It confirms our suspicions that Guy Martin financed the importation of cocaine from Colombia via international online bank accounts, claiming they're investments. The spreadsheets also showed that he'd set up ten dealers along the south coast, including Carlos.'

'That makes sense,' Flood said. 'Martin's wife is Carlos's sister. There's the connection. How come no one at the bank spotted it?'

'It's a sophisticated operation. Most of Martin's business income is in cash. A sharp-eyed employee of the bank queried the high sums being deposited and informed the National Crime Agency. The dealers, on average, earned between two and three grand a week. Carlos used an international money transfer bureau to move his share to an account in Costa Rica. That goes a long way in San José.'

'Have the NCA finished their investigation?'

'Close. They've tracked down all the dealers and charged them with possession and intent to supply, except one account is still outstanding. Samuels told me the spreadsheets showed a payment of a thousand pounds a week from Martin to a numbered account in Switzerland. The only reference is "Bill". The bank says the money's passed through a maze of shell companies and can't, or won't, identify the owner of the account. Samuels is questioning the dealers, including Carlos, to see if they'll give up "Bill's" identity.'

Flood's brain whirred, making a connection. 'Some time back, Bobby, you told me that Carlos's main concern after he confessed was having to serve his entire sentence in the UK and then being deported. You could offer to support an appeal to the Human Rights authorities to get a transfer to Costa Rica for family reasons if he gives up "Bill's" identity. You'd get your man and save the taxpayers some money.'

Bridge thought for a moment. 'That's a good idea. I'll put it to Samuels.' He gulped his drink and wiped his mouth with the back of his hand. 'You know Carlos's sentencing hearing is at Southampton Crown Court next week.'

'Yes. I'll be there. I want to see justice for Mandy.'

'Me, too. By the way, I hope you don't mind me asking; how is your daughter's case progressing? The trial date must be getting close.'

'It's in late October at Winchester.'

Bridges stood. 'Good luck. I hope you get a good result.' He paused before saying, 'Oh, I haven't told you about Ashford, have I? Professional Standards found him guilty of breaching the code of behaviour. He should have interviewed Fleming at the station under caution. He's been given a final written warning and transferred to Havant. The bosses thought a change of nick would be in the best interests of everyone concerned.' Bridges paused before asking, 'What did you think of him?'

'He pissed me off at first. He thought he could handle the Bradshaw case without my help. He changed, to be fair. When he interviewed Gary Fleming, he really got stuck in, certain that he'd been responsible for Mandy's murder.'

Bridges replied, 'I didn't like Ashford much. He took too many shortcuts for my liking. I can't complain, though. His fall from grace has been good for me. Since I passed my inspector's exam, I've taken over his job.' He grinned. 'You'll have to call me *DI* Bridges in future.'

Flood picked up his glass and clinked it against his. 'Congratulations, Bobby. Well deserved, if I may say so.'

'Thanks. I appreciate that, coming from you.' Bridges glanced at his watch. 'I'd better be getting back.'

They both finished their drinks and placed their empty glasses on the table. 'I mean it,' Flood said. 'I'm sure your dad would be proud of you, *Detective Inspector* Bridges.'

●▲●

CHAPTER THIRTY-SEVEN

The heatwave had given way to a moody, humid day as Flood drove down to Southampton Crown Court to see Carlos sentenced. He'd visited the modern, yellow-brick buildings many times in recent years, giving testimony as a result of his private investigations. This time, he sat in the visitors' gallery, joining a dozen others sitting on hard, unforgiving, wooden seats facing the judge's bench.

Although the courtroom lacked the gravitas of the Old Bailey, the presence of the gowned and wigged barristers and clerks in the well of the court created a hallowed ambience.

Within minutes of Flood's arrival at Court Five, a uniformed security officer led Carlos into the dock. He wore a navy blue suit, white shirt and plain tie to impress the judge. The glowering expression on his face suggested the imminent end of the world. The court clerk said, 'All rise,' as his honour, Mr Justice Stanhope QC, entered, resplendent in his red robes. Everybody stood, and the solemn atmosphere ratcheted up a notch.

The prosecuting barrister, a fair-haired, slim and earnest man in his mid-forties, spent the morning outlining the facts of the case, confirming that Carlos had pleaded guilty to murder and the possession and supply of Class A drugs. He rammed home the seriousness of the offences, finishing with, 'A young woman lost her life because she didn't pay the offender for the drugs he'd supplied. The defendant committed a reckless, intentional act knowing that death or serious bodily harm would be a virtual certainty. Your Honour, these offences call for the maximum sentence laid down by law.'

The youthful defence barrister, looking as if he'd only recently passed his bar exams, stood and spoke in a submissive tone, stopping short of actually doffing his wig to the judge.

'Your Honour, the defendant came to the UK as a tourist. His sister is married to an Englishman and settled here. He planned to spend time with them. However, he saw an opportunity to provide cash for his impoverished family in Costa Rica by joining an organised crime gang dealing in drugs. He now admits he made a stupid mistake. At the earliest opportunity, he confessed to pushing Mandy Bradshaw from the balcony of her sixth-floor hotel room. In mitigation, Mr Ramirez claims that the victim provoked him by failing to pay for the drugs and taunting him about it. It resulted in a moment of madness, which he deeply regrets.'

The defence barrister paused, letting the last sentence hang in the air. 'Mr Ramirez has shown considerable remorse for his actions, which he acknowledges were both foolish and reckless. I ask Your Honour to take these facts into account when arriving at your sentencing decision.' He bowed to the judge with a flourish and returned to his seat.

Flood glanced at Carlos who maintained his sorrowful look, no doubt designed to arouse the maximum amount of pity from the judge, who'd remained stony-faced throughout the proceedings.

His honour addressed Carlos. 'Before I pronounce sentence, do you have anything to say to the court?'

Carlos, as he'd no doubt been instructed by counsel, stood up straight and said in his distinctive accent, 'I am sorry for what I did and know I deserve to be punished. This is going to be hard on my family in Costa Rica. I will not see them for some time.' He maintained eye contact with the judge throughout.

His honour scribbled a note before brusquely announcing an adjournment, adding that he'd pass judgement on the sentence immediately after lunch.

Flood needed to stretch his legs. He made his way to the exit and bumped into the newly-promoted DI Bridges heading in the same direction. He'd been sitting in the space reserved for police officers at the side of the courtroom.

'What do you think he'll get?' Flood asked.

'Carlos's mitigating circumstances didn't amount to much so it could lead to a significant sentence. The judge will know from the tapes of the police interviews that the only reason Carlos confessed is because of the weight of evidence we produced. And I've never heard him say he's sorry for what he did until now. Do you fancy a bite to eat?' Flood nodded.

They headed for a café a hundred yards from the courts, ordered coffees and sandwiches and carried them to a seat in a quiet corner. As Bridges took the wrapping off his sandwiches, he said, 'Without your intervention, we wouldn't be sitting here today getting justice for Mandy. How do you feel about her now?'

'To be honest, I've got mixed feelings about her. When she first visited me, I didn't believe her story and turned down the job. You can imagine how guilty I felt when I found out she'd been largely telling the truth.'

Bridges frowned. 'But she persuaded Gary Fleming to help her kill Michael Bradshaw.'

'I know. That's when my opinion changed. She had the knack of getting men to do exactly as she wanted. I'm certain she provoked Carlos, too. It doesn't mean he should get away with murder, though.'

'I agree,' Bridges said.

'And it's more than likely that Mandy killed Lisa Black in Florida to get her passport. That's why I don't feel quite so badly about her now.'

***

The court reconvened and his honour asked Carlos to stand. Speaking in a measured tone, the judge said, 'Mr Ramirez. You have pleaded guilty to two serious crimes. One resulted in the death of a young woman. The other, no doubt, caused misery to many people to whom you supplied drugs. I have used the appropriate sentencing guidelines laid down by law for both charges and, as I am duty-bound, applied a one-third reduction in your sentence because you pleaded guilty. I have also taken into account the mitigating circumstances, such as they are, presented by your defence barrister.

'You are hereby sentenced to eighteen years, reduced to twelve for the murder charge and seven years, reduced to four years and six months for the possession and supply of Class A drugs. The sentences are to be served consecutively. Under the Border Act of 2007, you will be deported after serving your sentence. Also, under the Proceeds of Crime Act 2002, the authorities will seek confiscation of the profits you made from your drug dealing. Take him down.'

Flood watched as Carlos defiantly glared at the judge with eyes which could pierce a bank vault. He yelled something uncomplimentary in Spanish before being led to the cells.

Bridges looked up towards Flood from the well of the court, caught his eye and gave him a thumbs up. Flood nodded back and smiled. *Justice has been done.*

***

A week later and two weeks before Gemma's trial, Monty called Flood and asked him to meet her barrister, Robin Porter QC at his office, located just a few steps away from Flood's office. 'We thought it may be a good idea to include you in our discussions,' Monty said.

Wearing a dark, tailor-made suit, grey silk tie and crisp sky-blue shirt, Porter offered a sympathetic smile when they met. 'This must be a difficult time for you and your daughter.'

'It is. I still haven't come to terms with her being charged with murder.'

They all sat and Porter, checking his notes frequently, said, 'I've reviewed Gemma's case with Monty and discussed a strategy to convince the jury that Gemma didn't *plan* to kill Simon Saltus, but reacted on the spur of the moment after he'd provoked her. It would have been helpful if we had evidence to back up her claim that throughout the short time they were together, Simon caused her a great deal of physical and mental pain. But we only have Gemma's word that it happened. To prove abuse, we'd need doctor's notes, a record of hospital visits, that sort of thing, but there's nothing. Did she tell you or your wife what was going on?'

'Sadly, she didn't.'

'That's a pity. If we had physical evidence of abuse, we'd be able to say that when Simon confronted her at the pub, she lost control due to the risk of serious violence of what he'd do next. That could be regarded as the trigger. However, that's not the case. The standard of proof is almost impossible to achieve.'

Porter ran a hand through his mop of his silver hair and pushed his notepad to one side. 'As I see it, the verdict will turn on two major issues. The first is the provocation. We'll have to prove that Simon provoked Gemma on the evening of the offence, causing her loss of self-control. The eyewitness testimony is crucial. I understand from Monty that you've met the man who came forward and was responsible for him serving time at Her Majesty's pleasure.'

'Yes. That's true.'

'We'll have to see how that plays out in court.' He added, 'The second issue is the *reasonableness* of Gemma's reaction to the provocation. The prosecution will call an expert in knife injuries to prove that the degree of force used to kill Simon showed she *meant* to kill him. We need to prove otherwise.'

Flood's stomach turned somersaults at the mention of the words, *knife, kill* and *Gemma* in the same breath. *How did it come to this?*

Porter continued. 'We could major on Gemma's mental health issues, but it's risky. If she's regarded as not being safe to be released, it could result in a lifetime spent at a mental institution.'

The possibility had crossed Flood's mind. Every time it bludgeoned its way in, he forced it out, being too upsetting to contemplate. *Could it get any worse?*

Monty chipped in. 'The prosecution has already disclosed that they will be calling an independent expert to assess her state of mind. We'll be calling Doctor Rogers who treated her at the mental hospital.'

Porter said, 'If we can get a manslaughter verdict, she'd serve a relatively short time in custody. We need to create doubt in the jury's mind that Gemma's motive wasn't revenge and that she didn't go to the pub where she knew her husband would be, carrying a knife, intent on killing him. In other words, premeditated.'

Monty added, 'What do we know about Simon, Andy? You must have met him.'

'Yes, I have. He seemed perfectly normal whenever we got together, not that we saw them much. As you'd expect, I checked his background before they got married and found nothing sinister. Despite Gemma taking the plunge so quickly, Laura and I thought marrying Simon would be good for her. How wrong can you be?' Flood shook his head and stared at the floor.

'No one ever truly knows what goes on in a relationship. I see it every day in court,' Porter replied.

Monty asked, 'Did you find out whether Simon had any previous relationships?'

Flood told them about Zara Warwick. 'She was his girlfriend immediately before Gemma. I wanted to ask her how he treated her, and whether he acted in a way to support Gemma's allegations, but she's proving difficult to find. I traced her mother, who told me she quit her job and spends time aboard. I often call her asking if Zara has returned.'

Porter nodded. 'That's a positive line of enquiry. It could prove significant. Good luck with finding her.'

'What are the chances of getting Gemma off the murder charge?' Flood directed the question to Porter.

'There are too many variables to give you a definitive answer. If you pushed me, I'd say we've got a 50/50 chance of getting a manslaughter verdict. Sorry, I can't be more positive. I can assure you that Monty and I will do everything in our power to defend Gemma.'

Flood left Monty's office with mixed feelings; encouraged by Robin Porter's final words but depressed by the possibility of Gemma never being a free woman. *And it's my fault.*

A week later, Monty called Flood at his office. 'I've got good and not-so-good news, Andy. The good news is that the judge has ruled that Carlos's murder conviction will not be admitted in court on the grounds that it is not relevant to his role as an eyewitness. That should help with his credibility.'

'Excellent!' Flood replied. And the not-so-good news?'

'I visited Carlos in Belmarsh prison to go through his testimony. He doesn't want to appear in court.'

'Why the fuck not?'

'He told me he's thought about the incident since being in prison and says he's no longer sure of exactly what happened. He wants nothing to do with the case.'

'Can he do that?'

'No. We can get a witness summons. If he still refuses to attend, he'll be charged with contempt of court. The maximum sentence is two years. He won't want that added to his time inside.'

'Then what?'

'If he refuses to testify or says something different to the original statement, we can ask the judge to regard him as a hostile witness. That means Robin can cross-examine him, ask leading questions, dig deeper to find out why he's changed his mind. It's risky because it could confuse the jury.'

'Shit! Is there anything we can do to make him stick to what he said?'

'I don't think so. Robin's considered not calling him as a defence witness, but that plays right into the prosecution's hands. We have to prove beyond a reasonable doubt that Simon provoked Gemma; otherwise, she's facing a life sentence for murder.'

Flood slumped down in his chair as if a heavyweight boxer had punched him below the belt. Again and again.

CHAPTER THIRTY-EIGHT

That evening, Flood received a call from an upbeat DI Bridges. 'I've got two bits of good news. Gus Martin has finally been charged with money laundering, the importation and supply of Class A drugs in addition to the passport forgery. He's facing at least fifteen years.'

'Fantastic! What's the second bit?'

'Do you remember The NCA were working on Gus Martin's spreadsheet which showed a thousand pounds a week being paid to a numbered account in Switzerland with the reference, "Bill"?'

'I do. The analysts were having trouble locating it.'

'On your suggestion, they offered to support an application from Carlos to the Home Office which would allow him to serve his sentence in Costa Rica if he revealed "Bill's" identity.'

'I know he was desperate to get back home so his family could visit him in prison.'

Bridge's voice increased an octave. 'The Home Office have an early release scheme for foreign prisoners. If they behave themselves in prison and cooperate with the police, they can be deported after serving less than half their sentence. Samuels put this to Carlos's solicitor who, in turn put it to Carlos. He agreed.'

'Great. So, who is "Bill"?'

'DI Ashford.'

'Ashford? Bloody hell!'

'Yes. Once Carlos spilled the beans, Samuels got his team to track the off-shore money trail which led to Ashford's bank account. He's been charged as an accomplice to Gus Martin's criminal activities. Ashford knew what was going on but turned a blind eye in return for receiving hush money. This confirms he and Carlos were part of the same gang.'

Everything slotted into place in Flood's mind, like scratching the last piece of foil off a lottery card to reveal the winning number.

Flood said. 'I mistook his corruption as incompetence. It's obvious now that Ashford got me to work with him so I could witness Gary Fleming's arrest. That deflected suspicion away from Carlos.'

He thumped his desk with a fist. 'The bent bastard! I reckon it was Ashford who tipped off Carlos when we went to Heathrow to arrest him.'

'Yeah. Bloody Ashford.'

'Now I'm certain Ashford told Carlos that I was responsible for getting him arrested. That's why he wants to change his statement, to take his revenge.'

'That makes sense,' Bridges replied.

***

On the Thursday before Gemma's trial was due to begin, Flood and Laura visited her at the prison.

'How do you feel about the trial next week?' Flood asked.

'Better now after Mr Montgomery and Mr Porter visited me earlier this week and told me what to expect in court. They said that if all goes well, I could be out of here within a few years.' She gave a weak smile.

Laura said, 'We've brought you some clothes to wear in court. We've left them with security. Hope they're OK. Is there anything else you need?'

'I don't think so.'

Flood didn't have the heart to tell her that Carlos had second thoughts about his eyewitness testimony. He needed to see her smile more often.

Gemma added, 'I'm being taken down to Winchester Prison on Sunday for the duration of the trial. Hope it's better than this place.'

'I'm sure it will be, Gemma,' Laura said.

Flood added, 'We won't be allowed to see you during the trial. But we'll be in the visitors' gallery every day, rooting for you.' He paused before saying, 'Laura and I have been thinking, Gemma. It's not worth keeping your flat in Southampton. You can't afford the mortgage now you've got no income. When you get out, you can live with us for a while until we can sort something out. What do you think?'

'But what about my stuff? And my car?'

'Don't worry about that. We'll go to the flat and arrange to have your furniture put it in store. You won't need your car, either. Do you want me to sell it?'

'OK. If you don't mind.'

'Of course, we don't mind. I'll need the keys to the flat. Do any of your neighbours have a spare?'

Gemma nodded. 'Yes. Judy next door, number 26, has a set. I'll call her when I'm allowed and tell her to expect a visit from you. Thanks, Dad. I don't know what I'd do if I didn't have you and Laura to help me.'

'All we I want is for you to get better, make something of your life when you get out. We'll always be here for you, princess.' He hadn't used his pet name for her in a while.

When the time came to leave, Flood and Laura hugged Gemma tightly, not caring what the prison officers would do. They must have known her trial was imminent; they turned a blind eye.

**

Winchester's imposing law courts hadn't changed since Flood's time in the Hampshire Constabulary, almost twenty years ago. The brick and flint building now blending with the nearby Great Hall, built on the site of a medieval palace.

Flood and Laura made their way to the public gallery in Court Two at 2.00 p.m. after Monty had called to tell them that the jury selection had been completed that morning.

They joined twenty others in the visitors' gallery. Flood tried to guess their reasons for wanting to attend his daughter's murder trial, other than having a connection. *Law students? Morbid curiosity? To gawk at an ex-copper's daughter who could be a murderer?*

Looking around, Flood recognised three of the visitors: Simon's mother, father and sister, sitting at one end of the gallery. He'd only met them a few times, once at Gemma's wedding. *Was that only nine months ago?*

Not knowing how to react to them, Flood chose to sit with Laura as far away from them as possible. He noticed Simon's sister nudging her mother and whispering something in her ear. The family turned to face Flood and Laura and glared at them as if they'd been personally responsible for Simon's death. Flood nodded awkwardly in their direction. *It must be hard for them, but it's hard for us, too.*

A few minutes after they'd arrived, the jury filed in. Seven women and five men, most carrying notebooks, sat down after picking up a manila folder which had been placed on each seat. From their elevated position, Flood appraised each of them in turn, although he wasn't sure what he was looking for.

Robin Porter QC, his spotless white bib gleaming under his chin, turned and checked a detail in one of his papers with Monty who sat directly behind him.

The babble of voices hushed as Gemma, looking older than her twenty-seven years, entered from a side door and walked the short distance to the dock accompanied by uniformed female prison officers either side of her.

She wore the black slacks and white top Laura had taken to the prison. She'd tied her hair back tightly against her head, revealing a faded, pink scar on her forehead, which contrasted with her pasty, unmade-up face. Flood ached to rush down to the dock and stand next to her in a show of love and support.

She gazed up at the gallery through the glass partition built around the dock. Flood and Laura put on their most encouraging of smiles, and gave Gemma a thumbs up. She managed a wan smile.

The respective legal teams peered into their laptops or flicked through the mountain of files on their desks in last-minute preparations. Several members of the jury, now seated, quietly chatted to each other.

The clerk shouted, 'All Rise' and the courtroom fell silent. The judge entered from her chambers opposite the dock. Her honour, Rachel Godwin QC, strode towards the bench, wearing a short wig, black and violet robes and a red sash. Her lined face, swan-like beady eyes and prominent nose, inferred a woman not to be crossed.

She sat down, those eyes sweeping the entire courtroom before nodding to the clerk of the court. He approached the dock. 'Gemma Louise Saltus, you are charged with the murder of Simon Anthony Saltus on the 18th of March 2018 at the Blue Anchor public house in Southampton. How do you plead?'

Laura reached for Flood's hand and gripped it as Gemma whispered, 'Not guilty.'

Her honour's cultured voice boomed, 'You'll have to speak up. The jury needs to hear everything you have to say.'

'Not guilty,' Gemma repeated, this time sounding more defiant.

The clerk continued, 'You are also charged with the manslaughter, due to loss of control, of Simon Anthony Saltus. How do you plead?'

After a short pause, as if she couldn't bring herself to say the word, she answered, 'Guilty.'

Her honour invited the chief prosecutor to begin his opening speech. Arthur Murray QC stood and pulled his black gown around his ample girth with both hands. He approached the jury, and stood a few feet in front of them, exuding confidence, his bulky frame dominating the area. Every member's eyes latched onto his.

'This is a straightforward case of a young woman who has admitted killing her estranged husband. The prosecution will prove that the defendant had a clear mind and an evil intent. Which is the very definition of murder.'

Flood could never imagine *his* Gemma acting so aggressively; it simply wasn't in her nature. She'd always been a calm, sometimes fearful child.

Finding his rhythm, Murray continued. 'She will claim that Simon Saltus physically and mentally abused her during their short marriage. She will also claim that he provoked her on the night in question, causing her to react in self-defence. You will have to decide whether the evidence and testimony you hear over the following weeks substantiates that claim.'

He paused theatrically, before saying, 'The prosecution case is that after the victim informed the defendant that he wanted a separation, they had a fierce argument, one of many, which took place in the victim's home where they lived after the marriage. Two weeks later, armed with a carving knife stuck down the inside of her boot, the defendant visited the pub where she knew her husband would be, sought him out and, using *substantial* force, fatally stabbed him in a clear case of revenge for wanting to break up the marriage. Following her arrest, the police carried out tests to determine whether the defendant was under the influence of alcohol or drugs. They found only small quantities of both, not enough in the experts' opinion to affect her rational judgement.' Murray paused again, long enough for the jury to consider what he'd said.

'This was a planned attack on her husband. You will hear from an expert witness who will testify that even if the defendant did act in self-defence, as she claims, the level of force used was disproportionate. Note the word, *disproportionate*. Not reasonable. *Disproportionate*.'

In the stillness of the courtroom, Murray spoke slowly and more precisely now, warming to the purpose of his opening address. 'You've heard the defendant pleading not guilty to the murder of Simon Saltus, but guilty of manslaughter, due to loss of control. The prosecution contends that it was more than a loss of control. It was a premeditated, vengeful attack with a lethal weapon, wielded with such force that the victim died.' Murray looked away from the jury and up at the judge. 'That is the case for the prosecution, Your Honour.'

Out of the corner of his eye, Flood noticed Simon's mother dab her eyes with a handkerchief.

Murray returned to his seat and sat down with a 'clunk', tucking his gown underneath him. Flood wanted to yell, *You're talking about my daughter. She's not a vengeful person. She isn't capable of murdering anyone.*

CHAPTER THIRTY-NINE

The judge scribbled a brief note and then nodded towards the defence team. 'Mr Porter, would you please make your opening statement?'

Considerably shorter and slighter than Murray, Porter spoke with quiet authority. 'Yes, Your Honour.' He turned to the jury and said, 'My learned friend has highlighted the key questions in this case: did the defendant *plan* to murder Simon Saltus? Was the *degree* of force she allegedly used with the knife, *reasonable* in acting in self-defence? And most importantly, was the defendant *provoked* into defending herself, having previously suffered at the hands of her estranged husband?

'The defence will produce evidence and witnesses to prove that the defendant reacted on the spur of the moment, believing she might be in danger. It's important to bear in mind that, as you will hear from experts, the defendant has a personality disorder which has led to her fearing men in general. But this does *not* mean she automatically wants to *murder* them. She is of impeccable character and profoundly regrets the result of her actions.' He turned back to face the judge. 'Thank you, Your Honour.'

All eyes in the courtroom switched back towards the prosecutor. The judge nodded and asked him to begin his examination.

Murray stood and fiddled with his gown, yet again. This time, he addressed the jury from behind his table so that he could refer to his notes. 'In your bundles, you'll see statements from several neighbours who say they heard the defendant and the victim arguing on many occasions at the marital home. You'll also find statements from witnesses who knew Simon Saltus and refer to his good character. Those statements have been accepted by the defence, except for one. I call my first witness, Mr Frank White, a close friend of the victim.'

Flood had met White once before. He'd been the best man at Gemma and Simon's wedding. With his gelled-back, blond hair and tanned face, White would have looked more at home acting as a lifeguard on Bondi beach. Flood's impression was that he was a smart-arse.

After being sworn in, Murray asked him to describe his relationship with Simon. White said they'd attended school and university together, played in the same rugby team and been best man at each other's wedding.

'Knowing each other for over twenty years, you must have a very good idea of what Simon Saltus was like?' Murray asked.

'Yes. We were best mates.' White shook his head. 'I can't believe he's dead.' He said it as if he meant it.

'Can you tell the court exactly what Simon Saltus told you on the night before he decided to end the marriage?'

'He told me that he and Gemma had got on well at first. He thought she was beautiful and loved her bubbly personality. But after a while, he said he couldn't understand why she constantly picked fights with him for no apparent reason. The arguing grew so intense, he couldn't handle it any more. He told me that Gemma was incapable of living a normal married life.'

'What do you think he meant by that?'

'He knew before they got married that she was into drugs and suffered from some kind of personality disorder, which made her not trust anyone. Particularly men. But he said that he felt confident all that would change once they were married. Sadly, it didn't.'

Flood wasn't shocked by Gemma taking drugs. These days, it had become an acceptable lifestyle for young people.

Murray continued. 'Did Simon tell you how she reacted when he told her he wanted to split up after just two months of married life?'

'He said she went ballistic, wouldn't accept that the marriage was over and refused to leave the house. In the end, he kicked her out. He told me he stuffed her clothes in a couple of suitcases and called a cab to take her to the flat her father helped her buy some years ago. Simon and Gemma put it on the market after she'd moved in with him but it hadn't sold.'

'Thank you, Mr White. I have no more questions.'

Porter rose to the judge's invitation to cross-examine Frank White. 'Did Simon ever suggest to you that his life might be in danger if they split up?'

'No.'

'If you were such good pals, he would he have discussed this with you, wouldn't he, if he thought it was a possibility?'

'I presume so.'

'Is that a yes or a no?'

After a moment's hesitation, White replied. 'Yes, I think he would have mentioned it to me.'

'So the fact that he *didn't* mention it to you, his best mate, suggests that he didn't expect the defendant to attack him with a knife. That's a reasonable supposition, isn't it?'

'I suppose it is.'

'Would you agree, therefore, that it's safe to assume that although the couple argued a great deal, the defendant had never *threatened* Simon Saltus with violence?'

'If she did, he never told me.'

Porter paused before asking the next question. 'Knowing the victim well, how would you describe his character?'

White visibly relaxed; his shoulders became less hunched. 'He was a great guy. I always found him even-tempered, amiable and a great friend.'

Porter picked up his notebook from the table in front of him and flicked through to a particular page. 'That's in complete contrast to the statement made by the defendant.' He read from his notes. 'She says that after they'd married, Simon became increasingly physically abusive and demanding, that he harassed her and displayed an explosive temper. Did you ever see that side of his character?'

White replied with an edge to his voice. 'No. I didn't.'

Porter referred to his notebook once more. 'Well, several neighbours did. They testified to hearing Simon forcefully arguing with her on many occasions. How often were you in touch with him in, say, the past two years?'

White appeared momentarily to be caught off-guard. 'I don't know, maybe three or four times. We weren't as close as we used to be after I got a job working in Manchester.'

'Three or four times? So you've not exactly been that close a friend in recent times then, have you? It's not the same as living with someone in the same place seven days a week. Nobody knows what truly goes on behind closed doors, do they?'

The judge intervened as Porter held White's gaze for a second. You don't have to answer that, Mr White.'

Porter placed his notebook on the table in front of him. 'One final question; did you witness the defendant being aggressive on any of the occasions you met her?'

'No. I didn't.'

Thank you, Mr White.' Porter looked up towards the judge. 'I have no further questions, Your Honour.'

The judge closed her laptop and said, 'I think this is a good point to adjourn for the day. The court will resume tomorrow at ten a.m.' Before heading for her chambers, she reminded the jury not to discuss the case with anyone other than their fellow members.

As Flood and Laura drove home, Flood broke the silence. 'Thank God, we've got that first day over with. Murray is no pushover, is he?'

'He made Gemma sound like a lunatic. She's nothing like the way Murray portrayed her. Robin Porter's got a heck of a job on his hands.'

Flood looked across at her as they stopped at traffic lights. 'I hate not being able to help her.' He angrily punched the steering wheel, not for the first time. 'We've got to hope Porter can convince the jury that she's incapable of such behaviour.'

***

Back in the courtroom the following morning, Murray stood and once again referred the jury to their bundles. 'They include an independent medical report showing that the defendant suffered from borderline personality disorder. I call a psychiatric expert, Doctor Elizabeth Stratton.'

A petite, bespectacled woman with short, no-nonsense, silver hair and a ruddy complexion entered the witness box. After the clerk to the court swore her in, Murray asked her to run through her impressive medical qualifications.

'Doctor Stratton, can you please explain to the court, in laymen's terms, the symptoms of borderline personality disorder?'

She spoke so confidently, she must have acted as an expert witness before, Flood thought. 'The main symptoms are: feelings of emptiness, sadness, anger and anxiety. People suffering from BPD usually do not feel good about themselves. Another common symptom is constantly being afraid that the people they trust will abandon them.'

Murray raised an eyebrow. 'Fear of abandonment?'

'Yes. BPD sufferers often develop paranoia of being left alone, especially if the person leaving is someone they care about.' The answer sounded so contrived to Flood, he thought that she must have been coached by Murray, strictly against the rules, but impossible to prove.

'Thank you, Doctor Stratton.' Murray sat down with a hint of a smirk across his lips. Flood wanted to punch him on the nose.

The judge nodded to Porter who stood and said, 'We don't intend to cross-examine this witness, Your Honour.' In a dig at the prosecution, he said, 'We'll be calling a medical expert who has the advantage of *personally* treating the defendant for BPD.'

Doctor Stratton left the witness box and the judge nodded towards Murray who, in turn, said to the court usher, 'Please call Mr George Mercer.'

A short, balding, smartly-dressed man in his fifties entered the witness box. The clerk swore in Mercer and Murray asked him, 'Would you please outline for the jury your particular expertise and relevant qualifications.'

Mercer's baritone voice reverberated around the court. 'After gaining a master's degree in Forensic Science, I've spent twenty-five years working for a forensics company which has a contract with Hampshire Police. I specialise in analysing pathologists' reports following knife crimes and worked on over a hundred cases.'

'Thank you, Mr Mercer.' Murray turned to the judge. 'Your Honour, I would like the jury to inspect exhibit one, namely the weapon used to fatally stab the victim. It will help put my witness's testimony into context.' He picked up a clear plastic wallet containing the knife and presented it to the court clerk who, with almost religious deference, handed it to the nearest member of the jury. He peered at the knife before passing it to the other members.

Murray asked, 'Mr Mercer, what, in your opinion, are the key factors that would make a knife capable of causing a fatal wound?'

'It's sharpness, the thickness of the blade and the force used. We also have to take into account the relative movements of the people involved.'

'You've inspected the knife used by the defendant. What can you tell the court about it?'

'Most people would describe it as a carving knife. It is 20 cm long and made of steel. It's designed to cut meat, so is particularly sharp and has a small radius at the tip. The blade is thin, which would ease penetration.'

'And the degree of force used? What can you tell the court about that?'

'Without a video of the altercation, it's difficult to say with certainty. The pathologist's report showed that the knife caused a single three-inch wound which penetrated the left chest wall and passed through the right atrium of the heart. This led to profuse bleeding, which was the cause of death.'

Murray shifted his weight from one foot to the other and cocked his head to one side. 'Using your considerable experience of knife wounds, would you describe the force used in this case to be slight, moderate or severe?'

'In my professional opinion, the force used was somewhere between moderate and severe.' Flood noticed Gemma shaking her head.

'Could that level of force be applied by, say, the defendant simply lashing out with the knife in her hand?'

'No. The wound indicates something much more than a laceration.'

'So, to be absolutely clear on this point, for this particular knife to be capable of a fatal strike, it would have to be used with a moderate to severe degree of force?'

'Yes.'

'Thank you, Mr Mercer. That is all, Your Honour.'

Flood couldn't believe they were talking about his daughter. *She isn't capable of sticking a knife into anyone. This is only one man's view. Trials ebb and flow. Every time a witness speaks, things change.* He reminded himself that all the defence had to do was to prove reasonable doubt.

He looked down at Gemma again. She looked paler than ever and Flood grew concerned that she might pass out at any moment.

CHAPTER FORTY

Porter stood, still with his notebook in hand. He'd scribbled profusely during Mercer's testimony. He opened his cross-examination with, 'Mr Mercer, in response to the question, "what are the factors which make a knife capable of causing a fatal wound?" you mentioned several.' Porter looked down at his notebook. 'Amongst them, you stated, "the relevant movements of those involved." What if the victim's body position was such that he'd leaned or bent *towards* the defendant in an intimidating or aggressive manner? Would that make a difference?'

'Unfortunately, as I've said, there is no CCTV footage of the clash between the defendant and the victim. No one, other than the people involved, knows precisely the relative movements.'

Porter nodded. 'That is correct. We have to make assumptions based only on the evidence.' He turned to the jury. 'The defence will be calling an eyewitness to the stabbing who made a statement regarding the victim's movements during the altercation.'

He faced Mercer again. 'Of all the factors you mentioned, which would you say is the *most* lethal?'

Mercer paused, thinking about his answer. 'They're all important, but I'd say the sharpness of the tip of the knife.'

'Because?'

Mercer spoke slowly, as if addressing a five-year-old. 'It's obvious. The sharper the knife, the easier it is to penetrate vital organs.'

Porter consulted his notebook yet again. 'You've just told the court that this particular knife, exhibit one, is especially sharp. So, surely it is logical to presume that a lesser amount of force would be required to fatally penetrate a body. Wouldn't you agree?'

Mercer sighed. 'As I keep telling you, in these situations, you need to take into account *all* the factors.'

Porter snapped back, a hint of annoyance in his voice. 'But, just now, you informed the court that the sharpness of the knife is the most important?'

'It is.'

'I put it to you that it is perfectly plausible for the combination of an *especially* sharp knife, together with an *aggressive* move by the victim *towards* the defendant could cause a fatal wound. That's correct, is it not?'

Mercer, looking visibly flushed, paused before saying, 'It is a possibility.'

'Thank you, Mr Mercer. That's all I wanted to know.'

Flood's appreciation of Robin Porter soared. He'd surely planted a modicum of doubt in the jury's mind.

Her honour thanked Mercer and added, 'You are free to go.' As he left, she briefly typed on the keyboard of her laptop and peered at the screen, checking the information.

Murray waited for her to finish before standing and saying, 'Your Honour, I'd like to call the final witness for the prosecution. Mrs Kathy Church.'

Monty had informed Flood that the prosecution would be calling her. She'd be a key witness, he'd said.

Kathy studiously avoided looking in Gemma's direction as she approached the witness box. Gemma sat forward, unsuccessfully trying to make eye contact with her.

The clerk swore her in and Murray stood and faced the jury. 'The defendant's statement, reference P56 in your bundle, states that she went to the pub that fateful Saturday night as part of a hen party organised by this witness, a friend of the defendant.' Murray turned to Kathy. 'Why did you choose that particular pub?'

'I didn't. I don't go to pubs much, but knew Gemma regularly went out pubbing with her other group of girlfriends. I asked her which would be best for a girls' night out before my big day.'

'And which pub did she suggest?'

255

'The Blue Anchor in Southampton, near the docks. Gemma said it would be a good place to start.'

Murray turned to the jury again. 'I refer you to the defendant's statement in which, she admitted that she knew her husband *always* went to the Blue Anchor on Saturday nights.'

Turning back to Kathy, he asked, 'Did you recognise Simon Saltus when you got to the pub?'

'Yes. He was standing at the bar with a few other men.' Kathy began twisting her wedding ring with her other hand.

'Did you see the defendant making contact with him?'

'No. We were sitting at a table some way from the bar. As far as I could tell, she made a point of ignoring him.'

'So you didn't witness the altercation?'

'No. I saw Gemma going to the Ladies at around half nine. That's when it happened. The first we knew anything was wrong was when someone told us a man had been stabbed outside the toilets. I hoped that Gemma wasn't in any way involved, so I pushed past a couple of people and was surprised to see her sitting down, not far from the loos, in a state of shock, next to Simon. I sat next to her and put my arm around her.'

She paused before continuing. 'It wasn't a pretty sight. Gemma and Simon were both covered in blood. I noticed a bloody knife on the floor.' Kathy's voice trailed off as she recalled the scene. It took her a moment to recover. 'A man had used his jacket to stop the bleeding from Simon's chest, while I held Gemma's body close to mine, trying to comfort her. When the police and paramedics arrived, they took over.'

In that moment, Flood felt his heart flip with more compassion for Gemma than he'd felt before. *She must have been so shaken up by what she'd done.*

Speaking slowly and deliberately, Murray turned to the jury. 'It is the prosecution's case that the defendant went to the pub that night armed with a lethal carving knife knowing he'd be there, intent on taking revenge for him abandoning her.

Seeing Simon leaving the bar and heading for the toilets, she followed and took the opportunity to stab him to death.'

Bile stuck in Flood's throat. *That can't possibly be true.* He also became aware of Simon's family glaring at him again. He ignored them, not sure how he should react. Instead, he glanced at Laura sitting next to him. She'd closed her eyes and let out a sigh.

'Thank you, Mrs Church.' Murray turned to the judge. 'I have no more questions, Your Honour. That concludes the case for the Crown.' He returned to his seat.

Porter stood and addressed Kathy. 'How many pubs have you visited in the last year, Mrs Church?'

'I've already said. Pubs are not my thing, but I wanted to have a good night out and some fun with my girlfriends. That's why I asked Gemma to recommend one.'

'How long have you known the defendant?'

'Three years.'

'Did she tell you about her relationship with the victim?'

'She told me she was excited about marrying Simon, happy to have found someone to share the rest of her life.'

'And after they'd separated? What did she say about that?'

'She said the marriage hadn't worked out and that they violently argued every day. She didn't go into details.'

'When she suggested the Blue Anchor, did she say Simon would be there?'

'Yes. I asked Gemma if she was OK with that.'

'And her response?'

'She shrugged and said she's free to go anywhere she wanted; why should she have to avoid him? She told me the Blue Anchor's a lively pub and usually has a group playing great music, so it would be a fun place to kick off the evening.'

'Thank you, Mrs Church. That's been most helpful.' He looked up at the judge. 'I have no more questions, Your Honour.'

'In that case, as the prosecution have concluded their case, we'll adjourn until tomorrow morning at 10.00 a.m. when we'll hear the case for the defence.'

The court became a hubbub of noise as the judge, jury, Gemma and the legal teams slowly left the courtroom. Before the visitors' gallery emptied, Flood and Laura waved at Gemma as the prison officers led her back to the cells. Gemma nodded back towards them, offering yet another pitiful smile in return.

As Flood and Laura made their way to the exit, he turned to her. 'I hope the jury believe Gemma's reason for choosing the Blue Anchor. If they do, it's all about *why* she carried the knife.'

***

Early the following morning, as Flood prepared breakfast, his mobile's shrill ringtone startled him. He picked it up. The screen showed the time as 8.10 a.m. and a caller's number he didn't recognise.

'It's Zara Warwick. I understand from my mother that you want to talk to me.'

It took Flood a nanosecond to realise who Zara was. An image of her photos on the wall of her mother's house flashed before him.

'Zara, yes, of course. Thanks for getting in touch. Where are you?'

'I'm back here in the UK, staying at my mother's house. Why do you want to see me?'

'I'd like to talk to you about your ex-boyfriend.'

'Are you talking about Simon? Simon Saltus?'

'Yes. I'm working on a case involving him.'

'My mother told me he was stabbed by his wife.'

Every time someone referred to the murder case, Flood wanted to put his hands over his ears, blank them out, pretend it never happened.

'I know, but I would still like to meet up soon. Today, if possible. It's urgent. It would be great if you could see me in my Winchester office.'

'I can be there by ten.'

'That's great. See you then.' He gave her the address, thanked her again, and hung up.

Flood yelled, 'Yes', so loud, Laura shouted down the stairs from the bathroom. 'Are you all right, Andy?'

He rushed to the foot of the stairs and saw Laura standing at the top, wrapped in a towel. He told her about the conversation. 'I'd almost given up trying to trace her, but I'm seeing her this morning. You can tell me what happened in court whenever I get there. We've got to hope Zara can confirm Simon's abusive nature. It's the breakthrough we need.'

***

Zara had inherited her mother's sallow complexion and brown eyes which peered through designer spectacles. She wore a dark-blue, suede jacket which zipped up at the front and blue jeans. With her deadpan, unsmiling expression, Flood thought she'd make a good poker player or an ideal undercover agent; the sort of person you'd pass in the street and not notice.

He motioned to Zara to sit opposite him at his desk and asked if she'd like a coffee. She nodded. Flood poured out a cup for Zara and topped up his. He handed her the cup and said, 'I appreciate you coming to see me. You were impossible to trace.'

'I know. I've been travelling in Europe with a friend for the past year or so, trying to decide on a new direction for my life. Unfortunately, my mother became ill with cancer. She died a week ago. It happened quickly. I came back to be with her in her last days.' Teardrops filled her eyes. She reached for a handkerchief from her handbag and gently dabbed them.

'My mother told me you'd visited her and wanted to contact me to talk about Simon Saltus. She gave me your business card. I'm intrigued.'

'I'm sorry to hear about your mother, Zara. Please accept my condolences.'

'Thank you. What do you want to know about Simon?'

'You met him at work and had a relationship, I understand. Let's start there.'

Zara bit her lip before saying, 'Simon and I dated for around six months before I left the company. I suppose you could say we fell for each other. It got serious. Even discussed getting married, although he never got round to buying me an engagement ring. I told all my friends about him and our plans.'

'What happened?'

'One of my workmates tipped me off about Simon having another girlfriend. I told her she must be mistaken. Then she showed me a video she'd taken on her mobile. It showed him with his arms around another woman and kissing her neck at a Southampton nightclub the previous week. I couldn't believe my eyes. It got worse. She filmed them leaving together.'

Flood screwed up his face. 'Oh! What did you do?'

'I got my friend to send me a copy of the video and I played it over and over, looking for anything to suggest he'd simply been flirting with her. But he wasn't. His hands were all over her.' Zara spat out, 'Why would he go to a nightclub without me? We were practically engaged.'

'Did you confront him?'

'I did. Simon denied it at first, but when I showed him the video, he admitted it, said he was sorry, giving me all the usual excuses.' Zara rocked her head from side to side as she mimicked Simon. '"I was pissed. It was only a bit of fun. She came on to me." I told him I could never trust him again, and that as far as I was concerned, it was the end of our relationship.'

'That's understandable.'

'When I spoke to the other girls in the office, they said Simon was renowned for dating dozens of girlfriends over the years. It seems he can't resist women.' Zara let out a deep sigh.

'So that's why you left the company and went travelling?'

'Yes. I couldn't face working in the same place as Simon. Our splitting up became the only topic of gossip at the water cooler. People started looking at me, nudging each other, as if to say, "Simon's dumped her." That's why I needed to get away.

'Another friend of mine had always regretted not taking a gap year between college and uni, so I joined her, backpacking around Europe and deleted all my Facebook and Twitter posts. They're far too invasive.'

Flood raised the question he'd been aching to ask ever since he knew Zara had been in a relationship with Simon Saltus. 'During the time you dated Simon, did he ever harm or abuse you?'

Zara shook her head. 'No. Quite the opposite. Always the smooth-talking charmer.'

Flood's big break snapped in two, like a weathered twig.

Zara continued. 'Anyway, why do you want to know about me and Si?'

Flood took a deep breath. 'The woman who stabbed Simon Saltus is my daughter.'

Zara gasped and put her hands to her mouth. 'What?'

'I hoped that you could support my daughter's allegations about Simon's abusive nature.'

'I'm sorry, Mr Flood. I can't. He's a lying, cheating womaniser, but he was never violent or abusive to me.'

CHAPTER FORTY-ONE

Flood ambled to the courtrooms, less than half a mile from his office, with slumped shoulders. He entered the main concourse and noticed Laura sitting on a bench having an earnest conversation with Monty. 'Are you alright, Andy?' Laura asked. 'You look upset. How did you get on with Zara?'

Flood blew out his cheeks and shook his head. 'Not good. We've got nothing on Simon.'

She reached for his hand. 'Oh, Andy, I'm sorry.'

'Why aren't you in court?'

Monty replied. 'The judge called a comfort break.'

'Did anything important come out of this morning's session?'

'No. Mainly taken up with legal points,' Monty added. 'Robin will be calling Carlos to the witness box next. Last night, we discussed the best way to deal with him. You should know that we've disclosed his conviction for Mandy's murder to the prosecution.'

Flood, already in a bad mood, exploded. 'You've what? That's his credibility shot.'

Monty put up a pacifying palm. 'Robin believes it's the only way to winkle out why Carlos wants to change his statement. I admit it's a gamble, but we have to trust Robin.'

'It's obvious why he wants to withdraw it, 'Flood scowled. 'He's trying to get back at me for helping to put him away.'

'We want the court to hear that.'

Laura put a hand on Flood's arm. 'Monty is right, Andy.' At that moment, an announcement came over the loudspeaker stating that all interested parties should return to Court Two immediately.

'I'd better be going. Chat later.' Monty dashed off, clutching several files under his arm.

Flood turned to Laura as they made their way to the courtroom. 'I bloody-well hope our team know what they're doing.'

As they entered the public gallery, they had difficulty in finding a seat. Interest in the trial had increased following the press coverage. The only spaces available meant they had to shuffle past Simon's mother, father and sister, all looking deadly serious. They stood to let Flood and Laura past. Flood felt their eyes drilling into the back of his head. He concentrated on looking down at the dock, trying to catch Gemma's eye to reassure her that he wasn't far away.

Robin Porter called Carlos to the witness box. A burly, uniformed prison officer accompanied him. Carlos's expression implied that he'd rather be anywhere else but in this courtroom. He wore a creased, open-neck, black shirt and jeans. His former designer stubble had been replaced by a scruffy, dark beard. Porter had failed to persuade him to wear a suit and tie to make him appear more credible.

Flood willed Carlos to stick to his original statement, crucial to Gemma's defence.

The clerk asked him to take the card to swear the oath. He shook his head and spat out in a thick Latino accent, 'I don't want to swear an oath.'

The judge swivelled her head and faced him. Focussing her beady eyes on his, she ordered, 'Mr Ramirez. As a witness for the defence who has already made a statement to the police, you will swear to tell the truth. Otherwise you will be in contempt and I will seek the maximum prison sentence of two years.' She nodded to the clerk to continue.

Carlos shrugged, like a naughty schoolboy. The clerk handed him the card with the oath written on it and asked him to read it out loud.

In a bored, deadpan voice, he read it.

Porter started gently. 'Mr Ramirez, you made a statement on 26th March 2018, just over a week after you'd witnessed the victim, Simon Saltus, harassing and physically abusing the defendant. I have a copy of it here in my hand.' He waved it at

Carlos then turned to the jury. 'There are copies in your bundle, Reference D23.'

He turned to face Carlos. 'Do you stand by that statement? If you can't remember what you said, I can read it out to you.'

'I know what I said but now, I'm not certain what I saw.'

Here we go. Just as Flood expected.

'But you came forward voluntarily. You also said in your statement that you felt sorry for the defendant. That she shouldn't be tried for murder because she acted in self-defence. You signed the statement in the presence of police officers, didn't you? So you must have been sure of what you'd witnessed then?'

'I've told you. I'm not sure anymore.'

'So you cannot or will not confirm the contents of your original witness statement?'

Leaning forward, Carlos looked at the judge. 'I'm not answering any more questions.'

Flood closed his eyes and bowed his head, impotent to Carlos's stubbornness.

Her honour glared at Carlos. 'I am losing patience with you, Mr Ramirez. You've sworn on oath today that you will tell the court the truth.' Carlos silently stuck out his chin in defiance.

Robin Porter looked up at the judge. 'Your Honour, may I see you in chambers? I'd like to speak to you about something which cannot be discussed in court.'

Glaring once more at Carlos, the judge nodded and said, 'Court adjourned.' She rose and left by the side door as the clerk uttered, 'All rise.'

Flood wanted to scream at Carlos. *For God's sake, just confirm that your original statement is true. Then we can all move on.*

***

As several visitors left to stretch their legs or seek a drink, Flood and Laura remained seated in the gallery. Flood stared vacantly down at the emptying well of the court before turning to Laura. 'If the jury don't accept Carlos's original statement, Gemma's had it.'

'Let's wait until we hear what Porter comes up with. I'm sure he knows what he's doing.' She squeezed his hand.

When the court resumed, the judge directed her comments to Carlos who'd been brought back into the witness box. 'I have received an application from defence counsel to treat you as a hostile witness. As your testimony today differs significantly from the statement you made shortly after the incident, I agree with the defence. You signed your statement, saying it was true. Now you're saying it was not true. The effect of this ruling is that defence counsel may cross-examine you and ask leading questions. Do you understand?'

Flood watched Carlos balling his fists. 'I don't have a choice, do I?'

'No. You don't, Mr Ramirez. Please continue, Mr Porter.'

He rose and said, 'Thank you, Your Honour,' and turned to face Carlos. 'Let me ask you again, Mr Ramirez. Why do you want to change your statement?'

'I've told you. I'm not sure what I saw.'

Porter exaggerated a sigh and cocked his head to one side. 'Well, are you *lying* to the court now or were you *lying* when you made your statement?'

Carlos shifted his weight from one leg to the other and pursed his lips. Her honour prodded him. 'Please answer the question.'

Leaning forward again, Carlos said, 'I didn't lie the first time, and I'm not lying now. All I'm saying is, I'm not sure what I saw.'

Flood resisted the urge to run down to the witness box and punch Carlos squarely on the nose. He wasn't sure how much more of Carlos's shilly-shallying he could take.

Porter remained his usual unflappable self and asked, 'I want you to think carefully about the answer to the question I'm about to ask you.' He paused, before saying, 'Did you discover, *after* making your statement, that the defendant's father is Mr Andrew Flood, a private investigator? The same private investigator largely responsible for providing the evidence leading to you serving sixteen years and six months at Her Majesty's pleasure?'

Flood heard a gasp from several people in the visitors' gallery. He glanced at Laura, then watched Carlos's face twitch before he answered. 'I didn't know.'

Porter turned to the jury. 'Because of Mr Flood's intimate knowledge, Hampshire Police invited him to cooperate with them as a special advisor on the case in which this witness,' Porter pointed at Carlos, 'was convicted.'

Turning back to face him again, Porter added, 'You came forward as a good citizen to ensure justice would be done and signed a statement giving, what the defence believes, is an accurate version of what happened in the early hours of March 8th. I put it to you that once you discovered that Mr Flood is the defendant's father, you wanted to exact your revenge on him. That is the reason why you want to change your statement. Am I correct?'

'In your opinion.'

'It's not my opinion that matters, Mr Ramirez. The jury will decide. I have no more questions, Your Honour.' Porter sat down, a solemn look on his face. Flood looked at each member of the jury. *Had Porter done enough to convince them?*

Murray for the prosecution stood and, in a theatrical manner, readjusted his gown for the umpteenth time. With an exaggerated look of puzzlement on his face, he peered at Carlos.

'I'm confused, Mr Ramirez. And I'm sure the jury is, too. First, you say you witnessed the victim being provoked. You came forward and made a statement to that effect, which is highly commendable, if I may say so. Now, in this courtroom, you no longer stand by your statement. The defence has put forward a barely plausible reason for your change of heart but offered no *actual proof* of you wanting to take revenge on Mr Flood.' Murray spoke the next words slowly. 'So, did you see Simon Saltus provoke the defendant? Yes or no?'

'I've told you. I thought he did at the time, but now I've had time to think, I'm not so sure of what I saw.' Flood's pent-up anger threatened to overtake him. His nails dug into his palms so tightly, he thought they might bleed.

Murray looked up at the judge for support. When none came, he sighed and continued. 'Clearly, I cannot force you to commit yourself. Perhaps you will be more explicit on another matter. The defence have disclosed that you are currently serving time for murder and related drug offences. According to the transcripts of the police interviews undertaken during the investigation into your crimes, you emphatically denied the offences at first, didn't you?'

'Yes, but I admitted it later.'

'But only after the police produced overwhelming proof of your guilt. That's correct, isn't it?'

Carlos sighed. 'I told you. I admitted it.'

Murray addressed the jury. 'Here we have a defence witness who admits to lying to the police following his arrest. Who is to say that, for reasons best known to himself, he made up his statement and now wants to withdraw it. I suggest this witness's testimony cannot be relied upon.' He turned back towards the judge. 'Thank you, Your Honour. I have no further questions.'

Flood looked closely at the members of the jury again. They appeared transfixed by Murray's oratory. He whispered to Laura, 'This is not looking good.'

The judge said with a resigned voice, 'Please take Mr Ramirez to the cells. I shall consider his contempt of court shortly.' Then she asked Porter to call his next witness for the defence.

'I'd like to call Doctor Matthew Rogers.'

Doctor Rogers' imposing frame towered over the witness box. After swearing his oath, Porter asked him to explain his role. 'I was the Senior Clinician for the defendant immediately after she was sectioned following the murder charge.'

'And following your examination of the defendant, what did you learn about her medical condition?'

Adjusting his glasses, something he did often, Doctor Rogers replied, 'Our initial examination confirmed a diagnosis of borderline personality disorder. She has all the classic symptoms: impulsive behaviour, extreme emotional swings and a need for closeness, love and affection.'

'Did you discover what caused this disorder?'

'When Gemma was three years old, a criminal gang of men killed her mother in a hit and run in retribution for her father, a DCI in the Metropolitan Police at the time, being responsible for putting away their boss. Two years later, another gang abducted and tortured her and her sister in another act of revenge. These experiences will have had a major effect on her personality.'

Flood closed his eyes recalling both painful events.

'Would this affect her attitude to men in general?' Porter asked.

'In my experience, it would be a major contributory factor. No one fully recovers from something like that, especially as it happened when she was so young. Gemma also told me she'd had several relationships with men who didn't treat her well. Despite this, she believed her marriage would resolve everything.'

'Why was she sectioned?'

'When she arrived at the Intensive Care Unit after the altercation, she displayed deep feelings of guilt at what she'd done. We were concerned about the possibility of self-harming or attempting suicide.'

'In your opinion, has the defendant shown remorse?'

'Yes. Gemma repeatedly said that she couldn't believe she'd stabbed her husband to death and deserved to be punished.'

'She never sounded triumphant, or gloated over the fact that her husband was dead?'

'No. Quite the opposite.'

'Thank you, Doctor Rogers. I have no further questions.'

Flood hoped the jury would warm to Doctor Foster's no-nonsense, authoritative testimony. *A definite plus in Gemma's case.*

The prosecution declined the judge's invitation to cross-examine him. Flood assumed Murray didn't think he'd gain much.

The judge said, 'This will be a good point to adjourn for the weekend. The court will reconvene on Monday at 10.00 a.m.' She pulled down the lid of her laptop and made her way to her chambers as the court slowly emptied.

As Gemma was led back to the cells, Porter looked up into the gallery and gesticulated to Flood and Laura to meet him and Monty on the concourse.

Monty opened the conversation. 'Robin and I have been discussing whether we should put Gemma in the witness box. We've decided it's best *not* to put her at the mercy of Murray.'

Flood frowned. 'I disagree. She can explain everything from her point of view. I think the jury will believe her. She's looking vulnerable; I can't believe they'd think that she *deliberately* went to the pub to kill Simon.'

Porter replied. 'Our major problem is how the jury will judge her. We need to present her as the victim. If we allow Murray to cross-examine Gemma, he'll treat her as the perpetrator. I think it's better to rely on her statement and the police transcripts of her interviews.'

Flood opened his mouth to say something, but Porter got in first. 'I'm also worried that the prosecutor's questions will reveal the weaknesses in our case.'

Laura asked, 'What do you mean?'

Porter replied. 'The prosecution will ask Gemma *why* she carried a knife. If she wanted to ward off any harassment, why didn't she carry a Mace spray or something similar? And why visit a pub where she knew Simon Saltus was a regular?'

Monty added, 'Even worse, what if the jury don't believe Carlos's original eyewitness statement? It could look like Gemma lied about being provoked. See what we mean?'

Flood turned to Laura. 'What do you think?'

'I think Robin and Monty are right, Andy.'

'So, it's three against one, is it?' Laura, Porter and Monty nodded.

Flood glared at each of them before storming off towards the exit without saying a word.

'Sorry about that,' Laura said, before running after him. When she caught up, she shouted, 'For Christ's sake, Andy! You've got to let the professionals do their job.'

●▲●

CHAPTER FORTY-TWO

Over the weekend, Flood hired a van and took several suitcases, cardboard boxes and plastic bags to take Gemma's possessions back to his house. Laura insisted on going with him. She thought she'd be much better at packing Gemma's personal belongings.

When they arrived, Flood said, 'Why don't you start in the bedroom, I'll start in the kitchen.' He began emptying the contents of the cupboards into various boxes. When he opened the cutlery drawer, he winced as he recalled Gemma telling him it's where she'd taken the knife she'd used to stab Simon.

He took out the last of the cutlery and tried to push the drawer back into place. It wouldn't close so he took the complete drawer out. He got down on his hands and knees to see what the obstruction was. Taped to the back of the unit were half-a-dozen clear cellophane packets. He instantly knew what they contained.

Prising the packets away, he peered at them. Each one had a logo of a scorpion printed in the corner. His mind raced as he made the connection.

He dashed into the bedroom to find Laura. She was neatly folding Gemma's clothes on the bed before placing them in one of the suitcases.

'Look at this.' Flood held open the palm of his hand to reveal the packets.

'Where did you find them?'

'Taped to the back of the cutlery drawer.'

'It's probably cocaine. You're not surprised, are you?'

'No. I'm not, but see that scorpion logo? Crime Scene Investigators discovered the same branded cocaine packets at Carlos's flat and Mandy's hotel room. It was the first time the drugs unit had come across this particular logo. It looks like Carlos supplied Gemma as well as Mandy with the gear.'

'Couldn't she have got them from a middle man, someone Carlos supplied?'

'That's not how it works. According to the spreadsheets found at Gus Martin's house, it's clear that he financed the importation of the drugs and supplied the dealers; Carlos being one of them. There is no middle man.'

Laura looked thoughtful. 'Surely the police would have searched her flat. How come they didn't find the drugs?'

'They probably did, but didn't need to be very thorough. There was no reason to conduct a full forensic search: they had the weapon and her mobile phone. She also admitted the stabbing and that the knife was hers.'

'But if Carlos was working here illegally, why would he give a statement to the police?'

'That's a good question. I can only think he came forward in order to wrong-foot the police after he'd murdered Mandy. Put him in a good light. I need to know more about the relationship between him and Gemma.'

Something clicked inside Flood's head. 'I'll get Bridges to look at Gemma's mobile, see if there were any calls or texts between them. He can also get forensics to check for fingerprints on these packets; see if they match Carlos's.'

'You can't do that. Suppose it proves that Gemma and Carlos *did* know each other? Bridges would have to inform the CPS who'll want the court to hear about the connection.'

Flood bit his lip. Laura was right. She added, 'And you'd have to inform Porter and Monty about your suspicions. They couldn't rule out the possibility that Gemma went to the pub to kill Simon and Carlos was in on the act.'

Flood sat down on the foot of the bed and placed his head in his hands.

Laura asked, 'Did you ask Gemma whether she'd met Carlos?'

'I did. A while back when she was on remand. She said she hadn't.'

'Do you think she lied?'

'I don't know what to think.'

Laura remained standing and put her arm out onto Flood's shoulder. 'Andy, listen to me. If everything goes well, Gemma could be home living with us in a few years. We'll never know the truth. If you want to continue your relationship, you'll have to accept things as they are.'

Flood shook his head. 'I'm not sure I can live with that, Laura. If I'm right, Gemma's no different from Mandy Bradshaw. She had a ruthless streak, too. If they're to be believed, they both took revenge against abusive husbands. I didn't have much sympathy for Mandy. What am I supposed to feel about Gemma?'

'What's the alternative? You can't challenge her. If you do, you run the risk of losing her forever. Is that what you want? You've already lost Pippa. She doesn't want anything to do with you. You'll have to decide whether you want Gemma in our life.'

Laura sat next to Flood on the bed and turned to face him. Speaking softly, she added, 'When Gemma gets out of prison, she'll need our unconditional support. That girl's had a lot to deal with in her life. You should be making it up to her.'

'I'm not sure I can do that, Laura, not without knowing the truth.'

*****

In court on the Monday morning, the impassioned closing speeches from the prosecution and defence barristers left Flood no nearer to predicting a verdict.

Murray majored on Carlos's lack of credibility and repeated his suggestion that the jury should ignore his original eyewitness statement. The last thing he said, designed to stick in the jury's minds before they'd retire to consider their verdict, was, 'The defendant carried a knife to the pub where she knew Simon would be. She wanted to take her revenge for him rejecting her and forcing her out of the matrimonial home. I'd remind you all that a medical expert stated in court that one of the effects of the defendant's disorder is that she cannot handle being abandoned.'

Flood turned to face Laura and shook his head realising that Murray had summed up his fears precisely. Laura placed a consoling hand on his arm.

Porter pushed back hard on the absence of CCTV footage at the pub, stressing that nobody, apart from the eyewitness, the victim and the defendant knew what happened. He emphasised that Carlos had valiantly came forward and made a statement supporting the defendant's claim that Simon Saltus harassed and abused her. 'Whatever Mr Ramirez's motive for wishing to amend his statement, the very fact that he made it should place a *reasonable doubt* in your minds, enough to acquit the defendant of a murder charge.'

As the judge began her summing up, Flood leant forward in his seat concentrating on every word. Occasionally, he glanced at the jurors trying to judge their mood.

'Members of the jury, this is a serious case. A young man has lost his life. In deciding whether the defendant is guilty or not guilty of murder, you must consider the following: did the defendant go to the pub to seek out her estranged husband to kill him in a planned attack, motivated by revenge? If you believe this to be the case, then you must find her guilty of murder.

'If you believe the defendant acted in self-defence, then you must find her not guilty of murder. However, you must also consider whether the action she took in the circumstances was disproportionate or reasonable. If disproportionate, this too would constitute murder. That is the law.

'It is essential for you, the jury, to assess the state of the relationship between the victim and the defendant, both before and after the breakup of their marriage. This will establish motive. The defendant's statement alleges that the victim physically abused her throughout the short time they lived together, although her counsel produced no evidence to support that view. However, you heard testimony confirming many violent arguments between the defendant and the victim.

'You heard from two medical experts, one suggesting that the defendant's fear of abandonment *may* have caused her to act the way she did, the other saying that she showed remorse rather than triumph at the outcome.

'You must also consider whether to believe the defendant's statement in which she claimed that carrying a knife as a deterrent would help her cope if she found herself in perceived danger from *any* man who attempted to harass her. You will have to decide whether her personality disorder and her experiences as a young girl had any bearing on her behaviour that night.

'Regarding the evidence from the expert in knife crime, you will have to determine whether the force of the blow caused the fatal wound or, as the defence alleges, an aggressive movement by the victim contributed towards his death. Without CCTV footage, you must decide whether the defendant lashed out with the knife simply to ward off her estranged husband or whether she thrust it into his chest with deliberate intent?'

Flood closed his eyes in an attempt to block the thought. *My daughter would never do such a thing. She isn't capable.*

'A further issue for you to consider is why the defendant suggested to her friend that they visit the pub knowing her husband would be there. Was it to show him that she was a free agent? Or was it part of a deliberate plan to murder him?

'A great deal will depend on whether you rely on the testimony given by the only eyewitness, Mr Ramirez. He came forward and signed a witness statement saying that the victim provoked the defendant who acted in self-defence. However, he decided, for whatever reason, to withdraw his statement. You will have to make your mind up which version is correct.

'I cannot guide you as to how much weight to apply to the evidence and testimony you have heard from each of the witnesses. You will have to determine that in your discussions. Please take your time over this and remember; if you have any reasonable doubts in your minds about whether you believe the defendant is guilty of murder, you must acquit her of that charge.

'I remind you that the defendant has pleaded guilty to manslaughter due to loss of control. It is now time for you to debate. The court usher will take you to the jury room.' Her honour nodded to both legal teams and the jury before retreating to her chamber.

The jury filed out, clutching their bundles. Gemma stood silently still, staring at the ground yet again. One of the security guards signalled that they should leave the dock. For the first time at the end of a sitting, Gemma didn't look up to the gallery to acknowledge her father and Laura.

Flood's eyes welled up, fearing the worst but willing the jury to find Gemma not guilty. He had no idea how they'd vote. This feeling wasn't alien to him; he'd attended many trials and given up trying to outguess the jury's verdicts.

CHAPTER FORTY-THREE

'That's it. There's nothing more any of us can do,' Laura said, as they stood looking down at the empty courtroom. She put an arm around Flood's waist.

'I wish we could be with Gemma. She must be going through hell,' he said.

They made their way from the courtroom to the concourse to meet Porter and Monty who were stood, talking to each other.

'What do you think?' Flood asked them both.

Porter answered. 'It's a hard one to call. A great deal depends on whether the jury accept Carlos's original statement and our reason for why he wanted to withdraw it. It could go either way.'

***

Thinking a change of scenery might improve their downbeat moods, Flood and Laura spent the afternoon drinking coffee in the nearest café to the courts. Flood checked his mobile frequently, anxious not to miss a call or text from Monty telling them the jury had reached a verdict.

Late afternoon, Monty did call, saying the jury would be staying in a local hotel and deliberating overnight. 'I'll buzz you tomorrow as soon as I hear something.'

Flood and Laura had no appetite but decided to go to a pub for a drink for something to do. As they sat in a quiet corner, Laura asked, 'Have you thought anymore about how you'll handle your relationship with Gemma?'

'Only all the time. For all my adult life, I've fought for justice. I expect Simon's parents will want to see justice, too.'

'That sounds like you want Gemma to be found guilty to prove you're right.'

'Of course I don't,' Flood snapped.

'Well, you'll have to do what most other parents would do in these circumstances; choose between loving Gemma but hating what she's done, or rejecting her. I'm going for the first option.'

Her words seared an impression in Flood's brain.

***

Following a sleepless night and with his mind still in turmoil, Flood got up early and went for a jog; something he hadn't done in a while. By 10.00 a.m. he and Laura were again sitting in the nearest coffee shop to the court, awaiting Monty's call.

Three cups of coffee later, Flood's mobile pinged. He listened to the message then hung up. Turning to Laura, he said, 'They've reached a verdict.'

They hurried to the courtroom just in time to see the jury filing back into their seats. Flood stared at each of their faces once again trying to interpret their thoughts. He'd read once that experts could predict a jury's verdict by their demeanour. If jurors didn't look at the defendant as they returned from their deliberations, they'd agreed a guilty verdict. Some looked at Gemma, some didn't.

The judge entered last. After she'd sat down, she said, 'Would the defendant remain standing for the reading of the verdict.' A palpable tension spread throughout the courtroom and the over-flowing visitors' gallery. Flood noticed Simon's family sitting a few seats away from them, their eyes glued to the jury.

He looked down on Gemma to see that she'd closed her eyes and crossed her fingers. Her honour nodded towards the clerk who asked the jury, 'Have you elected a foreman?'

A juror sitting closest to the judge stood. Middle-aged and wearing a check sports jacket, he said, 'Yes, I am the foreman.'

'Have you reached a verdict upon which all members of the jury are agreed?'

'Yes, we have.'

'Do you find the defendant guilty or not guilty of murder?' Flood repeated under his breath, *not guilty, not guilty, not guilty.* His palms started sweating and his heartbeat went into overdrive.

In a courtroom quieter than a graveyard in the dead of night, the foreman answered, 'Not guilty.'

Flood and Laura simultaneously gasped and turned to each other. Flood uttered, 'Yes!' under his breath.

He looked at Gemma again. She'd gripped the bar on top of the dock with both hands to stop collapsing, relief etched on her face.

'And that is the verdict of you all?'

'Yes, it is.'

Flood heard Simon's mother, sitting a few spaces away, utter in a barely audible voice, 'That's not right.' He concentrated on looking at Gemma.

The impassive judge, said, 'The defendant has pleaded guilty to manslaughter due to loss of control. Before sentencing, I will hear any mitigating circumstances from the defence. Mr Porter?'

'Thank you, Your Honour. The defendant has never denied stabbing Simon Saltus and pleaded guilty at the earliest possible time. She has no previous criminal record, is of good character and presents no threat to the public. She is prepared to undergo rehabilitation and further treatment for her personality disorder. Her family are supporting her.'

'Thank you, Mr Porter. I will consider the sentence and announce my decision tomorrow morning. The court will sit at 10.00 a.m.' The judge turned to the jury, thanked them for their deliberations and dismissed them.

Down on the concourse, Flood and Laura met Porter and Monty in their usual spot. Shaking their hands enthusiastically, Flood beamed. 'You both did a great job. We're so grateful for all you've done.'

'What do you think Gemma's sentence will be?' Laura asked.

Porter replied. 'The guidelines suggest anything between two and ten years. The judge will take into account the mitigating circumstances, so I'd guess about four to five years.'

Flood pulled a face. 'That long?'

'Yes. But Gemma will be out on licence after she's served half that time.' He added with a smile, 'Assuming she behaves herself.'

Flood did the maths. Taking into account the six months she'd already served meant she'd be out of prison in less than two years. *That's a bloody good result.*

***

Porter's forecast proved accurate. The following morning, the judge sentenced Gemma to four years and three months. Flood blew out his cheeks in relief. Gemma looked up at Flood and Laura in the visitors' gallery and smiled.

They floated out of the courtroom as if on top of a cloud to congratulate Porter and Monty. On the way, Flood felt an arm clutching his elbow from behind. He turned to face Simon's mother.

Her small, flushed, unmade-up face twisted into a snarl. 'I always knew your daughter would be bad news for my Simon.' Her eyes blazed at Flood as she flicked a stray blonde hair away from her eyes and tucked it behind her ear. 'She should have got life for what she did.'

Flood thrust his head closer towards hers. 'That's not what the jury thought.'

Laura tried pulling Flood away. 'Don't get involved, Andy. It's not worth it.'

Simon's father, bald and well-built, butted in. 'Thanks to your daughter, my son is dead. We'll never see him again. But that piece of trash will be out in a few years. How can you live with that?'

Flood's breathing quickened, and he gritted his teeth. Brushing Laura's arm away from his sleeve, he took a step towards his tormentor. Laura anticipated Flood's move and squeezed between both men. Facing Flood, she said, as if commanding a dog, 'Andy. No!'

For a moment, he stood his ground. His body tensed as the adrenaline surged and he glared at Simon's father. Laura snapped, 'C'mon, Andy. Let it go.' She dragged him towards the exit.

CHAPTER FORTY-FOUR

On the drive home, Laura said, 'Have you thought any more about your relationship with Gemma?'

'I'm still thinking about it. I'll go and see her as soon as I can.'

Two days later, Monty called to say that Gemma would serve her sentence at the same prison she'd been on remand and that she was now allowed visitors.

When they met, Flood hugged Gemma tightly. She responded in the same way, saying, 'It's great to see you, Dad.'

As they sat opposite each other in the visitors' hall, he noticed that her smile had returned and her complexion showed more colour.

'Thank God the jury found you not guilty of murder, Gemma. How are you feeling?'

'Much better, Dad. I'm so glad the trial's over. I feel like I've been through a wringer. Monty and Mr Porter were wonderful. I can't thank them enough.' She paused before adding, 'Oh, my writing's coming on. It's only a few scraps about my childhood so far but the therapist says it's good for me.'

Flood smiled. 'That's great. If you can't remember stuff, ask me. The old grey cells are still working. Just about. Are you OK serving your time here?'

'Yes. At least I know the regime and know who I can trust. I've made a few friends, too, despite being an ex-copper's daughter.' Flood didn't need reminding about the effect his serving in the police force had on his family.

They talked about her early childhood memories and Gemma scribbled notes for her writing project. When there was a break in the conversation, Flood took a deep breath and said, 'There's something I need to talk to you about, Gemma. When Laura and I cleared your apartment, we found packets of cocaine hidden at the back of the cutlery drawer. I'm sure they were provided by Carlos Ramirez. Was he your dealer? I want to know the truth. You told me you'd never met him.'

Gemma looked sheepish and bit her lip. 'Sorry, Dad. I should have told you before, but I didn't want you to know about my habit. That's why I lied.'

'So you *did* know each other?'

'Yes. We met to trade the drugs. We got on well. He liked me.'

'Why didn't you tell the police that it was Carlos who witnessed Simon harassing you?'

'You must believe me. I didn't know it was him. And anyway, he dashed off quickly not wanting to become involved. At the time, I was in a hell of a state. I was covered in Simon's blood and I guess I was in shock. After Simon died, I can only think Carlos felt sorry for me.'

'Was he part of your plan? Did he come forward and lie about Simon provoking you, giving you the excuse to stab Simon?'

Gemma's eyes narrowed. 'Dad! How could you think that?'

Flood looked around to make sure he couldn't be overheard and whispered, 'I need to know, Gemma. Did you go to the pub with the intention of killing Simon?'

Gemma looked downwards for a second before facing her father. 'Yes. I did. Carlos wasn't involved.'

'Oh, Gemma! How could you?'

'You don't know what's it's like to be molested, sexually abused and then kicked out of your home. Simon's actions that night made me more determined than ever to carry out my plan. He made me feel utterly worthless. I wanted him dead. I didn't care what became of me.' She sat back in her chair. 'There. I've said it.'

Flood outwardly remained calm although he wanted to scream at her. Tell her how stupid she'd been. Laura's words about acting like a proper parent swirled around in his mind. The enormity of the effect on Gemma of losing her mother and being abducted, leading to her consequent mental condition finally hit home. *And it's my fault.*

The sound of a klaxon blasted around the room signifying the end of visiting time. 'OK,' Flood said. 'It's going to take me a while to come to terms with this, Gemma. I'll come and see you next week. We can talk some more then.'

'I'd really like that, Dad.' Her eyes began welling up.

Flood stood and hugged her again before making his way to the exit. He had a lot of thinking to do.

THE END

ACKNOWLEDGEMENTS

Grateful thanks to the following who helped create this novel.

    Sarah Davis

    Kathy Day

    Hannah Duffy

    Rod Ellaway

    Di Ingram

    Roy Lambert

    Barbara Needham

    Dave Renwick

    Susan Swalwell

    Dee Waterman

Special thanks go to Brendan McCusker who started me on my writing career.

Extra special thanks must go to my wife, Lorraine, and my ever-supporting family for their encouragement.

OTHER BOOKS BY DAI HENLEY

B Positive!

This is not a celebrity memoir. Nor is it a tear-jerking depressing journal – it's quite the opposite. This is the inspirational story of someone determined to succeed in business, sport and life. It encompasses the social, technological and economic fortunes of the country from the end of WW11 to the present day. With great resolve and spirit, the writer tackles everything thrown at him with positivity and enthusiasm. It's no coincidence that B Positive is his blood type.

Blazing Obsession

What would you do if your wife or husband and your two children were murdered in an arson attack and the killer got away with it on a technicality? And the 800-year-old law of double jeopardy means he can't be tried again.

Grief-stricken James Hamilton, a successful and wealthy entrepreneur, is incensed with the judge and disillusioned with the legal system. Together with his wife's best friend and a canny private investigator, he plans the perfect retribution.

Will he get away with it?

Reckless Obsession

When DCI Flood's wife is murdered in a hit and run attack by a vengeful gang, his life is torn apart. The police fail to find the perpetrators. Two years later, the investigation is relegated to a cold case. Flood becomes obsessed, spending all his spare time hunting down his wife's killers, alienating friends and family.

After witnessing another shocking murder, he is plunged into the menacing world of organised crime. His investigations unearth startling similarities to the cold case, putting his life in danger.

For more details, sample chapters and reviews, and links, please visit:
www.daihenley.co.uk

Lightning Source UK Ltd.
Milton Keynes UK
UKHW010634291021
393035UK00002B/248